Praise for **Steph**

'Quirky, clever and unputdown

'A really delightful book ... lots of brilliant recommendations along the way' **Adèle Geras**

'So assured and gentle, full of compassion and replete with astute observations of human nature and behaviour'
Carys Bray

'Absolutely gorgeous ... compelling, compassionate'
Sarah Franklin

'Burns fiercely with love and hurt' **Linda Green**

'Intriguing and touching' *Sunday Express*

'A really moving read – with great book recommendations included, too!' *My Weekly*

'A beautiful book' *Prima*

By Stephanie Butland

The Second Chance Book Club
Found in a Bookshop
Nobody's Perfect
The Woman in the Photograph
The Curious Heart of Ailsa Rae
Lost For Words
The Other Half of My Heart
Letters To My Husband

Non-fiction

Thrive: The Bah! Guide to Wellness After cancer
How I Said Bah! to cancer

THE SECOND CHANCE BOOK CLUB

STEPHANIE BUTLAND

REVIEW

Copyright © 2025 Stephanie Butland

The right of Stephanie Butland to be identified as the Author of the Work has been asserted by her in accordance with the Copyright, Designs and Patents Act 1988.

First published in Great Britain in 2025 by
HEADLINE REVIEW
An imprint of HEADLINE PUBLISHING GROUP LIMITED

1

Apart from any use permitted under UK copyright law, this publication may only be reproduced, stored, or transmitted, in any form, or by any means, with prior permission in writing of the publishers or, in the case of reprographic production, in accordance with the terms of licences issued by the Copyright Licensing Agency.

All characters in this publication are fictitious and any resemblance to real persons, living or dead, is purely coincidental.

Cataloguing in Publication Data is available from the British Library

ISBN 978 1 0354 1605 9

Typeset in Baskerville by CC Book Production

Printed and bound in Great Britain by
Clays Ltd, Elcograf S.p.A.

Headline's policy is to use papers that are natural, renewable and recyclable products and made from wood grown in well-managed forests and other controlled sources. The logging and manufacturing processes are expected to conform to the environmental regulations of the country of origin.

HEADLINE PUBLISHING GROUP LIMITED
An Hachette UK Company
Carmelite House
50 Victoria Embankment
London EC4Y 0DZ

The authorised representative in the EEA is Hachette Ireland,
8 Castlecourt Centre, Dublin 15, D15 XTP3, Ireland
(email: info@hbgi.ie)

www.headline.co.uk
www.hachette.co.uk

For Lou,
my best friend

10 October 1990, London

April is holding a soundly sleeping baby in her arms when she opens the door. Lucia feels the love inside her double, treble, at the sight of them.

'Auntie L!' April says. 'I'm so happy to see you!' And then she hands baby September to her. She is just a few weeks old, and wrapped in the blanket Lucia knitted to welcome her.

Although Lucia has come to meet the baby, still the fact of her is the most glorious surprise. Her head is fuzzy, her skin clear, her nose the best little nose Lucia has ever seen. 'Hello, little one. Welcome.' Then she looks at her niece. 'Oh, April.'

'Isn't she the most perfect thing you have ever seen in all of your life?' April looks tired and her hair is unbrushed, but she glows with happiness.

'She's one of the two most perfect things.' It's twenty-one years since Lucia held April for the first time.

April leads the way up the stairs. The flat she shares with Rex, when Rex is around, is a tiny one-bedroomed nest of a place, and it might have been dingy, but April has decorated it with sequinned scarves and bright lamps. September has started to make little mewls and stretch her mouth. April sits on one end of the sofa, unbuttons the shirt she's wearing and holds out her arms for her baby. Lucia kisses the perfect little head before she hands her over.

'Should I make some tea?'

'That would be lovely.' April glances up from watching September at her breast. She seems so serene. Lucia exhales. This is what matters.

'You look so happy,' Lucia says.

April laughs. 'Rex is surprised too. I think I'm supposed to be an emotional wreck. But all I'm doing is sleeping when she sleeps and feeding her when she's hungry and it feels . . . easy. If she cries and she isn't hungry and doesn't need winding or a nappy change I just sing her a bit of Madonna.'

'I think that's exactly what the baby books say you should do. They might not specify Madonna.' Lucia thinks of when April was born, and how her sister, Mariah, had a long and difficult labour followed by a long and difficult transition into motherhood. Maybe it's just as well that she couldn't persuade her to come and meet this new baby. She puts a mug on the floor by April's feet, and sits at the other end of the sofa with her own tea. In the quiet she can hear September's soft breath against her mother's skin.

'How are things in Harrogate?' April asks.

Lucia says, carefully, 'Much the same.' The news of April's pregnancy was not well received by her parents and grandparents. It seemed to act like a magnet for all the anger and dysfunction of their family. Lucia has refused to have any part in it.

April shifts September so she is leaning against her shoulder. 'I'm not going to let them spoil anything for me,

Auntie L,' she says. 'I'm going to live my life. I'm going to do every single thing that I've planned. I'm going to finish my degree and go travelling and get an amazing job, and I'm going to share it all with Rex and September. If my parents don't want to be part of it then it's their loss.'

'Yes,' Lucia says. She looks at September, who is dozing again already, the skin of her eyelids so fine that the blue of her veins is visible. She thinks: *what a lucky child you are*.

April 2024

September uses her hair straighteners to tidy up the collar and cuffs of her uniform: it saves a bit of ironing and they're still hot, anyway, from sorting out her hair. Shaun says she looks like a sheepdog when she doesn't straighten it, and it's almost funny, but lately she's been wondering whether he was always so keen to point out what's wrong with her. Still, six of one and half a dozen of the other. She's threatened to bin his old band T-shirts often enough.

The banging on the door makes her smudge her eyeliner. There's only one sort of person who knocks like that: hostile, demanding. Maybe they learn how to do it at bailiff school. But if she hides and waits until they go, she'll be late for work.

September buttons her blouse, puts on some lip gloss and picks up her bag. She opens the door with a smile. 'I'm just on my way out, I'm afraid. And Shaun's not here.' She steps on to their scrubby front path and closes the door behind her. Debt collectors are like vampires: if you don't invite them in, there's nothing they can do to you.

But: 'It's September we're looking for.'

He's a smiling one, this one, but still twice as broad as September is, and a good head taller. Best to be nice.

'That's me. What's it about?'

The bailiff licks his thumb, riffles the grubby pages attached to his clipboard. Some debt collectors have iPads now. The paper makes her anxious. More anxious. There's something old-school about it, and that means not much of a chance of negotiation.

September hates that she knows enough about debt to think in this way. The thought of her parents flits across her mind; she closes her eyes against the memory of their careful saving, their horror of owing money.

'Moped, it says here. Three months behind on payments. Three hundred and ninety due today.'

'Moped? Are you sure?'

'I'm sure.' Of course, a bailiff is going to be used to people denying they've ever bought something. He might even expect it. But not only is September certain she hasn't bought a moped – Lord knows, she wouldn't be walking to work in all weathers if she had – but she hasn't seen Shaun with one, either.

She shakes her head. 'I promise. I don't know anything about a moped.' She hates that her voice sounds panicky.

'Not what it says here, love.' The man in front of her looks almost disappointed, as though such an obvious lie is a mark of disrespect to him, a deliberately lazy step in this dance they are doing.

September tries a smile. 'Look. This is the first I've heard of it. Honestly. And if I don't get to work I'll have nothing to pay anything off with, anyway.'

It's as though turning her smile on has turned his off. 'You should take this seriously, love.'

Her gut clenches. She's tempted, for a moment, to tell him just how seriously she takes it. How she wakes in the night from nightmares of choking. How she eats her discount cereal with water. That her boss at the supermarket thinks she's keen because she doesn't mind working an extra few minutes at the end of her shift, but really it's because if she goes out of the back door alone she can sometimes pull something that's still good out of the top of the rubbish storage bins, unseen. She's tempted to tell him how she doesn't know how her life has turned into this struggle; how she wouldn't have believed that it was possible to work and work and still feel as though everything you have is sliding away from you. That no matter how hard you try, you cannot seem to ever get on top of things.

But of course, September doesn't tell the bailiff any of this. Instead, she smiles again. He must realise that she means it this time; or maybe he sees beyond her words to how she's hurting. He sighs, rocks on to his back foot.

'Look, I'll put you down as a "no answer". But I won't be able to do it next time.'

September is so grateful at this small kindness that she almost cries. But she knows for a fact there's no point in crying. So she says thank you, and sets off down the road a little bit faster than is comfortable. She can't afford to be late for work.

It's one of those shifts with nothing to brighten it. A woman in a coat that probably cost more than September earns in a month tears her off a strip because they don't sell one particular type of potato. Before September got this job, she thought potatoes were only old or new. She knows better now, but she's pretty sure it's not worth shouting at someone about. A baby projectile-vomits in the jams and preserves aisle, and September is the one who cleans up after it. She doesn't get out of the way of one of their regular customers in time, meaning that he 'accidentally' rubs her breasts when leaning past her for a tin of marrowfat peas. The staffroom has a 'beware' board, with images from CCTV so the squeezers, feelers and other abusers can be avoided, though they never get barred.

But more than all of this, today it seems that no one has a kind word for anyone. Couples bicker as they shop; children run around screaming; wherever September parks a trolley or a cage on the shop floor, she is in someone's way. None of the colleagues she is friendly with are on shift. So September has nothing to do but think about how much she is earning, and how little it is compared to the money she needs to find to pay next month's rent and bills. Shaun doesn't have a regular job, though every now and then he gets a good run of gigs as a roadie, and when that happens, he's generous to a fault. And of course, there is the question of the moped. She didn't even know Shaun had bought it. She didn't know about the guitar he bought himself last Christmas, either, and he swore blind then that he'd never go behind her back again. So much for that.

This morning wasn't the first time September has spoken to a bailiff. It's a fact of her life that she is in debt and will never get out of it. But usually there's a way to manage it: a weekly payment that she can just about find if she gives up taking the bus, a raid on the scant amount of money that she's put by on the off-chance of being able to afford a haircut or a meal out on her birthday. But this time, she has nothing left to cut away or cut back on.

At least it isn't raining, September thinks glumly as she heads home. The April sky is bright and she walks slowly, kidding herself that she's enjoying the fresh air when really, she's putting off facing Shaun, and the discussion they need to have. She knows, from experience of their many conversations about money, that he will be infuriatingly calm. Calmness is something September once thought of as a good quality, but now she wishes that he would, just once, shout back at her. At least that way the air might clear, instead of clouding even more with ill-will and stress. 'It's not us,' Shaun is fond of saying, 'it's our situation. We're sweet, September, you and me. We're good, babe. It's just that life's a bit tough, yeah? We need to keep on and wait for the good times to roll. We've survived this long, haven't we? We've kept a roof over our heads?'

Once, September had loved Shaun's clear-eyed ability to see beyond their circumstances and remind her how precious their relationship was. Now, more and more, she thinks that a relationship that can only exist in either a vacuum or a place of no stress isn't really a relationship at all. Still, beggars can't be choosers. And he's a sweet man really, honest and true at his heart. They've just never caught a break.

When she opens the door, there's the sound of post scraping along the doormat, and her heart sinks. It can only be bills. She picks them up and adds them to the pile on top of the radiator.

'Hey,' Shaun comes through from the kitchen and takes September's bag from her shoulder. 'I thought I'd cook. Did you bring anything we could have for tea?'

September laughs. 'Milk and bananas.'

Shaun kisses her. 'Beans on toast it is, then.'

She sinks against his shoulder for a moment; the fact that she isn't holding up all of her own weight is a quiet pleasure. She breathes him in. It smells as though he's showered today, even if he has put his dirty clothes back on. She really wants to stay here, in this moment. But. 'We need to talk about the moped,' she says.

The clench-and-release of his muscles is almost imperceptible. 'What moped?'

September sighs and pulls away. She slips her shoes off. 'I got stopped by a bailiff on my way out today.'

Maybe it's the way she says it – she's too tired for blame, and all out of fight – that means she gets a straight answer, for once. 'I bought one a couple of months ago. Thought I could get some delivery work.'

'You put the loan in my name?'

'Sorry, babe.' He looks sorry. Properly sorry. 'I couldn't get it in mine. I thought I'd told you.'

'Well, you didn't. Because I haven't made any payments, and the bailiffs came. A hundred and thirty quid a month, Shaun? What were you thinking?'

'I just said. I thought I could get some delivery work.'

'And?' She touches his shoulder. This might not be so hard to solve. They can just let the moped be repossessed. That was what they did the time they bought the big TV, thinking that her Christmas overtime would be enough to cover it when the bill came in.

'I wanted to find the right time to talk to you about it. So I – I left it at my brother's.'

'Oh, God. How could you?'

Shaun sighs and doesn't reply. He doesn't need to tell her what happened next. His brother said he would look after it, and Shaun believed him because Shaun always wants to believe that his brother has really changed. Maybe Shaun's brother also thought, in that moment, that he had changed. September laughs, despite herself; she tries to remember that gambling is an illness. 'He sold it and put the money on a horse? Was it a dead cert?'

Shaun laughs, in the same not-laughing way as September did a moment ago. 'Apparently not.'

'Why didn't you tell me?'

'I didn't want to worry you.' He raises his arms: don't shoot me. 'I know I was stupid.'

September picks up the stack of bills. 'You're not the only one with their head in the sand.' She hears a wobble in her voice.

Shaun pulls her in, kisses her forehead. He takes the envelopes from her. 'These can wait, can't they? I'll make your tea.'

'I suppose.'

'That's my girl.'

September laughs. She'll be thirty-four this year. How long will she keep being his girl? 'Do you think we'll ever get ourselves sorted?'

'We seem pretty sorted to me,' he says. September watches as he goes into their tiny kitchen, takes a can of beans from the cupboard, then looks in all three drawers before finding the tin opener in the utensil pot on the worktop. Where it always is.

He can't really think the way they live is okay, can he? Even before the moped. Though she's the only one it's a surprise to. He just hasn't been thinking about it at all.

'I'm going to change,' she says, and he nods, clicks on the radio and gives a little bounce of delight when he hears Blur. Because she knows he isn't listening to her, she adds, 'Don't you ever get tired of all this?'

Four hours later, after beans on toast, a cup of tea for her and a can of cider for him, and a bit of reality TV that seems a lot better than their reality, September and Shaun are in bed. September is still awake. Beside her, Shaun is snoring in his uncomplicated sleep. September watches him and wonders how he does it. She's not sure whether she envies him or is furious with him. It's possible that it's both.

Knowing that sleep isn't coming for her any time soon – so much money, almost a week's wages, for a moped that they don't even have! – September goes downstairs, makes a cup of tea and sits down on the sofa with the pile of bills. There's nothing unexpected in the envelopes, just the usual statements: minimum payments due or sometimes overdue, and interest quietly ticking up. September does the monthly maths, subtracting her income from her expenditure, and works out that she should have thirty quid left over. That's before food; and before the moped. Still, it could be worse. It's been worse. She doesn't examine this thought too closely, in case it turns out to be untrue.

There's one unopened letter left.

The envelope is thick and heavy; if September knew anyone who was getting married she might have thought for a minute it was an invitation to their wedding.

But the name printed in the corner is that of a firm of solicitors. It's the second one she's had from Briggs & Associates. The first came in January, and she'd been scared when she received it. She had thought she must be in real trouble this time. Though if anyone had noticed her shoplifting, she would have been sacked on the spot, and anyway it had been months since she'd done that; since Shaun told her, when he had that cold he couldn't shake, that he'd rather get scurvy than see her lose her job over a bag of oranges.

When she'd opened that letter, her initial relief – no one was taking her to court – had been replaced by utter disbelief. The letter had read:

Dear Ms Blythe,
We are dealing with an estate of which you may be a beneficiary. Please send us any documents in your possession that relate to your birth and adoption, along with proof of identity (passport or driving licence). At this stage, copies will suffice, although if the matter progresses we will need to see and verify the original documents. You may also have relevant artefacts in your possession, in which case, please send detailed photographs in the first instance.
We look forward to hearing from you.

Then a scribble of a signature and beneath, 'Marina Mulhaney' followed by a lot of letters.

September had puzzled over 'artefacts'. The only thing she thought it might mean was the bracelet she was found with: impossibly tiny, a gold chain with a long gold plate and her name engraved on it. She had photographed it, front and back, and added those printouts to the envelope. There was no way she was letting the only thing she had from her birth family out of her sight.

Shaun had said the whole thing was a scam. September had laughed at the idea, and told him that if anybody wanted her identity and her shitty life they were welcome to it. She had photocopied the documents – such as they were – in the manager's office at work, addressed an envelope, and put it in the post tray. She had assumed she would hear nothing else.

But here she is, holding another thick envelope.

There's only one way to find out what it's all about.

September takes a deep breath and opens the flap. She unfolds the single sheet of paper, then closes her eyes to put the moment off a little longer. She didn't realise until now how much she was hoping that something – anything – would come of this.

The letter isn't what she was expecting.

No brush-off, no 'thank you and goodbye'.

Something else, entirely.

Dear Ms Blythe,

We wrote to you in January, when you were kind enough to provide us with copies of papers relating to your birth, adoption and identity, and photographs of a bracelet found with you.

We have now concluded our research and due diligence and would be grateful if you could come into our offices to discuss the matter of the estate of Ms Lucia Dawson of which you are a beneficiary.

Please contact us to make an appointment, and bring the originals of all documentation, as well as the bracelet.

Yours,

Marina Mulhaney

September folds the letter back into the envelope. Looking at it makes an old, old scar ache. She was abandoned when she was barely walking: found at a hospital in Nottingham. Her adoptive parents had told her this in a way that made her feel special, chosen, blessed: they had been unable to have a child of their own, but they had hoped, and on the day that they got the call from social services, they had seen a rainbow when they had looked out of the kitchen window, even though there hadn't been any rain. Her parents adored her, and she them: they had told her that if she wanted to look for her birth parents, they would help and support her. When she was eighteen, she had applied for her adoption file, not from any need for a family – she had one – but for the sake of knowing her own story.

The file was thin. And reading it, the important fact of her childhood became not that she had been a miracle given to loving parents who longed for her, but that she was a baby so unwanted that she was abandoned at a hospital; not even put into the care of a nurse, but left in the waiting area of an A&E for someone to find. When September read this, she imagined the screech of tyres as whoever left her there drove away. She read about how doctors, nurses, social workers had decided things about her, based on the quality of her clothing (high), the state of her teeth (good), the way she interacted (well, though she asked for her mama a lot). Someone had made a list of the words she knew: Mama, Daddy, Nana (assumed to be banana, which she ate very happily), woof, sun, bus. She liked to play with crayons. There was a note about how when others said their names and put their hands on their chests, Child A would put her hand on her own chest and say 'Bebemba'. Put together with developmental milestones and the bracelet in her pocket, it was assumed that her name was September, and she was allocated a birthday of 25 September, as she was found on 25 January. There were notes about how parents were looked for, connections sought out, but no one could be found with a connection to her and no one came to claim her. So she was put up for adoption.

Since she got her file – since she went through it, line by line, with her adoptive parents, who did all they could to reassure her that, whatever had happened, none of it was September's fault – September has tried very hard not to think about it.

Until now.

She tucks the letter into her bag. Whatever this is all about, it's nice to have something in your life that isn't the cheapest possible version of itself. She goes back to bed, where Shaun is still snoring. Her feet always seem to be so cold.

September makes an appointment to see the solicitor, three days from the day she received the letter, which she reads, sometimes, on her breaks, if there's no one else in the staffroom. She still thinks it's a mistake; it has to be. But she imagines inheriting something beautiful. Another bracelet, maybe, with diamonds along the chain, or the sort of china you see in period dramas, so fine you can almost see through it. Whatever it is, it will tell her that she was never forgotten.

That Thursday, she makes her way to the solicitor's office. It's a lovely day, and her shift finished at two o'clock. The bailiffs have been back twice about the moped, so she's in no hurry to go home; Shaun just keeps on watching TV, ignoring the knocking at the door. He has no ideas about how to find the money and is so unbothered that September wants to scream. Walking into town is a good idea anyway, in case there are any sales on and she can replace her work shoes, which have split along the side. 'Buy cheap, buy twice,' her adoptive mother used to say. September is glad, every day, that her mother – both of her mothers – can't see her now. Not that there's anything to be ashamed of in the way that she lives. She works hard, she does her best. But still. Her life is not the life she would wish for anyone's daughter.

The solicitors' office is on a street off Neville Street, and has a set of five stone steps leading up to a grand old door. September seems to remember from school that doors had to be this big, once, for women to get their skirts through them, though surely that can't be right. There are five bells; the third has the same name as the envelope. September rings it before she can think about it. She's buzzed in and makes her way up the stairs. The receptionist looks pleased to see her, in that professional way that September recognises from the times she has to cover the customer service desk.

She pulls the letter from her bag. It's got grubby at the corners. 'You sent me this.'

The receptionist – apparently you don't have to wear a name badge in this sort of customer service – unfolds the letter and reads it. 'You're September Blythe?' She looks at September, gaze searching her face, as though her name might be written on her forehead.

'Yes. I have an appointment. I brought my original papers, like you said.' September takes the file from her bag and holds it out. The bracelet is in her purse; she's holding on to it for now. The receptionist takes the file without opening it, smiles, and says, 'You took a bit of finding.'

'I assume there's a mistake. I don't have any relatives left. And anyway, I was adopted.' Her voice, unexpectedly, stumbles at the word 'adopted'. It's not as though it was ever a secret from her, just a fact of her life. She ploughs on. 'I mean, I suppose my birth parents could be alive. But I was—' September cannot bring herself to say the word 'abandoned' out loud – 'I was found on my own at a hospital. I'm thirty-three and no one has ever tried to find me. I've never heard of Lucia Dawson.'

She has said it 'loo-see-a'. The receptionist corrects her without seeming to, pronouncing 'loo-chee-ya': 'Lucia Dawson was one of our oldest clients. I'll see if Marina is ready for you. Please, have a seat.'

The receptionist disappears through a door. September hears the words 'Marina, she's here!' before it closes behind her. She sits down to wait. The chairs are comfortable. Everything smells clean. There's a low coffee table with magazines on it; they are all the current issues, and they look as though no one has opened them. September leaves them where they are and looks out of the window. The buildings opposite are just as grand as this one, with the same old-fashioned windows and built of the same uneven yellow-brown stone. September is comfortable and uncomfortable, all mixed up together. She will be glad when this is over.

Then another door opens and a woman about the same age as September erupts through it. She is all gleam and curve, from her black wavy hair to her emerald-green shoes, and as September stands to greet her she has the fleeting thought that no one has ever been as pleased to see her in her entire life as this woman is now. Marina beams a welcome. Her teeth are a perfect line. 'September Blythe!' She extends a hand, and September shakes it. 'Come through, come through.'

September says yes to coffee and then wishes she hadn't, because it's clear that she isn't going to be able to get things cleared up until the receptionist – Marina calls her Hilary – has made it. When it comes it's creamy and smooth, and there's a biscuit in a little packet on the saucer. The longer she stays here, the grubbier she feels. She's still in her uniform, which was clean on this morning, but a split yoghurt pot means she has a white mark on her thigh, and she can smell sourness coming up from it. She puts her bag in her lap.

'Well,' Marina says, 'I'm so glad you're here. I acted for your great-aunt—' September's face must say something, because she hesitates, 'What do you know about your birth family?'

'I don't know anything,' September says, channelling her best, no-sir-I-cannot-sell-you-any-more-alcohol voice. 'My adoptive parents died in 2014 and 2015. I was abandoned as a toddler. Social services tried to find my birth parents but they couldn't, so I was put up for adoption. I've always assumed that I wouldn't have been left if there was anyone in the family who could have taken me in.' She wonders how often she will have to repeat this – these four painful things, strung together like something as inconsequential as a shopping list – before she can be excused from this cocoon of comfort and plenty, and go back to her life.

Marina's gaze is fixed on September. 'That is a tough start in life. I'm sorry.'

'Yes.' September thinks about saying how she is lucky; she cannot remember anything before her life with her adoptive parents, she probably got a better deal with them, anyway. But she doesn't. Because it seems she had a family all along, and they chose not to keep her.

Marina continues, 'So you don't know anything about your birth family?'

'Nothing.'

'Nothing at all?'

'No.' September hears irritation in her voice. 'I sent you my adoption papers. That's all I have.'

'Right,' Marina says. She gets up from her desk and comes to sit in the chair next to September. 'First of all, I'm so glad we found you.'

September nods. Should she be glad, too? She supposes so. It seems it's too late to go back to being September Blythe who has one, occasionally rubbish, boyfriend. Except this previously unknown great-aunt, who is dead.

Marina takes a deep breath. She looks as though she might be nervous. 'I'm about to give you a lot of information. It might be a shock to you. You're my last appointment today, so we can take as much time as you need, and go over things as much as you need to.'

September nods. She is nervous too, now. This isn't going to be about jewellery, or a tea-set. It isn't going to be a mistake.

'I acted for your aunt. She was a lovely woman. Always immaculately dressed.' September curls her feet with their broken shoes under her chair, out of sight. 'She was smart up here, too.' Marina taps her temple, twice, then continues, 'She came to see us in 2020, after her older sister Mariah died. Mariah was a widow and she and Lucia had what are called mirror wills, where they left everything to each other in their lifetimes, and then they had a list of charities that would be beneficiaries when the surviving sister died.'

Marina looks at September. Something seems to be required of her. She says, 'My parents did the same thing. Mirror wills.'

Marina nods. 'When Mariah died Lucia became a very wealthy woman. She was anyway, in that she and Mariah shared their parents' estate. But Mariah and her husband were wealthy people too, in their own right.'

September hears Shaun, in her head, saying something about *the well-off sticking together* or *if you're born into it you're all right, Jack*. She brings her mind firmly back to what she's being told. Mariah. Lucia. A will. 'I still don't see what this has to do with me.'

'Lucia came to see me because she wanted to make a new will. She said she wanted to leave everything to her great-niece, September.'

'I don't understand,' September says. 'I told you. I was adopted because I was abandoned.' The words are bitter in her throat. 'No one came forward. No one came to find me.'

'Mariah was your grandmother. Lucia was your great-aunt.'

'But—' Somewhere deep inside September, the child left in the hospital A&E department in January 1992 starts to sob. Adult-September realises how cold she is, all through. She laces her fingers into a cradle. She waits.

'Lucia told me that there had been a rift in the family, not long after you were born. Lucia believed that your mother had taken you travelling. Her sister Mariah was – difficult – and

Lucia believed your mother had made the decision to take you and make a clean break. She was also sure that your birth mother and father had split up. She always hoped to hear from you, one day.'

'Hoped?' That feels like not enough effort. And then something else occurs to September. 'What do you know about my mother?'

Marina takes a deep breath and looks directly at September. She touches her arm. 'As I said, your aunt believed that she had taken you to start a new life—'

'No,' September says, 'that's not what I mean. I mean, is she alive?' She can tell immediately, from Marina's face, that she isn't. That there isn't going to be the smallest doubt. Suddenly she realises that the smallest doubt has sat in her heart for all of these years, a seed ready to spring to life.

'I'm sorry, no. She died shortly before you were found. In January 1992.'

'What happened to her?'

'The cause of death was meningitis.' Marina hesitates. 'I have her death certificate, if you want to—'

'No,' September says. Part of her whispers that anything, anything would be better than nothing, but she doesn't want a death certificate to be the first thing she sees of her mother. She realises that Marina is waiting for her to speak. She doesn't know exactly what she's going to say until it comes out of her mouth, but of course, it's the only question that her heart wants to be answered.

'What was my mother's name?'

'Oh, God.' Marina's eyes shine with tears. 'I'm so sorry. Yes. We think your father was called Rex – we don't know his surname – and your mother,' she steadies herself, 'your mother's name was April. April Alice Jane Merriwether.'

'April.' September starts to cry. Her name means more than the month she was born. It means a connection. It means belonging. It means – surely, it means being wanted.

'Do you want to stop?' Marina says. 'We can make an appointment for another day, or you can take a walk around the block, come back in half an hour. Do you want to call someone?'

'No,' September says. She wants to gobble down her history, as fast as she can. She wants to know. She wants to fill up the spaces that have been empty for thirty-three years. Her coffee is cold, but she drinks it. She eats the biscuit, for something to do with her hands, her face. She's shaking.

'It's a lot to take in,' Marina says.

'They thought my mother and I had – gone?'

'Yes. As I say, there was an argument. Lucia said it was on New Year's Eve of 1991. April said she was going and never coming back. Lucia tried to find you both – she went back to the place where you and your mother had lived – but then a box of your mother's things arrived at her parents' and Mariah took it as proof that she had gone off somewhere and would come home in her own good time.'

September bites back the questions: where did we live, where did we go, what was the argument about, why now? She thinks about the grandmother who said something so terrible that her own daughter, September's mother, left and never came back. September had four good, kind adoptive grandparents of her own, and she's grieved them all. They would have given her anything. And all the time, she had another grandmother, one who had money, and who was determined she should go unfound. The shaking grows. It's as though it's coming from her bones, her belly, her heart.

'When did she die? Lucia?' September says it carefully, correctly.

'In September 2022.'

'She had a lot of time to find me.'

Marina looks unsure. 'I feel as though you might have had enough for one day.'

September wills her shaking hands to stillness. 'No way,' she says. 'I want to know everything. Now. Please.'

Marina tells September how Lucia came to the office, not long after her sister died, with April's death certificate. Until then she had believed April to be alive and well somewhere in the world. She had thought that April had made a decision that she was better off without her family, though she hadn't really believed this until Mariah told her April had sent a box of her art and other possessions to her parents' house, for storage. At that point, Lucia said, she had accepted that April must have decided, for her own reasons, to sever contact with her family entirely. After Mariah's death, Lucia had found the box, and discovered April's death certificate in a sealed envelope in that box. The box had contained April's ashes in a wooden casket, and her identity bracelet, which matched September's.

Lucia believed that Mariah didn't know that her daughter was dead. Once she had absorbed the shock of the discovery – she had always hoped April would come home one day – she had wanted to know what had happened to September. She had asked Marina to find her. Marina spreads her hands. 'So we did.'

September cannot imagine finding a death certificate and a casket of ashes in a box. She hopes Lucia wasn't alone. She asks a question that she can cope with the answer to. 'But how? How did you find me?'

'Unusual first names are a bit of a gift. We have someone who traces people. Because we knew from Lucia that April lived in Notting Hill Gate and gave birth in London on the seventeenth of September, we had someone go through the birth records. Then we had them look for people called September of about the same age. Of course, if your name had been changed, it would have been harder.'

'Seventeenth of September?' It's as though she is becoming a new person, right here in this office. She has a mother with a name. A different birthday. She has always celebrated on the twenty-fifth, the birthdate on her adoption birth certificate.

Marina nods. 'Yes.'

'But Lucia died before you found me?'

'She did.'

'Why didn't you tell me all this in January?'

'This firm is named as the executor of Lucia's will, which stipulates that her estate goes to you, if you can be found, and if not, to her charities. So we had a legal duty of care to ensure that we had found the right person. By the way, did you bring the bracelet?'

'Oh – yes.' September takes it out. Marina goes to her desk and takes something from a drawer. She puts it on the table. It's another bracelet. It's bigger. It says, 'April', in the same script. Mother-daughter bracelets.

September picks up the bracelet that her mother must have worn.

Marina says, 'The hallmarks tell us they were made at

the same time, by the same maker. And they have the same lettering style.'

'So, you think it's definitely me.' September's voice feels – sounds – as though it isn't hers.

Marina nods. 'We do. I wouldn't have told you all of this otherwise. And,' she says, with a smile, 'you look like her. You have the same eyes.'

Before September can even begin to absorb this, Marina looks down at her hands, then back at September. 'And I know this is going to be another shock, but as you're the sole beneficiary of Lucia's will, you own a four-bedroomed detached house in Harrogate and all that it contains, and you have several hundred thousand pounds in the bank.'

September decides to walk from the station. Harrogate is the sort of town that's pleased with itself: there are fancy stone buildings and flowerbeds everywhere, and the tourists look every bit as delighted to be there as the buildings seem to expect.

She had hoped that Shaun would change his mind about coming, but he's remained steadfast in his position: he doesn't need to go and see a house that September is going to sell, and neither does she. It's funny – by which September means, it's not funny – that they have argued and bickered more in the week since she got the news of her inheritance, and her long-lost family, than they have in all of the eight years they've been together. Well, maybe they haven't argued more, but there's been an intensity to it, an unpleasantness, that September doesn't like. She hopes Shaun doesn't, either. It seems as though they aren't on the same side any more. Before, their rows were about managing their situation, mostly, about being tired and skint and trying to find their way along together. It isn't like that any more.

September checks the map on her phone and sets off. It's about a half-hour walk; there's a bus that gets her almost-there, but she wants to be quiet and think. Her route takes her along the edge of the town centre, past broad and leafy streets. The gardens are tidy, the doors painted in shiny dark blues and greens. The cars parked on the drives and by the kerbs have child-seats and bike-racks and generally speak to this being a good place for a family to be. Soon she comes to a park, which is called the Stray according to her phone, and heads across it. Lucia might have walked this way.

The entrance to Lucia's house – September's house – is down a lane on the other side of the Stray. The gates here are far apart and the houses barely visible; there are winding paths, trees in bloom, and a general sense of keep-away meant to deter passers-by from invading the privacy you can buy with a place like this.

When Marina told September how much the house was worth, the number had seemed impossible. It was almost ten times the price of the house she had grown up in, when she sold it almost a decade ago, after her parents died. And her childhood home had been a happy, solid, semi-detached house in a part of Leeds that the estate agent had described as 'desirable', in a way that had made September want the whole sale over with as quickly as possible. When Shaun asked her what the Harrogate house was valued at, she said she didn't know.

In deference to Lucia's reported immaculate dress sense, September has put on her best jeans, the blouse she saves for best, and the leather jacket that was her twenty-first birthday present from her parents, and still looks great. She bought a notepad and pen at the station, because this feels like the sort of day when you might need to write things down. There are going to have to be lists, September thinks, though she doesn't know what of, yet.

Unlike the other gates in the road, the one to number 5 is painted a cheerful orange. When September swings it open and steps into the garden, the first thing she notices is the smell. It's the scent of spring. It smells warm, and it smells . . . the only word September can think of, in that moment, is 'safe'. Which is ridiculous. But also feels true.

A gravel path leads September around the edge of a lawn, which is not square and scrubby with a set of football goals, like the garden she grew up with, but soft-edged and curving, with bushes and plants all around the border. It's a garden that begs for the sort of picnic you'd see on TV, with a hamper and red-and-white checked linen, and a white parasol for laughing under.

There are pink tulips under a tree. September doesn't know what sort of tree, but that doesn't matter. She steps up to it, placing her feet carefully so as not to squash the tulips, or anything that might not be a weed, and puts one hand on the trunk. Then the other. Then she leans her face against it. The tree feels – warm. Slightly scratchy.

The idea of owning a house is strange enough. But the idea of owning a tree – a tree that must be older than she is, a tree that has grown for all of these years without her – severs the last of any hold that September had on her emotions.

Tears start to run down her face. There's a cast-iron bench, painted white, on the other side of the tree and she sits down and gives herself to crying.

It feels the closest to grief that she's been since those first weeks after her mother died of a heart attack, less than a year after her father's fatal stroke. The tears come, and come, and keep coming, and September lets them. Her sobs are small and ragged, her breath not deep enough. She realises that she's on her own; that no one can hear her. Not Shaun; not the neighbours, who would bang on their thin party wall at any noise at all; not one of her colleagues, who might tap on the toilet stall door and say, *is that you, September? I'm right outside if you want to talk*. September never talked to them, though she said thank you, and meant it. There's no point crying over spilt milk, as her mother used to say. And she was right: there was no point in crying over things you couldn't fix. September was usually crying over how tired she was, how sick of everything being a struggle. She used to cry because her life would never be anything other than work and worrying. It wasn't as though she wanted to be rich. She just wanted the occasional night unbroken by anxiety, or to buy soft fruits, sometimes, even though you got twice as many apples for the price of four peaches. If she tried to talk to Shaun about these things or if her tears woke him in the night, he would soothe her; but then he would talk about how they had so much, each other and a roof and food on the table. September knew he wasn't wrong. And yet.

And now, here she is, sitting under a tree that is hers (she really isn't sure you can own a tree, or should want to, but still) on land that is hers, on which stands a house that is hers. She has hardly dared look at the house, except to note its solidity out of the corner of her eye. 'Georgian', Marina had said, as though that should mean something. Marina had shown her a picture which suggested that 'Georgian' meant square. It was a house from a book, with evenly spaced windows and chimney pots and some sort of plant growing up the walls. Marina had said something about roots and brickwork, but to September, the plant had been the best thing about the house. Imagine being so solid that a plant lives on you.

September cries for the fact that she will never have to cry about these things again. She cries because, sitting here, she knows she is safe.

There's a moment, half an hour later, when September puts the key into the front door and it won't turn, that she thinks it has all been a mistake – of course it's a mistake, this could never really be hers. But when she tries another key, the door – orange, to match the gate, with a knocker in the shape of a bumblebee – swings open, and she steps inside. September wonders whether she should take off her shoes, but she isn't sure where she would leave them, so she wipes her feet on the mat and steps on to the dark, polished wood floor.

The hallway is broad and long. There are doors leading off it, and a staircase that is not quite the sort you see in grand houses in period dramas, but definitely from the same family. There's a sideboard with a mirror over it, and an embroidered cloth on top. September opens one of the drawers and sees five pairs of gloves laid out in a row, all different colours. Another drawer contains a hairbrush, a stack of handkerchiefs and four lipsticks. September has never owned more than one pair of gloves or two lipsticks at a time, replacing them as they were lost or ran out. Then again, she's never owned a sideboard with an embroidered cloth on top and a mirror over it. She looks at her reflection, runs her hand through her hair, which has frizzed a little in the damp of the garden, and watches herself blink. This is all going to be very different. 'An adjustment', as Shaun said, though he said it as though he was having a dig at her.

September walks quietly through the house, barely aware when an hour has passed, and then two. She discovers that she owns a grand piano, which lives in a room that can only be described as a library. There's a living room (maybe she has to call it a sitting room or a parlour?) with three leather sofas and an unfeasible number of small, spindly tables, each of which bears a lamp. The kitchen is big enough to house a big, round table and four chairs, and there's a separate dining room. The kitchen has a door leading to a utility room that leads to a garage. September wonders how many motorbikes Shaun would put in there. Not that they are going to live here: that would be ridiculous. Upstairs are four bedrooms, two of which have their own little bathrooms; an airing cupboard which smells faintly of lavender – from the garden, September thinks; it doesn't have that air-freshener smell about it. It seems that there are more towels, sheets and duvet covers stacked here than September has owned in her entire life. Until now, anyway. There's a room that's lined with more bookcases, though these hold mostly files and papers, and contains a spiral staircase which September assumes goes into the attic. (This house feels too grand for a loft.) And there's a bathroom with one of those baths that have feet. Well, claws really, September thinks, as she sits on the chair and looks at it. (Who has a chair in their bathroom? Who has the space? And why? Do wealthy people have someone to sit next to them while they have a bath?)

She hasn't tried to count mirrors or pictures, which mostly seem to be paintings of some sort of nature or another. She hasn't opened any cupboards or drawers since the sideboard. It feels a bit like snooping, and anyway, she is having a hard enough job absorbing that she owns the outside of all the things in this house without delving into their contents. She closes her eyes. Even though she didn't know anything about her great-aunt – not even that she existed – this time last week, it's impossible to walk around the house without getting a sense of her. She imagines a woman who never wears trousers, who smells of something floral, who is kind to animals and goes to church. She is sure that somewhere in the kitchen there's a hand-written recipe book, that the books in the library are in alphabetical order.

When September has wandered through the house, downstairs and upstairs and downstairs again, she finds herself back in the kitchen. The cupboards there feel okay to open. They are mostly bare, though there's salt and pepper, a tin of tea bags, a cafetière and a teapot, and a shelf full of mugs so fine you can see the light through them. They are gold-edged and covered in flowers. If there's one thing – one manageable thing – that September knows for sure from today, it's that her great-aunt really liked nature, as well as books. Two things.

She takes out her phone to call Shaun, but the air feels so full of silence that she can't bring herself to touch his name on the screen. So she checks the balance of her bank account on her phone – the reception is terrible, maybe it's the thickness of the walls – and decides to walk to the supermarket that's two streets over, according to the map she downloaded. She dials Shaun as she closes the gate behind her.

'How's the great heiress?' he asks, when he answers.

She's told him she doesn't like it when he calls her that, but he either hasn't listened or hasn't remembered.

'I'm – I'm okay.' She's surprised by the wobble in her voice. 'It's . . . a lot. To take in.'

'Of course it is, babe. It's life-changing, isn't it?'

'I know. But it wasn't till I came here that I really got it, you know? In my belly.' It's the only way she can think of to explain it. 'Shaun, the garden. There are trees. I own trees.'

'Nobody owns trees.'

She laughs. 'That's what I thought. But you know what I mean.'

A sigh down the line. 'I know what you mean. So. Have you rung any of the estate agents?'

'Not yet.'

'I thought you were going to do it on the way.'

'I was, but—' September takes a breath, 'All of her stuff is in there, Shaun. Gloves. Tables. Towels.'

'So call a house clearance company. Actually, no, you should get some proper people. You know. Antique dealers. It's old, yeah?'

'Yeah. It's all old. But it's nice.'

'Course it is. I've been thinking. We can do all those things we talked about now, September.'

But September feels as though all they'd done until this last week was talk about how life never cut them a break.

'What things?'

'Buy motorbikes and do an American road trip. Get a guitar and some decent amps and a van for the band.'

'Pay everything off,' September says.

'Well, yeah,' Shaun says, as though it's barely worth mentioning.

'Buy a place, maybe.'

Shaun laughs. 'Buy two or three, by the sounds of it.'

September is outside the supermarket now. She is thinking of bedding that smells of lavender, the tree that held her up, a piano. 'I'm going to stay over tonight,' she says. 'Just to have a proper look round. My shift doesn't start until four tomorrow.'

September has been back in the house for half an hour when she hears the rattle of keys in the door and jumps up so quickly that the kitchen chair she was sitting on tips over. Her desire to run is overcome – just – by the need to stand her ground. This is her house. She is entitled to be here. And – an uncomfortable thought whispers in – if she runs now there is nowhere for her to go, except home, to Shaun.

So she walks down the passageway towards the front door. She is barefoot now. Already she knows that this house, its carpets, wood and tiles, will be kind to her feet.

The door pushes open, and September sees a figure silhouetted in the doorway. She reasons that a burglar is unlikely to have a key, and to be humming to themselves.

'Hello?' she says. 'Can I help you?'

The woman clutches at her chest, surprise propelling her backwards on to the step. 'Oh!' she says, when she has recovered enough to speak. 'I do not need to ask who you are. I see you are the relative of our dear Lucia. You have her eyes.'

Marina said that too. Until then, no one had ever told September that she looks like someone else.

Well, that's not quite true.

People who didn't know she was adopted said she looked like her mother; and she and her mother would smile at each other, secretly, as though they had played a great trick on the world.

But that is nothing compared to knowing what Lucia's eyes looked like, when she checked her lipstick in the mirror in the hallway.

Oh, how it hurts, to be so close to a living relative – to stand, literally, where they stood – and yet to have lived her entire life thinking there was no one living who shared her blood.

September starts to cry. Not a storm of tears; more an overflow of the well of sadness and strangeness that's inside her.

'Now, now,' says the woman. 'Please do not cry at me. I am Esin. I am Lucia's cleaner. May I come in?'

'Yes. Please.' September swipes at her eyes.

'Good, good.' The woman steps inside the house and stands, waiting; September realises it's up to her to lead the way. She walks back into the kitchen, wondering about the state of the soles of her feet.

'I didn't know there was a cleaner,' she says, sitting down. She has no idea of what she should do. Does she offer to make tea? Should she go out until the cleaning is done?

'When Lucia died, Marina asked that I would look after the house. She said Lucia left money to take care of it. Until someone comes for it. Have you come for it?'

'Yes,' September says, and then, 'I have.' Saying so makes her realise that it's true.

Esin takes off her coat and hangs it on the hook on the

back of the pantry door. She bows her head for a moment, and September notices that her dark grey hijab is fastened with a pin that is the same yellow as her dress. 'Always, it is a little difficult to come here, and to remember again that Lucia is not here,' she says.

September nods, though she is thinking of her childhood home, when her parents had died. 'I'm September.'

'I know who you must be,' Esin says. 'Lucia told me all about you, though of course you were . . .' she mimes rocking a baby, 'so very small, then. And your mother was April.'

'Yes,' September says. Her throat is closing at how easily her mother's name – a name she didn't know until a week ago – is spoken by Esin.

Esin nods. 'Your great-aunt, she missed you both very much,' she says.

September can feel the tears coming again, but she decides not to cry any more. Not here, in this old-fashioned kitchen where her great-aunt heated soup and made tea. Not now, in front of a woman who knows more of her family than September herself does.

Esin puts on an overall, then hesitates. 'I am sorry. Is it convenient for me to clean today?'

September, to her own surprise, laughs. It feels good; loud, in this quiet house. Rich people have it so easy. 'This is the cleanest place I've ever been. But sure.'

Esin smiles. 'This house has been lonely. The first few times I came, with no Lucia here, it was hard for me. So hard. But then Marina gave the permission for the book group to continue to meet here, and now I feel that Lucia lives on. And now, you have come, and I can see it with my own eyes.'

'Book group?' September asks.

'Yes, we meet every three weeks. We are Lucia's friends. When she was alive she would choose the books. She was a librarian, you know.'

September nods. But she didn't know. 'I don't read much,' she says, with a shrug.

Esin nods. 'Some of the others, also. Really it was an excuse to be friends, I think.'

September goes back into the garden. She scrolls through her phone and finds the documents Marina has sent her: deeds for trusts, deeds for the house, bank statements. It all feels – not even too good to be true. Too strange to be true. September can have anything she wants, now. Shaun is talking good sense, about selling this place and choosing somewhere together, but September sits on the bench under the tree and thinks: *I came here. When I was a baby I came here. My mother was here, and my grandparents, and my great-grandparents, and Lucia, who loved me.* That feels like too much to give up without a thought. She breathes in; it's the smell of her garden. Hers. There is barely any traffic. She hears birdsong, the sound of children in the garden next door. Perhaps she dozes, because the next thing she knows, Esin is standing in front of her.

'I have made dinner for us,' she says with a smile, 'because book group will be here soon. This is what I used to do with my dear Lucia.'

September checks her phone: it's 6 p.m., and she has a missed call from Shaun and another from Marina. Marina has left a voicemail which asks her to arrange to come in and sign some paperwork; September holds her breath as she listens to the message. She has to keep reminding herself that this inheritance, this family, isn't a mistake. And that it isn't going to turn out to have been a mistake. Marina has looked at all the information that she had from Lucia, and found the birth records of a baby named September born to a mother called April. She has discovered that only three babies named September were born in England in 1990; two remained with their families, the third was found in a hospital in Nottingham with an engraved gold identity bracelet. Electoral records led to September Blythe, who knew nothing of her history. And now two people have said that she looks like her aunt.

September doesn't really know whether she is hungry or not. Strangeness, excitement and overwhelm could all feel a bit like hunger. Since she met with Marina, September has made more meals than she has eaten, and lost all sense of what, if anything, she is actually hungry for.

On the kitchen table are two plates of beans on toast. 'Your aunt's favourite meal,' Esin says, 'though she did not know that I would put a little cheese between the toast and the beans. Just to give her a little bit of something. She was always so thin.' Esin shakes her head, smiling.

'*This* was my aunt's favourite meal?' September used to dream of a life that had no beans on toast in it. But now they fill her mouth with sweet warmth; they take exactly the right amount of effort to eat. For the first time in days, her stomach feels as though it's in the correct place in her body, and comfortingly full, and calm.

'Your aunt, she did not like things to be complicated. Quick to make, quick to eat, quick to wash up and be ready.'

September laughs. She wonders if this is what Shaun is

eating, too, though he won't have a knife and fork that feel as heavy in the hand as the ones she is using. The thought of him stabs at her, though she's not sure why. She'll call him back later.

Esin has arranged seven dining chairs in a circle in the library. September realises she will have no chance of going unnoticed. Also, though Esin seems kind and helpful, she has very clear ideas of what is and is not correct, and what Lucia would and would not have wanted: September decides against testing her by excusing herself from book group. September herself is certain that Lucia would have Strong Views on being hospitable to guests, and would have very little time for the idea that September still feels a little like a visitor in Lucia's – and, very possibly, her own – life.

Esin shoos September away from her preparations. She is laying out biscuits on plates, bringing jugs of milk and cups and saucers from the kitchen.

'I can do everything. Except—' she looks uncertain for the first time since she came through the front door.

'Except?'

'When everyone comes. Will you want to say something? An introduction? Everyone will want to know about you.'

Just the thought of it is enough to make September want to lock herself in the bathroom until it's all over, but then she reminds herself that this is her house, and that these people were her great-aunt's friends, and that she may as well get all the awkwardness out of the way in one go. Her heart quakes at the thought of so many more people who might say she looks like Lucia. 'Of course,' she says.

Esin nods. 'Sit, sit,' she says. 'They will be here soon.'

September chooses a chair close to the window, so she can look out over the spring sky if she gets bored. Which she probably will, because she hasn't read the book they are going to be talking about, which is called *The Color Purple*. She has a feeling that her mum might have read it, but her parents used the library, so there were no books for her to clear out from their home. There's a copy of the book on the piano stool, and she reads the first page, which is a letter to God about some sort of horrible abuse. And September is no academic genius, but she knows that it's spelt 'children', not 'chilren'. The words 'modern classic' are on the cover. No, September just doesn't get what's so great about reading.

She closes the book and looks out over the garden. She can see the top of her tree from here. There are so many shades of green in a garden.

It seems as though everyone arrives in a clump. The room goes from quiet to full in moments. September smiles at everyone as they come in, and they all say hello, and September tells herself, *They are only people, like me*. Esin brings in a teapot and a coffee pot and two jugs of water. Everyone helps themselves to drinks and biscuits, and they start to settle themselves into chairs.

A man who introduces himself as William takes the chair next to September. His skin is dark, his eyes brown. He smiles as though he means it. He's wearing a pin-stripe suit, white shirt and blue tie, and his shoes are polished. September notices that the shoes are old but the laces new. They exchange a few words and then he goes quiet, watching September, who goes back to looking at the tree. William clears his throat. 'Ah, the ash,' he says. 'I'm watching it for dieback. And that lawn.' He shakes his head. 'Terrible for daisies.'

September is about to ask what's wrong with daisies when Esin stands and the room settles to quiet.

'Well,' Esin says, 'when I came to the house today I found the September that our dear Lucia looked for. She is here!' She beams, and September takes this as her cue.

She stands, and then immediately wishes that she hadn't. Six serious pairs of eyes regard her. She takes a breath, straightens her shoulders, and imagines that her mother – her adoptive mother – is listening. Which may be a mistake, because now she is full of the urge to cry.

'Hello,' she says. 'My name is September Blythe. I just found out that Lucia,' she remembers to say it properly, 'was my great-aunt and she left me this house. I don't know what I'm going to do yet.' She's about to sit down when she realises everyone is waiting for her to say something else. 'I'm glad you're all here,' she says, 'you're very welcome. If you can help me to learn about my aunt I'd be very grateful. I'm a bit . . . to be honest, I'm quite lost.'

She sits down. William, next to her, says, 'Your aunt set up this book group. She made a long, long reading list and she died before we read everything. So we kept going. We think she would like that.'

September nods. Then he adds, 'I have known Lucia for a long time. I cared for the garden when she was alive and I have been doing it still.'

'Thank you,' September says. She's not sure whether she's grateful for the garden or the kindness in his face.

A young man with sprawled legs and a goatee goes next. He's wearing jeans and a hoodie; his trainers are immaculately white. 'Zain. Lucia got in touch with my school and said there was a piano here if anyone wanted to come and play it. No room for a piano at my place, man. No room for me, most of the time. She said I should come to the book group, so I did. I mean, I do. I was fifteen when I started.' He shakes his head at the idea of his own youth, though he seems like a child to September.

'Dan,' says the man/boy next to him, who has a similar sprawl but a slighter frame. He's wearing a black shirt, black trousers, black sliders. His hair is long and tied back, his eyes wide-set and brown. 'Same as Zain. Me and him are going music college together. After A-levels. Our teacher said we could count book group towards our Duke of Edinburgh.'

William laughs, and says to September, 'The only reason to be in a room full of old people.' September smiles, in a way that she hopes isn't going to make Zain and Dan feel slighted.

'I'm Johnny,' says a man in jeans and a check shirt who looks as though he's always expecting it to rain. His hair is short and wavy. His skin is pale and September thinks of how easily he would burn in the sun. He could be anything between thirty and fifty. 'I did some valuations for your aunt when she cleared her sister's house, and helped her to clear it out.' He pauses, as though deciding whether or not to say what he's thinking about. September likes how everyone waits. 'It was a hard time for her. But she was still so kind to me. People aren't, always, when they are bereaved.' He shrugs. 'I suppose she adopted me.'

September feels herself flinch. 'I was adopted,' she says, before she can stop herself.

'Ah,' Johnny says, looking at her with a serious expression.

His eyes are a washed grey. 'Then I'm sorry. I should have said, she made me feel welcome. Like part of a family.'

September nods. She doesn't trust herself to speak. People talk about adoption as though it's a trivial thing, and they shouldn't, because it isn't. Especially if you've spent more than thirty years of your life not knowing where you came from.

Esin is next. 'We have met, and talked a little, but I do not think I said that Lucia was my first friend when I came to this country. Until then it seemed that everyone else saw first that I was a Muslim, and many of them thought that I was a terrorist. But really I was afraid. Only afraid. Lucia helped me.'

She looks at September expectantly. September reaches for something true and says, 'I wish I had known her.' Her words might have an edge that she doesn't intend, because Johnny looks at her with a question on his face.

'I'm Kit,' says a young woman in jeans and a crumpled white shirt with its sleeves rolled up. She has perfect eyeliner and dark brown hair cropped short, which shows off her chunky silver earrings beautifully. September feels dowdy, even in her best top. 'I used to volunteer at the food bank and so did Lucia. She saw that I had a book in my bag and she invited me to this group. That was four years ago.'

That's all of them. 'Thank you.' They all look at each other for a minute, and then Esin says, 'So, this time, William chose *The Color Purple* by Alice Walker.'

William clears his throat. 'When this book came out, my wife read it. It made her weep. I read it too. It made everything we went through in this country feel . . .' he shakes his head. 'The woman in this book, she was treated so badly. And so were the Black folks around her. I think at first it made us feel we were lucky. But then we talked more and we realised that disrespect is disrespect.' William looks at his hands. 'The way that we were treated in this country made us people we did not always want to be.'

Kit clears her throat. 'But you were the victims.'

September is surprised by how heated the discussion gets. Dan, who is studying sociology as well as music, argues passionately for the story to be seen in context; Esin says that context doesn't excuse anything. Johnny wonders how much of a fairy tale the novel is: even though a lot of bad things happen, there's something like a happy ending that might be unlikely. Kit says that only a straight white man would think a novel in which a gay Black woman is raped, beaten and oppressed for the best part of thirty years before catching a break is a fairy tale. September holds her breath, but Johnny only laughs and says, *fair point*. Kit smiles at him. September is, for a moment, back in her childhood home, listening to her parents and their friends arguing about something; she would sometimes sit on the stairs and listen, half-afraid and half-fascinated, as words like 'solidarity' and 'sellout' and 'power' were thrown around with what felt like fury. Then, someone would make a joke or go to put on the kettle, and the tension would be broken, and September's mother or father would find her on the bottom step and say, *Go back to bed, darling, we're just working out the best way to save the world*.

William talks about how things have changed, but not so long ago as you might think. He has marked a passage in which a Black character notices, with surprise, that when she went to a white family's house she ate and drank from the same china that they did; he reads it out, and then recalls how there were times when he first came to the UK when he was given second-class things, and expected to give way to white people in all sorts of ways. 'Even at school,' he says, shaking his head, 'there were parents of my friends who would not have me in their house.' September tries to do the maths. If William is, say, eighty, then he'll remember things from the 1950s or 1960s. Finally, Zain observes that for an old white lady, Lucia had a lot of books about Black people and being Black. Next to September, William coughs and blows his nose, the books are put aside, and September realises she has a little stretch of headache across her eyes, where she's been concentrating. She hasn't worried about a single thing during the discussion. Except how a woman named Celie, who actually only exists on paper, was treated by her father and her husband, and whether Celie would ever see her sister again.

When everyone else has left, September and Esin wash up the cups, saucers and plates. 'I'm surprised there isn't a dishwasher,' September says.

'Oh, no. Lucia liked to do things with her own two hands,' Esin says with a smile.

'Except, she paid you to clean?'

'Ah,' Esin is still smiling, 'but after book group, we would stand, just like this, the two of us, and wash and dry. And anyway, things like this, they are too delicate for a machine.'

September already dislikes the china, which is covered with overblown roses and leaves. And it can't even go in a dishwasher, when she gets one. She also dislikes the pans, which are heavy, and the kitchen table, which has drawers under the surface that she banged her knees on when she sat down to her beans on toast.

And then she thinks: *I can replace it all. I can just replace it all.*

Esin empties the sink, rinses it, and wrings out the dishcloth and lays it over the tap. 'There!' she says, pleased. 'We are done. Johnny says I should add you to the book group WhatsApp.'

Esin's phone is nicer than September's. That's something else she can do something about.

And suddenly – this keeps happening – September is tired enough to weep, sad enough to want to slump in a chair and never get up. Maybe Esin sees this in her. She looks September full in the face, touches her shoulder. 'I am glad you are here,' she says earnestly, as though she thinks September may not have believed her when she said so earlier.

And now, September does cry the tears that almost came when she opened the door to Esin. It's loss and gain and tiredness; new life and grief for the fact that the people she should share her good fortune with – her parents, Shaun – aren't here to experience it with her. She cries in fear and in anxiety; in the relief of never having to worry about having a place to live again. She cries because all of these people at the book group knew her great-aunt better than she, September, did, and that seems so very unfair.

Esin takes September by both shoulders, then hugs her in. She murmurs words that September does not understand, but knows as comfort. When her tears stop, September pulls away and says, 'Thank you.'

'You are welcome,' Esin says. 'To cry is important. To mourn.'

'But I didn't even know Lucia.'

Esin touches September's face. 'And that is why you are mourning. You can mourn for what you did not have.'

It looks as though Esin might say something else – looks as though she might cry, too – but instead she takes her palm from September's cheek, smiles and leaves.

September is alone.

She doesn't sleep in the main bedroom, which feels too occupied, with a hairbrush on the dressing table and a wardrobe full of clothes. She wonders at a life that requires having three different straw hats, and two little ones (blue and black) with nets.

She makes herself comfortable in the other bedroom with an en suite. The bed is made up; she takes towels from the airing cupboard and a hot-water bottle from the cupboard under the sink, fills it and slides it between the cold sheets. She has peeked into the most likely looking cupboards and cabinets downstairs, but none of the rooms seem to have a TV, so she brings *The Color Purple* to bed and decides to see if she can understand what all the fuss is about.

And then she sleeps. Oh, how she sleeps.

Shaun has been looking up houses that border the Stray with the dedication of an estate agent trying to win a competition. 'So much money!' he says, over and over. He's studied the photos of the house on September's phone. 'And then, whoever buys it will probably just gut it and start again, new kitchen and all that. How the other half live.'

'It's nice the way it is,' September says. 'I mean – old fashioned . . .' Shaun is watching her, waiting, but she doesn't say any more. Because it would sound as though she was knocking their life if she talked about sofas that you sank into and baths deep and long enough to be truly relaxing and the patterns the tiles on the kitchen floor make.

Shaun says, 'Or it might make sense to convert it into flats. I mean, big, posh flats. If we made it into three flats then sold them, we could double our money. Treble it.'

September closes her eyes. Everything is different. Or is Shaun the same? She isn't sure. They've never had to deal with anything this big before. 'I just don't know.'

He comes close, kisses her forehead, touches her face. 'I know, love. It's a lot to take in. And a lot to do. But you can let me help. We're partners, yeah?'

She wants to say, *we weren't partners when you bought a moped in my name and didn't tell me*, but that would sound petty. And anyway, partner or not, it's not as though Shaun knows anything about converting a house into flats. It took him three goes to get the shower rail straight. Well, straight-ish. 'Marina said she'd help me to work things out.'

Shaun makes a face. 'A solicitor you've known for ten minutes? What does she know?'

'Well, she knows the . . . the legal things.'

'And she'll charge you for it.'

'Don't be like that,' September says. 'Marina's really nice. And anyway –' she almost doesn't dare say it, '– what things cost doesn't matter now, does it?'

Shaun rolls his eyes, but then he grins. 'Money no object. That's my girl.'

Then, because she doesn't have the energy to cook and now she has the luxury of not cooking, she suggests they get a takeaway.

* * *

Since that night of blissful sleep in Harrogate, September feels as though she hasn't had a moment's rest. She's covering shifts for someone else's holiday at work this week: when she signed up for it she was so pleased to be earning extra money. She still is. Sort of. But everything has got complicated, and even though she is tired to her bones and aching for rest, as soon as she closes her eyes, she starts to think.

And to wonder.

Is it possible to sell an entire house with the contents still in it, so she never needs to go there again? What if she rented it out and had the extra income, which would be like having a job she never had to show up for? Then, before she's got to the end of the logistics of that thought, her mind bounds off in another direction. What if she lived there? And she imagines herself, taking a book from the library, sitting on the bench under that tree, reading. Sometimes, in her imaginings, there's a dog curled up beside her, dozing in the sun. Her parents had always said no to a dog, on the grounds that it was too expensive. September had thought that was crazy: what difference could tins of dog food and the odd visit to the vet make? Now she knows what living on a budget is like, she understands. Sometimes, if she's lucky, she can drift off in that moment when she's imagining herself, the tree, the book, the dog. More often, a noise in the street or an especially loud snore from Shaun jolts her back to wakefulness, and she's thinking of all the things that Shaun is talking about buying. He's sent her links to drum kits, amps, a guitar, a van, a motorbike, another motorbike – 'we don't have to have the same one, so long as they've got about the same size engines' – a TV with surround sound and a games console. Also, oddly, a set of pans and another of Japanese knives, which appear to cost more than the moped did. 'I've always wanted to learn to cook,' he'd said when she asked him about it. She'd wondered what was stopping him now. They had beans on toast, or microwaved baked potatoes with tuna, when he cooked; and they had pans already, good enough to cook pasta, which September usually did, or an omelette, which Shaun considered 'too much faff'.

September lies awake and thinks about all of these things. She tries to imagine her and Shaun in the house at Harrogate, but she can't seem to make him fit in there. She feels bad, for a moment, but then realises that it's just that it's not his kind of place. She doesn't think he would like the quiet. Dogs make him nervous. He might want to convert the garage into a recording studio and invite his musician mates around. They're not awful, but she has nothing in common with them. And if she objected to any of it, she knows he would turn it against her. He already has, when they've argued: *It was all about the two of us when we didn't have anything, but now you're the one who makes all the decisions?*

Most of all, though, what September thinks about is Lucia, and how she couldn't find September when she was alive.

And then she will turn over, and try not to think of the parents who raised her. It still hurts, to miss them. And she knows what they would say about the house if they were here to ask. 'Just do what's right.' Which is no help at all. September's father had worked for local government; her mother had helped out in a friend's shop. But their life had been all about the things they did outside work. September remembers going on marches, hoisted on her father's shoulders, waving a flag even though her arms were tired, because she knew what they were doing mattered. She spent her weekends helping to sort jumble for church fetes and sitting behind trestle tables in shopping centres while her parents and their friends tried, earnestly, to persuade passers-by to sign petitions for this and against that. When they died, there weren't many savings to speak of – they had always believed in giving their money to charities. But September had the money that was left over from the house sale when the mortgage was paid off. She had enough for a deposit on a place of her own but she couldn't get a mortgage, so she rented, and her savings leaked away.

Her parents would have known what to do with a fortune. But here's the thing: although September knows that there are so many people in the world worse off than she is, she really likes the idea of being able to spend money, and not worry, and be comfortable. She doesn't think that makes her a bad person. Just a person who has never had much of anything.

In the end, the only thing that helps her drift into sleep is making mental lists of all the things she's going to buy, once she and Shaun have decided what they're going to do and where they're going to go. Top-of-the-range hair straighteners. Three pairs of jeans and a new leather jacket. Maybe a car. She might get her teeth whitened. Shaun says she can get the three weird moles taken off her stomach, because they freak him right out. And she can definitely afford a dog.

'I think,' September says the next evening, 'we need to look at what we owe. So we can pay it off.' She uses the word 'we' deliberately; if Shaun came into money and excluded her, she would be really hurt. Maybe that's why things have been so weird. For the eight years they've been together, they have never had money to spare. Even moving into Shaun's place came about because September couldn't manage when her landlord put the rent up on her little studio flat. She'd loved having her own tiny space, where everything had a place. She had been able to walk from her home to work, as a receptionist at an ad agency, in twenty minutes. She'd loved her job, too: the way serious-looking people with expensive sweaters spent a day talking about ideas, and sent out for coffees and lunches, and when they had agreed on what they would do, they would shake hands and hug and everyone would be so delighted. Granted, their ideas were to do with things like refreshing an orange juice brand or persuading people to buy a particular sort of bike; but after all the years of helping her parents to create world peace or solve global hunger, achieving anything at all gave September a buzz. She misses that job, still: misses helping people, misses working with people she likes. There will be no need for a job now, though.

She'd met Shaun when she was working at the agency. He was part of a team setting up for an event, and she'd noticed how tall he was and loved that he wore bright green Doc Martens when everyone else was in black from head to toe. He'd had a wicked twinkle in his eye when he looked at her, and his hair was back in a ponytail. They'd hit it off straight away. She'd fallen for his easy-going ways: the fact that he thought it was okay to live outside the rat race charmed September. She had thought, with a pang, that her parents would like him, because he didn't much care about what they used to call 'trappings'. When she'd explained to him, on one of their first dates, that her job didn't pay much but it had good prospects, he'd shaken his head and said, *Screw prospects: the question is, do you like your life today?*

September hates to admit it, but she hasn't liked her life much, since she heard about her inheritance. Taking control of things is bound to help. 'I thought if we paid everything off, that would be a good start.'

Shaun nods, though he seems a bit hesitant. 'Everything we owe? Me as well?'

'Of course.' Love rushes through her. As though she would ignore his debts. She takes his hand. 'Let's deal with this. Then we can work out what to do.'

'What do you mean, what to do? We can't go and live in Harrogate.' He says it with such scorn that she almost laughs. But instead, that tide of love rushes out of her as swiftly as it rushed in.

'Well, I'm sorry that my massive inheritance is such an inconvenience. I'm sorry having options for the first bloody time in our lives is such a burden to you.'

'All right, all right,' Shaun says, and gets up off the sofa. He says something that might be 'La-di-da' as he walks into the hallway, but September decides to ignore it. She's got out her notebook and written 'Debts' at the top of a page. There isn't a lot on her own list, but it still mounts up. She bought her hair straighteners and her winter boots from a catalogue, and her credit card is only for emergencies but there seem to have been a lot of them lately. Most of her outgoings, though, are her contribution to the rent and bills. She pays slightly more now than she did when she lived in her little studio; earns slightly less, except for when there's overtime. She dreads to think how people without a partner are managing. If they are. She knows she's not the only person at work who turns a blind eye to the shoplifting of baby formula, tampons, other small things that all add up. She reasons that the expert shoplifters – the real criminals – are the ones that you don't notice. The ones that you see slipping something into a pocket are the desperate, and she isn't going to make things any worse for them.

Shaun comes back into the room, carrying an old satchel that September has never seen before. He looks something akin to nervous. 'Don't lose your mind, babe,' he says as he sits down next to her. 'We're all doing our best, yeah?'

'Of course,' she says.

Shaun upends the satchel and a cascade of envelopes covers their laps.

'Your filing system's terrible, Shaun.'

He doesn't laugh.

She starts to put the envelopes into piles, but he interrupts her. 'You need to look at these first,' he says. He's taken the sheets of paper from the envelopes. British Gas, London Electricity, Thames Water. He passes them over.

They're statements. September doesn't understand. The amounts on them are lower than anything she's paying Shaun. 'Shaun—'

'When you moved in,' he said, 'I hadn't had a lot of work and I didn't realise how much I'd been spending. So when you said you wanted to pay towards the bills I—'

'You thought I may as well pay them all.'

He nods, though he won't look at her.

She waits for him to say something else, but he doesn't. He just looks at his hands.

So September waits to feel something new: some revulsion, some distress, some fury. But instead, it's as though everything around her deepens. The sense of discombobulation that she seems to have been breathing in since the day she went to the solicitor's office grows. Nothing in her life is what she thought it was. Nothing in her life is what it should have been. This is just another one of those things. She feels herself sink a little further. Surely, given her inheritance, she ought to be rising?

'And the rent?' she asks.

'What about it?'

'How much is the rent? Do I pay it all?'

Shaun nods again. He still won't look at her.

'So where is all the money going? I take two slices of bread to work for lunch some days, Shaun, and if there's anyone else in the staffroom when I eat it then I pretend it's a sandwich.'

'I'm sorry, babe.'

She shakes her head; she's not so much rejecting his apology as refusing this entire situation. Not Shaun. They have never been love's young dream but she thought she could rely on him. She wonders when the pain will hit.

'What have you done with the money? You must have had a lot left over. Seeing as I'm paying all our rent and more than the cost of our bills.'

He hands her another stack of papers. 'Credit cards. I was in a hole when you moved in and I thought I could get out of it. But—'

He owes thousands. Tens of thousands. She scans. Minimum payments, every month. But also . . . ah. Here comes the fury. 'You told me your mate gave you that leather jacket because he's gone vegan. Three hundred quid, Shaun. That's thirty hours of me filling shelves and answering questions about bloody food miles and, if I'm lucky, getting an hour on the tills so I can sit down.'

He takes her hand. She lets him. It would be petty not to. 'I just – I didn't know how to tell you. I got so used to . . .'

'To lying.' The words come out harshly. She shakes her notebook at him. 'I thought twice about buying this bloody notebook, Shaun. I owe forty quid on some hair straighteners and it really worries me. I told you when I got my boots from the catalogue so I could pay for them on credit.'

'I know, September. I'm so sorry.'

Again, that harsh laugh that doesn't sound like her, but it must be. Shaun looks as though he's about to cry. 'Not sorry enough to get a job. You've watched me go to work, all these months and years, and you've got your cash-in-hand and your here-and-there work because you want to be free. When do I get to be free? Once I've paid off the moped that your brother put on a horse?' Something else strikes her. 'Oh God, Shaun. You've been gambling as well, haven't you?'

'Not the way Adam does.'

'Am I supposed to be grateful?'

'No. I'm not asking you to be grateful, babe. I know I've done wrong and I'm asking you to forgive me. And this is a fresh start, isn't it? We'll be millionaires! We'll look back on this and it'll seem stupid. Something to tell the grandkids.'

September snorts and gets up. Enough is enough. 'You haven't even wanted to get engaged. And now we're having kids, and they're having kids? Come off it, Shaun.'

He takes her by the shoulders. 'It's just that . . . pressure's off, isn't it? I can see more clearly. I've been worrying about all this, September. It's been getting to me.'

She thinks of him, sleeping through the night. 'No,' she says. 'No.'

Lucia, 1967–70

Lucia has always loved Harrogate library. It is high and wide and has a carving of cherubs on the front; it has places to sit and read if you don't want to go home yet; and she could never quite get over the fact that you were trusted to take books home, read them, and bring them back. She got her first library card at the age of seven. Of course, she used the school library, too; but that was part of her education. The books she took out of Harrogate library were just to please her. She could read adventure stories that her father, Jacob, thought she was too old for, and Jilly Cooper novels that her mother, Alice, would have told her she was too young for.

When Lucia left school at the age of eighteen, she dragged her feet about going into her father's office for a 'try out' as a secretary and instead applied for a job as a library assistant. She got an interview. And then – she felt as though her whole body fizzed when she got the letter – she got the job. Her parents congratulated her, though they seemed puzzled about why she wouldn't have gone to work for her father. 'You do seem determined to make life difficult for yourself,' her mother said. She wasn't just referring to Lucia's working life: she despaired of her ever having a steady boyfriend, and clearly thought there was something odd about Lucia's assertion that she would rather be on her own than have a boyfriend for the sake of it. Lucia had been on some double dates with her older sister Mariah and whichever boyfriend she was seeing. 'How did it go?' Alice would ask Mariah when they got home. Mariah would roll her eyes and say, 'She asked them what their favourite book was.'

It wasn't that Lucia disliked the young men she went out with. She just liked books more. She loved the sense of possibility that came with opening the cover. It was wonderful, the way time flew past as she read. She even liked the way library books smelled, sometimes of cigarette smoke, sometimes of flowers, as though they had been kept in a handbag where a perfume bottle had leaked. Lucia's mother would wrinkle her nose and say, *We would buy you books, you know. You could buy them yourself, now you're working. Or you could read the ones we've already got.* But Lucia would rather a library book, any time; it made her feel as though she belonged, part of a chain that linked to the reader who had just returned it and the one who would borrow it next.

So a job at the library was perfection. She got to know the regular customers, the popular books. She recognised the girls from the years below her at school as they came in to study, and she always did her best to help them. Her colleagues were kind and hard-working, and mostly older than her; she felt as though they treated her like part of their families. She even went on some dates with men she met at the library. Her mother was palpably relieved when that happened and said things like, 'Well at least he will understand you.' When these relationships ended, her mother seemed resigned, as though Lucia was an impossibility when it came to men. But Lucia didn't want to be married, if marriage was the bad-tempered tolerance that her parents had for each other; when Mariah got engaged to Richard, Lucia was even more certain that marriage wasn't for her. Mariah seemed to be in a state of constant annoyance with Richard, who was clearly besotted with her, but appeared puzzled by a great deal of what she said or did. Some of her friends on the library staff seemed happily married, but Lucia couldn't imagine such a thing for herself. It would be like having only one book to read for the rest of your life.

And then came Billy.

It starts quietly, gently.

The man on the other side of the enquiries desk – the same height as Lucia, she notices first, then that he is smiling, dark-skinned, wearing a sports jacket and a trilby – would like to join the library. He is especially interested in books about planes and the history of the RAF. Lucia gives him the form and a pen and, when he returns them both – the pen re-capped, the block capitals careful and strong – she writes out his library card.

When he thanks her for her help, she looks into his eyes and feels a small 'oh!' ripple through her: enough to make her startle, not enough for losing sleep. When he comes back, a week later, she makes a point of saying hello, and making sure he had liked the books he'd taken the week before. He says he did, they were very helpful, and then he asks her for her name. She gives it, with the oddest feeling of never having spoken her own name before now: it is full of promise, in her mouth.

And so it continues, gently, gently, until one day, four months on from that first encounter, Lucia is in the dingy basement staffroom with her soggy tomato sandwich when her colleague Peter comes in and says to her, quite matter-of-factly, 'Your man is here to see you.'

She blushes and thinks about protesting, but she finds that she likes the idea of Billy being 'hers', even if it isn't true. And when she goes up to the foyer he is holding a bunch of yellow carnations, and when he hands them to her he says, 'Lucia, I would like to know if you would do me the honour of having dinner with me.'

Their first date is, at first, if not exactly stilted, then at least halting. Lucia is afraid to ask too many questions about his life, his background, for fear of sounding racist by accident. She herself lives in a mainly white world of her parents' church friends and her own school cohort of Harrogate Grammar School. Her colleague Celeste at work, who is Black, has matter-of-fact stories of people touching her hair without asking, and strangers on buses asking where she is *really* from, as though 'Harrogate' cannot possibly be the true answer. When news of Lucia's date spread through the library staff, Celeste had told her of the three restaurants where Billy was likely to take her 'because he will know where to go so you don't get stared at or God-knows-what in your food'. Apparently a lot of white people don't like to serve Black ones, something that makes Lucia feel ill. So their date begins with Lucia determined not to do or say anything that might make Billy uncomfortable. She has read *Bird at My Window* by Rosa Guy, a novel about a Black man from Harlem who wakes up in a mental institution, which has confirmed to her that racism is something that she has only the most simplistic understanding of; and *Of Love and Dust* by Ernest J. Gaines, set on a plantation, and so full of oppression that it gave her nightmares about drowning in heat and earth. But she doesn't think Billy has brought her here so she can explain to him what she thinks being Black is.

Billy throws her a lifeline, asking her where she lives; she tells him here in Harrogate, with her parents, her older sister having just got married and moved out. 'A little more space, hey,' Billy laughs, and Lucia says, 'Well, yes,' but then adds, because already she knows that she wants this man to know only the truth about her, 'It's a big house. We were all rattling round anyway.'

Billy shakes his head. 'We are like peas, all squashed in,' he says. 'Rent is expensive, and more expensive for Black folks, and we get paid less. So . . .' He shrugs, smiles, a 'what can you do' expression on his face. 'But my mama, she says that even if we all rich as kings, she like us all at home, where she can keep an eye on us.' He laughs, slapping the table, and then they are talking about siblings and parents, expectations and constraints, and at the end of the evening, Lucia wonders whether she has ever spoken so freely or been heard so thoroughly. Billy had seemed to understand that when she spoke of her frustrations with her parents, her difficulties with her sister, all amplified by Mariah's recent wedding, she wasn't trying to be unkind. She was just telling the truth. Lucia has not realised, until tonight, that her mother's 'if you can't say anything nice, don't say anything at all', has tied Lucia's tongue. Not because she wants to say horrible things. Not that she wants to be unkind. But, she realises as she talks to Billy, looks into his serious eyes, it has always been her mother who has defined what is a 'nice' thing to say. She thinks, as Billy puts his hand over the bill and shakes his head at her, that even if she never sees this man again, he's given her such a gift by letting her say what she thinks and what she feels, as though her opinions are easily as worthwhile as those of her parents and her sister.

When they leave the restaurant, Billy tucks her arm into the crook of his elbow and walks her home, through the quiet streets, to her gate. He holds her face, kisses her mouth, and says, 'Lucia, I think we should do this again.'

'Yes,' she says, and she smiles and pushes her mouth upward for another kiss: she understands, in this moment, why books call this kind of longing hunger. When she gets to the front door she looks back and he's there. He waves, she waves, and she's glad her parents have already gone to bed so that she can go to sleep without having to answer their questions or hear a blow-by-blow account of what they've watched on television.

Yes, falling in love is as easy as apples.

At least until Lucia introduces Billy to her family, two months later.

She had met his parents, uncle, two brothers and sister the weekend before, at a teatime that involved eight of them around a table, a lot of laughter and passing of plates, and Billy's mother saying that Lucia needed to get some fat on her bones, and Billy's father, presumably in an attempt to make things feel smoother, laughing and saying that a mother could do a lot of things for her son but she couldn't tell him where to love. Lucia had blushed to her fingernails; Billy had squeezed her hand and given her a smile that felt all the sweeter for being just for her in a room full of others.

Sunday lunch with Lucia's parents, and Mariah and Richard, is a different thing altogether. No one is, technically, rude. But Lucia is shame-hot at the way her parents behave around Billy. She had wondered about whether she should mention that his parents were from the West Indies, that he was Black; but then she thought, *I wouldn't warn them if he was white.* And therefore, she thought, to tell them that he was Black would be to betray him, somehow.

Her mother gives a little 'Well!' of surprise when Lucia shows Billy in. He has brought her mother flowers, and she takes them, and tells him that he looks very smart in his suit, in a tone of mild surprise. Her father asks him which church he goes to. Billy says that he doesn't, much, though he helps at a church youth group, and that his parents are Pentecostals, and her father says 'of course, of course' in a tone that is both sympathetic and dismissive. Richard asks Billy what line of business he is in. Billy says he is working, for now, in his uncle's car repair business, but he hopes to go into the RAF. Richard says that's a good choice for a chap like him. And just when Lucia thinks she couldn't be any more mortified, Mariah leans over and asks Billy what on earth he sees in her boring little sister. 'I think Lucia is the best person I have ever met,' Billy says, without smiling. 'She is so kind and clever and she thinks about everything. She is determined. And of course, she is beautiful.' Mariah rolls her eyes.

After coffee, Billy excuses himself – the youth club he helps at is on Sunday afternoons – and Lucia walks him out. 'I'm so sorry,' she says, as they stand by the ash sapling in the garden.

'You have nothing to be sorry for,' Billy says gently, taking her hand. 'People are people, is all.'

She watches him walk down the street, his back straight and his shoulders broad, his hands in his pockets.

And Lucia takes a deep breath and goes back into the house, full of all that she has to say to her superior, condescending family. But she doesn't get the chance.

'Why didn't you tell us?' her father asks – demands – as soon as she steps through the door.

'Tell you what?'

'Don't be difficult, Lucia. You know what your father means.' Her mother's mouth is sour.

'I want to hear you say it.'

'Oh, do grow up, Lucia,' Mariah says.

Lucia crosses her arms and waits.

Jacob sighs. 'Why didn't you tell us you were seeing a – a coloured chappie?'

'Why does it matter?'

'It doesn't,' this from Alice, 'but it would have been nice to have been . . . prepared.'

'Ah. So you were only rude because you didn't have a chance to disguise your racism in advance.'

Her father takes on the expression that – the thought flashes in and out of her mind so quickly that she barely registers it, though her cheek muscles pinch with the effort not to laugh – he so often wore during Mariah's teenaged tantrums. So this is what answering back feels like! It feels like power. No wonder Mariah has always done it. He says, 'I am not racist! I played a round of golf with Charlie just the other day, and his mother's from Bangladesh.'

'Oh well, that's fine, then.' Lucia resolves to ask Billy if the youth group need any more help. She has better ways to spend her Sunday afternoons than listening to her parents' nonsense.

'You see?' her mother says. 'This is what happens, Lucia.'

Lucia doesn't know where to start. So instead she says, 'I'm going to go and read.' They can do their own washing-up for once. As she goes upstairs to her room, she hears Richard say, 'I thought he seemed like a good sort,' and Mariah respond, 'Oh, do shut up, Richard.'

Between fifteen and twenty-five teenagers attend the youth group, roughly equal numbers of boys and girls, black and white. That's Lucia's first impression, anyway. Afterwards she realises she has put the Korean children in the same category as the ones whose parents are west African, and she cringes at herself. Billy is one of three volunteers – four, if you count Lucia. For the first few weeks she doesn't feel as though she is much use at all. The vicar begins by welcoming everyone. His wife puts out drinks and biscuits: squash in jugs, pink wafers and rich tea. Billy and an earnest-looking white man named Miles arrange games: usually something physical, tag rugby or continuous cricket, after which they might get out the playing cards and play rummy or twenty-one. Then the record player comes out. The vicar allows any music the kids bring in to be played, so they listen to the Beatles, Otis Redding, Tom Jones or Diana Ross and the Supremes; he monitors the dancing, though, and switches off the music if he considers it inappropriate. Some of the kids sit around a table, with homework. At the end of two hours, everyone helps clear the chairs and tables away.

After three weeks, most of which Lucia has spent making

small talk with Melanie, the vicar's wife, while washing up glasses in the cramped kitchen, she plucks up the courage to walk over to the homework table, and sits down. Everyone stops talking when she does. 'Don't mind me,' she says. The conversation starts up again: the group is talking about *Ring of Bright Water*, which they have to read for school, and just don't get. 'I've read it,' Lucia says. 'It's about a man who moves to a Scottish island and works with wildlife, isn't it? Maybe I could help?' She's immediately hit with a deluge of questions. The first one is, 'What's an otter?' The second, 'Why can't we read books where proper things happen?' She asks what other books they are reading. There are poetry collections and Shakespeare's *Richard III* and *The Merchant of Venice*. No one seems to be enjoying any of them. Lucia says she will help, and goes away and re-reads the plays in her lunch hours over the next week. Soon, book discussions are a regular part of the youth clubs. 'You do great work with them,' Billy says, one evening as he walks her home.

'I know,' Lucia says. 'But all I'm doing is making school less awful. I wish I could make them love reading.'

They are at her gate. Billy takes both of her hands and smiles. 'If anybody can, you can.' And then the kissing starts, and Lucia forgets everything except the shape of Billy's body against hers and the way the skin on her neck feels when he slides his palm along it.

She consults her colleagues about books teenagers in Yorkshire might actually want to read. They come up with a list. First, there's *A Wrinkle in Time* by Madeleine L'Engle, in which adolescents travel through space and time to rescue their father and fight darkness. There's often a lot of discussion of the previous evening's *Doctor Who* at youth group, so Lucia thinks it will go down well. Then there's *To Kill a Mockingbird* by Harper Lee, a tale of racism and discrimination in the Deep South. Lucia had wondered about it but was worried about the fact that it dealt with a court case following an alleged rape; but she gives it to Billy to read, and he says he thinks it's a good choice, and what he's learned from her is that books are a way to talk about difficult things. *The Owl Service* by Alan Garner, which has just come out, is judged to be the right kind of scary for adolescents; Lucia confesses to Billy that she slept with the light on while reading it, and he kisses her nose and then says he knows exactly what she means. *The L-Shaped Room* by Lynne Reid Banks is about teenage pregnancy and community. Lucia buys ten copies of each book. There might come a time when she has to watch her money, but for now, she keeps all of her wages for herself. Now, every week, she and the group race through the homework questions so that they can talk about their reading. The vicar asks her if she would like to have a reading group on a separate evening; so on every other Thursday, she and Billy go to the church hall, and he sets out the drinks and biscuits while she sits with the group, answering questions, asking opinions, teasing out answers. Every now and then she catches Billy's eye and thinks of how he will walk her home and they will kiss in the dark of the quiet streets.

Between Billy and her readers, this could be the happiest Lucia has ever been.

Meanwhile, Billy is working on his application to the RAF. When he talks about his future career, she feels achingly proud of him. When she thinks of him in the great, wide sky, she aches again, but with worry.

Lucia's parents have a busy social life, and so it's easy for her and Billy to spend time alone. At first, she had thought about sneaking him in, but – especially now that she knows all of the difficulty he and his family have to put up with, the overt racism and the passing slights – she is ready to stand up to her parents if she has to. She was horrified when Billy told her how he was ignored in a cafe until he got up and left; how his mother is asked not to touch fruit at the market; that his neighbour's child has been put in the bottom set at school even though he gets top marks in every test. Billy refuses to hold her hand in the street, because he says he wants her to be safe. She's noticed the way people look at them, sometimes, with curiosity or hostility, and she knows he's right, though she thinks maybe they should be braver. And then one lunchtime when he meets her outside the library he has a black eye. When she asks him what happened, he will only say, 'White boys who think they are something.' Lucia is twenty-five, for heaven's sake, and if her parents start any 'our house, our rules' business then she will stop cooking and washing-up and they can see how they get on. But in the event, they only look mildly pained when she says Billy is coming for supper. She overhears her father saying to her mother that 'at least we know Lucia will behave herself', and although she's annoyed by this, they're right.

She and Billy have progressed from kissing to touch; she loosens her blouse, he his shirt, and she lays her head against his smooth chest, and he strokes her breasts through her bra and kisses her shoulders, which makes her melt. She touches him through his trousers, feels the pulse of him there. But anything more scares her. She thinks she would be able to keep out of trouble, but even so. Four months ago, no one had so much as kissed her. But by the time her parents come home, either Billy has left, or they are washing up together in the kitchen, or sitting side-by-side on the sofa, doing a crossword.

Billy has a successful interview for the RAF in August. He will start his training on the first of October. His parents throw a party. Lucia is overwhelmed by the sheer joy and pride in their house: the back-slapping, the singing, the utter delight. Of course, she feels these things too – that is, when she is trying not to think of what this might mean for her – but to see them expressed so freely is almost painful. When she told her parents he had passed his interview, on the other hand, her mother made the slightly pained exhalation which is her standard response to any mention of Billy, and her father said, 'Well, well.'

It's the middle of August when it all changes.

Billy has been quiet with her, at the youth club on Sunday, at book group on Thursday, though he has walked her home and they have kissed the way they always do. She is so hungry for more that she almost can't bear it, sometimes; then, when she goes to bed, she touches herself until she shudders. She has wondered whether she has been quiet too: whether the thought of their impending separation is weighing on both of them. Billy's training could take him anywhere. To begin with, he'll go to RAF Swinderby in Lincolnshire, almost a hundred miles away, for six weeks of basic training. After that will come training postings, most likely at RAF Halton, almost two hundred miles away, for anything up to a year. And after that, depending on the aircraft he specialises in working on, he could be sent anywhere in the world – Gibraltar, Taiwan, Germany, Cyprus. Until he is married, he'll live in barracks. Billy has said how he knows Lucia will be a wonderful letter-writer, and she has joked about needing a passport to come to see him, but they haven't really talked about what his new job means. Lucia cannot bring herself to start the conversation. She doesn't want to spoil anything for him. Sometimes, when she is sleepless, she wonders whether she should have been braver, and could have gone – could still go – to university, move away from home. Whether if she were stronger he would want to be with her more. But the fact is, she loves her job in the library, as Billy will love his in the RAF. Maybe they are incompatible, for practical reasons: life, she reminds herself sometimes, is not like it is in books. But a part of her whispers, *what if it was, Lucia? What if you and Billy are a fairy tale?* After all, despite the griping anxiety about the future, she wakes up happy, she goes to sleep happy.

That Saturday, she leaves getting ready for her dinner date until late, because she's more than half-convinced that Billy will cancel. The unfortunate result of this is that she's still getting ready when Billy arrives to pick her up. She finishes drying her hair as quickly as she can, blots her lipstick, and then ladders one of her stockings in her haste to rescue Billy from her parents. When she gets downstairs, the three of them are standing in an awkward triangle in the kitchen. Her mother reaches out a hand, as though she wants to stop Lucia from going, but she only says, 'Take a scarf. The evenings are getting chilly.'

'My mama, she say the same,' Billy says. 'Mothers know.'

And then they're walking through Harrogate in the warm September evening. Billy takes her to the place they had their first date; Lucia is surprised, because he's confessed since that he finds Italian food boring.

Once they've ordered, Lucia leans over the table and says, 'Please, Billy, tell me what's wrong. Did my parents say something just now?'

Billy shakes his head and smiles. 'Nothing wrong,' he says. 'I'm just a bit nervous, is all.'

And then she knows exactly what he's going to say.

He goes down on one knee. The restaurant falls silent. And Lucia sees the smallest bit of uncertainty in his eyes as he smiles. *He really doesn't know what I'll say*, she thinks. *He really thinks I might turn him down, but still he's at my feet.*

'Lucia—' he says.

And, because she loves him, because she wants this, and, more than anything – *so this is what love means*, she thinks – she doesn't want her darling Billy to have a moment of worry if she can help it, she says, 'Yes!'

There's a round of applause and laughter from the other diners, and Billy opens the velvet box that's in his hands. But all Lucia can think about is his face, his darling face, and how she will look at it for every day of her life, and so every day of her life will be like a birthday. She puts her hands on either side of his jaw and kisses him; nips at his bottom lip with her teeth, and laughs as his hands find her waist. 'My girl,' he says, 'my dear, sweet Lucia.'

The engagement ring that he's chosen is a fine gold band with tiny emeralds formed into the shape of a star. It fits perfectly; it seems like a miracle, until she remembers the girls in book group a couple of weeks ago saying that she should wear more jewellery and offering her their rings to try on. Lucia hadn't thought much of it at the time; they were always giving her advice of one kind or another. She should learn to drive; if she dyed her hair blond she would look cool; she'd got good legs, she should get herself a miniskirt, she's not too old. She takes it all in good part, although she does wonder what age the girls think she is: obviously more than twenty-six. Or it could be that, to them, twenty-six is ancient. Anyway, the surreptitious ring fitting had gone unnoticed. 'They are all very excited to see you tomorrow,' Billy says, with a twinkle.

Lucia laughs. She cannot stop looking at the sparkling ring on her hand. 'Does everyone in Harrogate know?' Then her heart, which has been somewhere above the rooftops, bumps back into her body: 'Have you talked to my parents?'

Billy takes her hand. 'Of course I have. What you take me for?' He laughs. 'My mother told me I had to do it right, and I did.'

'What did my father say?'

Billy shakes his head. 'He gave me permission. It was not what you would call a resounding yes, but he said he thinks I am a good man despite my situation, and he would not stop me from asking you. He even shook my hand.'

Lucia nods; this sounds like her father. 'Your situation? I'm sorry.' She wants to say, 'I'm sorry, darling,' but she feels too shy. Billy calls her 'sweetheart' sometimes, or 'my flower'.

Billy shrugs. 'I been called worse than a situation.' He takes both of her hands. 'You know marrying a Black man might not be easy?'

Lucia shakes her head. 'I can't imagine anything easier than being married to you.'

Lucia's parents are in bed when Lucia and Billy get home; Lucia makes coffee, loudly, in the hope that she'll wake them and they can just get the whole thing over with. She and Billy kiss in the kitchen, pressed hard together, and for a wild moment Lucia imagines sneaking him upstairs to her bedroom, letting him out before the sun rises. But he leaves just before midnight, and Lucia goes to bed and lets her thoughts leapfrog over her parents, a wedding, and to a place where she and Billy are in their own bed in their own home and nothing else will matter in the world.

'You said yes, then,' her mother says, at breakfast. She takes Lucia's hand and examines her ring. 'Well.'

Her father says, 'He's a good chap. It's a shame.'

Lucia laughs. The giddiness of last night is in her blood, and it makes her brave. 'It's a shame he's Black, or it's a shame he's marrying me?'

Her mother rattles the teapot as she pours, and says to her father, 'You see? I told you this would happen.' Then, to Lucia, 'Don't think you can have a wedding like your sister's.'

Lucia has no desire for such a thing. Mariah's wedding was a year of arguments and tantrums in the making; it seemed to be the sole topic of conversation in their house, and Richard the least important person in it all. The day itself Lucia remembers as an onslaught of all the people her parents knew, all at once, and all of Mariah's friends, who considered Lucia as below their notice as Mariah did. Now she thinks back, everyone there was white. Lucia imagines her own wedding. Maybe she will wear a minidress, and carry yellow carnations, and get married at Billy's parents' church.

Mariah arrives and says, 'Billy? Really? Well, beggars can't be choosers, I suppose. At least you've found someone. Let's see your ring.'

Lucia stretches out her hand. 'Sweet!' Mariah says. 'So

tiny!' She holds out her own hand with its great trio of diamonds that had belonged to Richard's grandmother.

'At least mine isn't second-hand.' Lucia knows that her sister and her mother will be raising their eyebrows at each other behind her back. Well, let them.

It's when Billy gets his first posting that the trouble begins in earnest. He's going to be based at RAF Halton to begin with. When they get married, they'll get RAF quarters. Lucia is breathless at the thought of it. To be with Billy, all the time, to have a home of their own, where they can put cheerful posters on the wall, rather than miserable landscapes. They can have floor cushions and Lucia will make macramé holders for plants. Her parents do not approve of macramé, or indoor plants, or indeed, cheerfulness. She'll have to hand in her notice at the library, of course, and the idea makes her heart hurt. Her lovely, lovely youth group will be a miss. But she will be with Billy. That's what matters.

Lucia's mother is less sanguine. Before too long he'll be working and she'll be at home, in a place she doesn't know, with nothing to do all day. According to her mother's version of events, she'll be fat, or an alcoholic, or both, before a year of marriage passes, and Billy will quickly come to regret marrying her. Lucia knows that for her mother – who tries on her wedding dress every year on her anniversary, and parades around the house as though forcing her body into a thirty-year-old shape is an achievement – the threat of weight gain is the worst thing she can come up with.

She has argued that, when they are living on an RAF base, Billy is likely to go to work and come home just like anyone else would – he's an engineer, she keeps telling her parents, not a pilot. And if he's posted away from her, then she will manage. She'll be with other women in the same situation. She stops herself from saying, *at least I won't be here*.

Anyway, if there are no jobs to be had in the local library when they move, she might work in a shop. She's good at helping people. But when she mentions this to her parents it's as though she's proposed that she might take up prostitution. Of course, these sorts of attitudes are exactly what she wants to get away from. There's no shame in work. And if her parents are worried about her being lonely when Billy is at work, they can't be horrified at the idea of her having a job. Except, it seems, they can.

Billy's parents are warm and welcoming. But Billy's mother has a sad look in her eyes when she looks at Lucia sometimes. Lucia plucks up the courage to ask her why. 'You are choosing a hard life,' she tells her. 'I can see you and Billy love each other, but you do not know how it is. Has anyone shouted at you in the street yet? They will. White people, they won't talk to you, and Black folks they look at you strange, and you will be in the middle, and you belong nowhere.'

Lucia feels her throat close. 'I belong with Billy,' she says.

Billy's mother gives herself a shake, and smiles. 'Of course, of course. I just afraid for you, is all. You don't know what your life will be, child.'

She tells Billy about this conversation. Billy shakes his head and says his mother just worries. Lucia ignores the voice that says if both of their mothers are worried, maybe there's something to be worried about.

They decide to hold their wedding at the church which hosts the youth groups. When Lucia tells her mother she wants it to be a small wedding, her mother says comfortingly, of course she does. This makes Lucia want to get married in a cathedral and have the wedding on television.

And then Lucia tells her family, one Sunday lunchtime, that they've set a date, and the onslaught proper begins. There's a moment of silence so complete that it's as though it's been freeze-framed. And then there's an exchange of glances that Lucia might have found funny if Billy had been there, rather than helping his brothers fix the wreck of a car they had bought. Mariah looks at Richard, then at their mother, who then looks at their father. He finishes his mouthful of roast beef, puts down his cutlery, and clears his throat.

'Lucia,' he says, 'we know you're very fond of this chappie—'

'Billy,' Lucia says. She doesn't know whether her father can't remember Billy's name or just chooses not to use it, but she's not going to put up with it. He continues as though she hasn't spoken.

'—and, I have to say, he seems a good sort. Honest. When he came to see me about marrying you he was very correct. Made his case.'

'He is good. And honest. I don't know why you think he wouldn't be.'

Again, it's as though she hasn't spoken.

'But this is all going too fast. You simply can't rush into marriage like this.'

'I don't think it's a rush.'

'I know you don't, Lucia, that's very clear,' her mother says, 'and of course you think it's the right thing now. It must be very exciting for you. Very – exotic. But it simply doesn't make sense to rush at it like this.'

'I like Billy,' Richard says. Everyone ignores him, except Lucia, who nods at him. He risks a smile back.

'Would you rather I went away with Billy without us being married?'

Mariah laughs. 'You wouldn't dare.'

Their father clears his throat again. 'It seems to your mother and me that if this chap is all you say he is, and if you feel the way you do, then there can be no harm in waiting.'

'Waiting for what?'

'Waiting to see what happens.'

'What's going to happen is, we're going to get married.'

Mariah touches the back of Lucia's hand, just below where the emeralds catch the light. 'I know you can't believe it now, but marriage takes work. The better you know each other, the easier it will be.' Lucia thinks of biting back at her sister, *Of course it's hard, being married to you, I've never heard you say one kind word to Richard – let's ask him how marriage is*. But, because Mariah seems to actually be sincere for once, she doesn't. But then Mariah adds, 'And anyway, you need to think about children.'

'What about them?'

'Don't be obtuse, Lucia,' her mother says.

Mariah says, 'If you and Billy had children, they would be—'

'What would they be?'

Mariah looks at Richard. 'You see? You take her side, but there's no talking to her.'

Lucia rolls her eyes. She doesn't see why Mariah should have the monopoly on it. 'I'll tell you what my children will be. They will be beautiful. They will be loved.'

'But the truth is,' her father says, 'they would have a hard life. They would be treated as second-class citizens.'

Lucia knows she's going to cry, and that she isn't going to do it here. She stands. 'Who would treat them as second-class citizens?' she asks. 'You lot?'

Mariah starts to cry. Lucia regards her suspiciously: Mariah's tears are rarely for anything but effect. But these look genuine. Richard reaches out and takes her hand, something else that suggests this is real emotion on Mariah's part: any such intimacy is usually frowned upon by her parents, whom Lucia has never seen touch, unless you count an accidental brushing-past or being side-by-side in a church pew. 'I'm sorry,' Mariah says, something else almost unheard of. 'It's my hormones.'

Billy goes away for basic training, and Lucia writes him letters, and hangs around at home at the times when he has said he'd try to call. She is glad of work, and of the youth group; she writes to Billy of how she is helping the kids with university applications and recommending additional books for the students who are keen to do well in their exams. It's not often that she thinks of her own decision not to go to university; once she had accepted her parents' arguments for it not being necessary, because she had no need to better herself and she would never need a career, she had put the very thought of it out of her mind. It creeps back now, though. Lucia finds herself fierce on behalf of the children around her, their potential and possibility if only someone can help them to get on the right road. The fact that no one did it for her makes her want to scream. She reads *I Know Why the Caged Bird Sings* by Maya Angelou, an autobiography in which the author develops into a formidable young woman despite the racism in her life, and *Fire from Heaven* by Mary Renault, a novel about the young Alexander the Great growing into his power. She buys copies for the book group, in the hope that it will keep their fires alight.

Missing Billy is a thrum of discontent deep within Lucia, but at least his being away has stopped her parents using his every visit to try to persuade her out of her marriage. Lucia only takes her engagement ring off when she does the washing-up or takes a bath. She cleans it with solution she bought from the jeweller. Whenever she mentions her wedding, her mother says, 'Let's get Mariah's baby out of the way first,' as though one cannot happen at the same time as the other. Lucia suggests that if it's an issue she and Billy can marry before the baby is born, but everyone seems to think this proposition is both hilarious and ridiculous.

Billy had made Lucia promise that she would go to see his mother while he was away. The first time, Lucia is almost afraid: the delight with which she is welcomed by Billy's family throws her off kilter, used as she is to being considered the most disappointing member of her family, whose arrival is usually greeted with 'oh, it's only Lucia'. But only his mother is at home, and she makes coffee that she stirs condensed milk into, and sits on the sofa and pats the space next to her. 'Sit by me, child,' she says, and when Lucia does – the worn springs of the sofa mean their bodies roll together, and they laugh – she has a bright, sad moment of wishing she could live in this house instead of her own big, stiff-furniture home. The moment was so shining that she cried; and Billy's mother said, 'Hush, now, he be home soon,' and she cried all the more for being so comforted, even if the meaning behind her tears was misunderstood. Since that day Lucia has felt confident knocking at the door; she's noticed that her footsteps travel to Billy's home quickly, and are much less willing to carry her away again. She cannot wait for her and Billy to have a place of their own.

Billy's first leave is strange; but, Lucia decides, it was bound to be. Three days together after three months of longing is too much to be able to manage; they are stilted, at first, and when they go back to their restaurant there is hardly enough conversation to sustain them through three courses, and they leave before coffee. Lucia's parents are away, on their annual week in the Cotswolds with their friends Roger and Daphne. Lucia brings Billy home, and asks him to come to bed with her. He rolls his eyes, exhales. 'You are killing me, sweet Lucia,' he says. 'But I think we should wait until we are married.' Lucia knows she should be pleased, but she feels longing prowling in her, the way it did when she read *Story of O*: it's a book that library patrons sidle up and ask about under their breath, and having read it, Lucia sees why. She didn't like it, exactly – she has no desire for the sort of strange sex games she read about in its pages – but it did make her long for sex for herself. Why is she always waiting for something?

Billy completes his basic training, has two weeks of leave, then moves to RAF Halton near Aylesbury, and comes home for the occasional long weekend when leave allows. Lucia is always so very happy to see him; always oddly disappointed while they are together; always sad when they part. They have set a tentative date for their wedding, in February, which will be six months from their engagement and seven weeks before Mariah's baby is due. Her parents are less than delighted, but they seem to have given up trying to dissuade her.

Thanks to the baby, Mariah and Lucia have found a closeness that they haven't had since they were small. Pregnancy seems to have mellowed Mariah; that febrile quality of dissatisfaction, that need to always be winning, are in abatement. She meets Lucia at work sometimes, and in Lucia's lunchtime they go and look at baby clothes that seem too small even to be possible. Mariah eats sandwiches and cakes and says, 'I am so glad to finally have an excuse to be fat, and Richard cannot say a thing about it.'

'I can't imagine Richard complaining about you,' Lucia says.

'Oh, no, everyone loves Richard, poor Richard, married to Mariah,' her sister says, but she says it with a twinkle of self-knowledge that Lucia would never have thought possible. Mariah even talks to her about her wedding, and says she will pay for the flowers if their father refuses. 'Richard and I have talked about Billy, and we've decided we like him. You can count on us.'

'Even though my children will be . . .?'

Mariah shakes her head and rubs her hand over her stomach. 'I shouldn't have said that,' she says. 'I don't know why I did. We're not racialist. And anyway, Richard says Yorkshire needs some decent cricketers.' Because Billy says they must pick their battles, Lucia decides not to try to explain why assuming the child of a Black man will be good at cricket is actually a bad thing.

Billy can't get leave at Christmas. Lucia whiles away the dullest parts of the day – her parents rapt at the film about the Royal Family before lunch, and then later snoring in front of *The Morecambe and Wise Show* – by imagining what her next Christmas will be like. She cannot quite picture her and Billy staying here, in this house, even if they are married, though maybe by then her parents will have become more accepting and she will be able to relax when they are all under the same roof. But perhaps they'll come for the day, or stay with his family. Or maybe it will just be too far for them to make the journey, so they will stay in their own place, wherever it is, wherever they are. It will be more of a home than this one.

Their wedding is six weeks away, when Billy next comes home. She can tell by the look on his face that something's wrong, though he embraces her just as closely, as warmly, as he ever does. He walks her back to his house, and when she finds that it's empty, she knows something dreadful has happened, or is going to happen. When he tries to make her some tea, she says, 'Just tell me. What's wrong?' All she can think is that he is hurt – though he looks well, apart from a greyness at the skin around his eyes which happens when he's tired – or that he's been diagnosed with some horrible disease. She knows there are medical exams, that the recruits' fitness is taken seriously. 'Billy. I'm going to be your wife. You have to tell me what's wrong.'

And he looks at her.

And that's when she knows she isn't going to be his wife, at all.

His reasoning is frustratingly unarguable. He has realised, he says, how hard life can be for a RAF wife; how hard life is for the white wife of a Black man. He fears for her safety, for her sanity. At first, Lucia tries to laugh him out of it. Hasn't he praised her for being strong? Hasn't he told her that he could not imagine life without her, that her 'sweet determination' is all that he needs? Lucia wipes the tears from her eyes, furious with them for betraying her.

In the end, although she knows she has lost the argument – lost the life she was going to have – she says, 'Love doesn't have to be easy. How do you know it's worth it if it is?'

'Ah, Lucia,' Billy says. 'I wish our life could be one of your books.' She knows then that he's made up his mind. She can see, too, that he's as sad as – sadder than, maybe – she is. But she knows him well enough to understand that he has made his mind up. And maybe she is as weak, as below notice, as her family think, because she begs. She actually begs.

'It would not be kind, for us to marry and for me to give you that life. And I want to be kind to you, Lucia. It is all I have ever wanted, since I met you,' he says.

'You should have thought of that sooner.' She hears her mother's bitterness in her tone, and wants to take that moment back. Then she wants to take all of them back, every single moment since Billy first came into the library. Anything, anything, for this to not be happening to her.

His mother coming home puts an end to it all. 'Oh,' she says when she walks in, wearing the first uncertain look Lucia has ever seen on her face. 'I thought you would be done by now.' She stretches out her arms. 'Lucia, my darling. I am so sorry. My boy, he can be a fool.' Lucia lets herself be held.

'You're his mother,' she gets out through her sobs. 'Can't you tell him? I could do it. I know I could.'

Billy's mother shakes his head. 'Maybe you could, maybe

you couldn't. But he made up his mind.' As Lucia leaves, she is aware of Billy walking into his mother's arms, into the space that she has left.

Lucia wears her engagement ring that evening, and lets her parents' conversation – the Rotary, the mess of leaves in the neighbours' gardens, the repairs that the car needs – wash over her. She does the dishes and goes to bed. She imagines that she'll cry but instead she stares at the light as it fades and darkens and brightens again round the edges of her curtains. She doesn't know if she sleeps.

In the morning, she waits until her parents have gone to church and then she gets up and takes a long bath. When she dresses she doesn't put her engagement ring back on, instead tucking it into the back of one of the drawers in the chest in her bedroom, next to the underwear she had started to buy in readiness for her honeymoon. When she sits down to lunch with her parents, she says, 'Billy and I won't be getting married, after all.' She has been determined that she won't answer their questions or satisfy their prying. But they don't ask questions, and they don't pry. Rather, they assume. 'I'm sorry, Lucia,' her father says, after a moment when Lucia has concentrated on her plate but been able to feel her parents' looks passing back and forth across her head. 'But you've done the right thing. I've no doubt.'

'Yes,' her mother adds. 'I knew you'd think better of it.'

The fight that Lucia has found since she met Billy seems to have gone. She says nothing. She doesn't even try to tell her family that he's the one who changed his mind, though she knows that she should. She eats enough of her food for her parents not to comment on her losing her appetite; she washes up; she goes to the youth group. Billy isn't there. She didn't think he would be. Not today, though he usually looks in when he's on leave. It seems as though he's let everyone know, though, because for the first time in weeks there are no questions about her wedding. Lucia helps with a practice essay about *Richard III*. The time goes quickly. When Lucia gets home, she goes straight to bed, and sleeps for a straight twelve hours. The next day, in her lunch hour, she goes to buy wool and needles and a pattern and, that evening, she embarks on a baby blanket for Mariah's baby. That's the next event in the family, after all.

The baby comes on exactly the day predicted, in what Lucia later thinks is the only compliant thing her niece has ever done. She weighs seven pounds exactly. She is the most perfect thing that Lucia has seen in her life. Richard is misty-eyed when he looks at her. Mariah says, 'I've told Richard, that's it, he's going to have to make do with a daughter,' but she says it with a smile in her voice, and she receives the gift of the baby blanket with a sincerity that Lucia didn't anticipate. She had pulled her knitting out again and again, determined that the blanket would be perfect; by the time it was finished, it wasn't fair to say that she had healed, but a scab had formed over her heartbreak.

April Alice Jane is named for the month she is born and both of her grandmothers, which delights everyone. Mariah doesn't take to mothering easily. Richard works long hours, and Mariah is the first of her friends to have a baby. Lucia sees, with a painful pang, that her sister is lonely. She goes to see Mariah on her Wednesday afternoons off. At first they talk and coo over April, and Lucia cleans out the fridge or makes a meal; Lucia takes April for a walk in her pram, so Mariah can sleep. Then, as Mariah recovers, their Wednesday afternoons change. Mariah goes out, to meet a friend for tea or go shopping; Lucia spends time with April, whose face glows with delight when her auntie walks into the room. Although Lucia has always loved her job at the library, her Wednesday afternoons soon become her favourite parts of the week. She still helps at the youth group; as time passes, and new people join, she feels her identity as Billy's ex-fiancée fade. But it is a duty, now, something that it seems necessary to do; and there's a surprising balm to that.

One Wednesday, eight months after April is born, Lucia arrives home with a hand-print of hers and April's hands. Her mother smiles at it, though she herself has shown little inclination to do anything with April except hold her for a few minutes on a Sunday or buy her old-fashioned pale pink dresses that froth with lace and make April claw crossly at them. (There is a surprising balm to this, too; Lucia realises that it's not that her mother isn't interested in her, specifically, but that her mother is not keen on any children, not even her own, although Mariah has circumvented this by becoming her mother's ally.) Lucia's father says ruminatively, 'It's a shame you didn't find someone else after that Billy chap, Lucia. You'd have made a good mother.' Lying in bed that night, Lucia realises that her father thinks that, although she is only twenty-seven, she will never marry; that her life, as it is, is all it will be. Of course, he is thinking of his own generation; he and her mother married when they were barely in their twenties, and that was the norm. And then she realises something else, with the certainty of a deep bell ringing. He's right. This is her life. She knows enough from her reading, from the church friends that her parents pity, from the way Mariah already treats her as someone less than her, that the life of an unmarried woman can fall between the cracks of the world, even now, in 1970. She knows that she is not someone who will do something spectacular – she has no desire for adventure, no thirst for achievement, not even much of a wish to be seen. Married quarters in a faraway town, children she would love with all of her heart and protect with ferocity, a job in a library: this life would have been all that she wished. She didn't get it. She has the one she has. But, that night, Lucia decides that she will not disappear.

She buys a notebook. It's navy-blue, A4, good for making lists in: it looks like one of her father's record-keeping ledgers for the Rotary Club. At the end of every day, she makes a list of things that she's done.

After a month, Lucia reads the lists back. If she was trying to prove to herself that her life was worth something, she realises, she's failed. She is starting to remind herself of a Barbara Pym heroine: dowdy, unseen, useful to more important people. So the next night, she turns to a fresh page, and writes, 'Kindnesses'. She makes a list of all of the things she has done which are kind. Not all of them are big things. Telling her mother she has lipstick on her teeth; spending time with a library visitor showing them how to begin tracing their family tree. But these are things she could have chosen not to do, so they count. Over the weeks, Lucia begins to feel, if not happy, at least content. She feels as though she belongs in the world: as though kindness gives enough weight to her feet to make an impression on the earth.

Soon, her kindnesses start to look too small. And though Lucia knows they make a difference, she knows she could do more. So she takes a day off work during the school summer holiday and takes two of her youth group students to Cambridge on the train so they can take a look around the city; their teachers are keen that they apply there for university, but they have never set foot outside Yorkshire. She buys more books for the youth group. She asks a woman with a deaf child who comes into the library to teach her some sign language, insisting on paying her. This way she is able to communicate, a little, with deaf readers.

And so Lucia reclaims her life after Billy, by taking back her sleep; making a shell that her family's inconsideration and pity can slide off. She has books, she has work, she has the kindnesses that she writes down and that remind her that she matters in the world. She is content.

And for happiness, there is always April.

May 2024

It's been three weeks since that awful evening with Shaun.

He might have lied to her, but he didn't try to defend himself. They had sorted the bills into piles, and she had made a list of everything they – well, Shaun, because it was mostly his debt and because there was no longer a 'we' – owed. It had added up to something close to fifteen thousand pounds. She had said she would give him the money, and he had said he would go and stay with his brother while September worked her notice and got ready to move out. He'd gone straight away, and she had lain on her own in their bed that night, looking at the ceiling, wondering why she hadn't realised he was playing her. Thinking about how uncomfortable the mattress was, how her pillows were flat and old. She had considered paying his debts directly and making him close his accounts as the condition of her bailing him out. But she didn't have the energy. And there was no point. She couldn't stop him from getting into debt again if he wanted to. She could only do the right thing, and move on. It sounded easy. It was hard.

She worked her notice quietly, and told her work friends

that she and Shaun had split up and that was why she was moving. There was a card, signed by everyone, flowers and chocolates, and an earnest entreaty from her manager that if September ever decided to come back to work, she would be very welcome. September did her best to look grateful, especially now that she knew she could have earned a reasonable living here, if Shaun hadn't been stealing from her – she can find no other way to think of it – for all this time. And then she might have made some proper friends here, too, if she'd been able to join in the nights out and she hadn't been so damned tired all the time. She hadn't realised that she was friendless; it had happened so gradually, as her life got smaller and more constrained. Everyone at the supermarket told her to keep in touch, and Georgie set up a WhatsApp group and made her promise to tell them what she was up to. September was so grateful she could cry; she could go into her new life feeling less alone.

When September's last day of work was done, she went back to the flat to pack. Though it wasn't really packing. There was precious little she wanted to bring with her. Shaun was welcome to all of life's necessities: the crockery, the pans, the bedding. She had a house full of them waiting for her. She left the tech, too – it was all Shaun's, really, and she could buy things to suit her when she settled in.

She threw most of her clothes away. They weren't worth saving. She bought a new suitcase – a big one, with wheels on, and a matching mini-case which apparently she could take as cabin luggage on her next flight. She had felt almost dizzy at the idea of getting on a plane: and at the thought that, just by making this purchase, she was, in the eyes of the woman who served her, someone who clearly made a habit of flying.

Back at home, she had filled the big case with the clothes she was keeping, the things she had brought from her parents' home, her toiletries and make-up and her trainers. She thought about bringing her CDs, but she has a Spotify account now. The small case was perfect for her papers and admin, her notebook and her cables and chargers.

When everything was packed, she slung her best handbag over her shoulder – though she planned to replace that, too – left the keys on the table, and walked out of the house and towards her new life. Once she was safely on the train, she texted Shaun: The place is all yours, and money should be in your bank account. Take care. She almost deleted his number, but it didn't seem necessary. She had loved him; he had betrayed her; she was gone.

A week later, and September is getting used to her new home. The space had seemed indifferent when she first stepped into it, but she has played music, loudly, and taken long baths, and found a ridiculous sort of giddiness in knowing that all of this is hers. She need never worry about money again. If she is sad she can book a holiday. If she's tired she can order takeaway. If she fancies a change, she can – well, she can do anything. Sometimes the thought scares her, but mostly it makes her laugh. Out loud. In her home. Where no one will hear her, or judge her, or accuse her of – well, of anything at all. And if they did, she would just say: I deserve this. This is my family home.

Most days, she goes to an ATM and requests her bank balance on a printed slip, then looks at all the zeroes. Marina has put her in touch with a financial adviser; they are going to meet the following week. Maybe she will have to make some decisions then.

September is keeping the notebook she bought on the day she first came to the house for anything official: whenever she speaks to Marina, she makes careful notes of what she says, and reads them back afterwards. She's gone through all the paperwork for the house, and written down the costs of council tax, of gas and water and electricity. They are the sort of bills that would once have made her weep. Now, they don't matter. But she looks at them every day, just to make sure that they haven't changed, or she hasn't miscalculated. They haven't. She hasn't. She is still rich. She can still do whatever she likes.

She can't change her past, but she has a future now. September wears April's identity bracelet, and every time she glances at it the knowledge of her mother's name warms her. Does every daughter feel like this, she wonders, or is knowing your mother's name so unremarkable for most people that you don't ever realise it's one of the foundation stones of your life?

Sometimes, sitting under the tree in the garden, September imagines another trajectory for herself. The ad agency closed, but she had a generous aunt who would cover her rent while she found another job. She might have looked further afield – gone to London, or Edinburgh, or even somewhere abroad. She imagines herself putting on lip gloss in an airport, walking along pavements while the sun shone, working in an office that had a courtyard. She knows Shaun wouldn't be in the picture. Lucia would come to visit her, and they would find that they had so much in common. They would be sad about all the time they had lost, but they would make up for it. Lucia would tell September stories about what her mother was like when she was a child, a teenager, a shining young woman. September would have persuaded Lucia to clear out her wardrobe, to paint the house in brighter colours, to get a TV so they could watch films together when September came home for Christmas.

She has plucked up the courage to google Lucia. There wasn't much to find: just a few local newspaper articles in which her aunt stood, smiling, at some charitable function or another. When September looks at them she sees the slant of her cheekbones, the shape and colour of her eyes, shown back to her. It hurts, and it makes her warm.

On a sunny morning a week after she has moved in, September takes her coffee into the garden and looks at all the green things she owns, wondering which are weeds.

From the general tidiness of the place, she thinks, probably nothing. From what William said at book group, he obviously doesn't think much of daisies; though if you're rich, September thinks, maybe you get to decide what's a weed. I could grow a whole lawn of dandelions and say, this is my golden dream-lawn, and everyone else would nod and go and grow dandelions of their own. She laughs. This is her life now: deciding what she thinks of dandelions and daisies.

She wanders around the side of the house, where there are rows of things she half-recognises from her grandad's allotment. She wasn't very old when he died, but she remembers loving helping him to plant and dig. There are canes for berries of some sort; she goes closer and recognises raspberries and gooseberries. The neat rows are carrots and potatoes and something else: broccoli, maybe? She sits with her back to the wall of the house and shades her eyes from the sunshine. Maybe these plants need watering. They will be trying to grow. She tries to remember seeing a watering can, or a hose; she hasn't really spent a lot of time in the garage or utility room yet.

And then she hears the sound of whistling, which is bigger, somehow, than the man who follows it from around the corner of the house. William is pushing a wheelbarrow, so only his top half is visible: a wax jacket that has seen better days, a black hat which struggles to contain his greying Afro, his kind, clean-shaven face. He comes to a halt next to one of the freshly dug trenches, puts down the wheelbarrow handles, and smiles to himself. 'Today we weed and we water, Lucia,' he says, and it's the fact that he clearly thinks he is alone that prompts September to get to her feet.

'Hello,' she says. William jumps, puts his hand to his chest with what September suspects is only a slightly exaggerated gesture. 'It's me, September. I'm sorry to startle you.'

'I am very pleased to see you again,' William says, walking over and shaking her hand.

'You too.'

'You don't mind me working in the garden?'

'Of course not!' Then she adds, 'If you want to.'

William laughs. 'Oh, I want to. Me and this earth, we are friends. We know what's what.'

September laughs back. 'I used to help my grandad. He used to say you need a gopher and a gaffer in the garden.' She had forgotten that, until this very minute. 'Do you need a gopher?'

'Always!' William says. 'Your grandad taught you how to water plants?'

September nods. 'Underneath the leaves, not too little, not too much.'

'Exactly so. I'll get on with the hoeing.'

After an hour or so, September goes into the kitchen and makes tea. She brings the mugs out, with a packet of biscuits, on a tray. They sit on the bench under the tree: September really needs to get some cushions for it. 'Thank you,' she says. 'I wouldn't know where to start, looking after a garden like this on my own.'

William shakes his head and smiles. 'It truly is my pleasure. I like to be here.'

'What do you do when you aren't here?' All September knows about William, and the other book group members, is that they read, and they knew Lucia. It doesn't feel like enough.

'Well,' William says. 'I wake up with the sun. I read my book, in bed, and then I go downstairs to have breakfast with my sister. She is a widow now, and I'm a widower.'

'I'm sorry,' September says.

'So am I. I miss my wife every day. But I get on. I do jobs in the house, and sometimes I cook. I look after this garden. I read and I go to the library. I start the crossword, but I do not often finish it.' He smiles and shakes another biscuit from the packet. 'I take my ease, you could say.'

September nods. She's not sure she should ask about his wife, so she stays quiet. It feels good, to be sitting here in the sun, the hem of her jeans wet from the hose.

'How are you doing, September?'

'Me? Fine.' But there's something about William that calls

truth from her. 'It's – I'm so glad of all this. I've done nothing but worry about money for ten years and now I never have to think about it again. I never thought I'd know anything about my birth family and now I know people who knew my great-aunt and say I look like her. It's everything I could want. But—'

She looks at William. He raises an eyebrow. 'Hmm?'

'It's hard. I don't know why. I didn't think it would be.'

William smiles. 'So many things are not what we expect. It's only after, they make sense. You look back, you think, I did the only thing I could do, or I was walking along a path I couldn't see.'

'Yes.' September is already seeing the path she walked with Shaun more clearly. Talking herself out of her unhappiness, because why admit to it when you can't afford to do anything about it?

'You know what your aunt used to do?'

'No,' September says. 'I don't know anything.'

William indicates the house. 'You know a lot, just from being here.'

September nods. She must stop feeling sorry for herself. She knows that her aunt liked baked beans, and white bedding, and paintings of nature; lipstick and gloves and A-line skirts. She knows Lucia loved books and reading. She knows she liked to help. 'True.'

William says, 'But something I don't think you know. She wrote down every kind thing she did, and every kind thing anyone did for her, in a book. She said it kept her sane when things were hard.'

'So – a list?'

'I think it was more than that. I never saw it, but she told me about it.'

'Do you have one?' September thinks of her own lists, of money in different accounts and things she needs to do. Lucia's sound much better.

William laughs. 'I like to do things with my two hands,' he says. 'When I told Lucia I missed my allotment, she said I could make one here. That was just like her.'

'My grandad had an allotment,' September says. It's a distraction from the other thoughts that rise.

'An allotment could be the very best thing on God's green earth,' William says. 'And you are here on just the right day for pulling the first carrots.'

'I like carrots.' September immediately feels silly for saying it. But if William thinks she's silly, he doesn't show it. He puts his mug back on the tray and says, 'Come on, then.'

And she does.

She gets so involved in the garden – the tug-and-give of the carrots coming up, their smell of green and sweetness – that she almost forgets about her haircut. 'I have to go,' she says, 'I'm so sorry.'

William smiles. 'No matter. The garden is always here.'

She had booked the haircut online in a fit of boredom and sadness yesterday. Leaving the house, her keys in her pocket and her old handbag over her shoulder – she hasn't decided on a new one yet – she strides out for the town centre. She chose this hairdresser because there was a cancellation, and she suddenly could not bear to look at her hair, all split ends and dryness from hair straighteners and cheap shampoo and not having been cut for months.

When she opens the door to the salon and sees the huge fresh flower arrangement on the reception desk, she has an urge to run. But before she knows it, she is wearing a gown that covers her scruffy old sweatshirt, and she has a glass of something the receptionist has called 'bubbles' in her hand, and a man she met not ten minutes ago is running his fingers through her hair, asking her if she would like highlights or maybe a balayage, and scrolling example haircuts on an iPad. 'Volume is in,' he tells her, 'and you're very lucky to have it naturally.' September isn't sure whether he is just being polite – is this how rich people are told their hair is frizzy? – but he shows her enough pictures of models with hair like hers and peculiar make-up to convince her that she could have left her hair straighteners behind in Leeds, after all. Maybe Shaun's next girlfriend could have used them.

The hair wash is followed by a head massage. Once the dye on her hair has been applied and she's sitting under a lamp, September is offered a manicure. She says 'yes' before she knows it: she really wishes she hadn't started thinking about what Shaun's new girlfriend will be like.

The manicure includes a hand soak – she apologises for the soil under her nails, explains about the carrots – then there is more massage, with a rich cream that smells like some extremely fancy flowers. The manicurist files September's shortish, blunt nails into smooth almond shapes, and paints them a pale pink, with white tips.

Two-and-a-half hours later, September leaves the salon, having spent what would have been an unthinkable amount of money two months ago on the haircut, colour and manicure, plus some shampoo, conditioner and styling spray. The two glasses of fizz, the coffee and the biscuits are all, apparently, complimentary, something September's father would have snorted at and said, *If it's free you can be sure you're going to pay for it another way.* Then she remembers something else about her father – not just something he said, but something he did. On the rare occasions that they ate out, he always left a tip, in cash. *You look after the people who do the work.* So September goes to a cashpoint, draws out twenty percent of the bill, and takes it back to the salon, where she leaves it for her stylist.

After the haircut, and the manicure, and the tipping, September feels different. Taller, somehow. Her hair is so soft that she cannot stop touching it. Her nails are so perfect that she cannot stop looking at them. It is easy, suddenly, to walk into a shop she has lurked outside on many of her daily walks and ask to look at a handbag, and have it explained to her by an earnest woman who wants September to be very clear on what the many internal pockets are for, and how much the bag can hold. September likes the fact that it has a dog on the label. She buys it and is about to say she will use it straight away, when the assistant puts the bag into another bag, and then wraps the whole thing in tissue. Then she slides the tissue-wrapped, bag-wrapped bag into a carrier bag, and ties it shut with a ribbon. 'It's a good idea to keep it in its dust bag when you're not using it,' she says, and September thanks her and walks out into the sunshine of the late afternoon. This is the life.

When September gets home, Esin greets her like a long-lost friend. 'Oh, my!' she says. You were beautiful before, but – oh, my!'

'Thank you.' She almost asks Esin what it's like to keep

her own hair covered while everyone around her doesn't, but she decides against it. Instead she says, 'That smell, Esin. It's not baked beans.'

Esin beams. 'I decided to make you something from my country. For a welcome. It is called aushak and it is dumplings with herbs and tomatoes. We make it for a celebration in Afghanistan. All the women, in the kitchen, all day long together.'

September thinks of the time and money she has just spent on her hair and a handbag. 'This is so kind. But you don't have to cook for me, Esin. Especially not something so elaborate.' Esin has taken a plate of dumplings from the oven – September realises that she has been waiting for her – and is dressing it with onions and yoghurt, then sprinkling chopped herbs on top. The table is set. September cannot remember the last time she felt so taken care of.

Esin smiles. 'I know. Let it be my gift. I would have liked best to make it for you and your aunt, together.'

'I would have liked that, too.'

'Then sit, please. Let us enjoy this food together.'

It's so tasty that September realises she isn't speaking; since she put the first forkful in her mouth she has thought only of the flavours, the textures, the pop and sting of garlic and ginger against the softness of the dumpling, the tang of tomatoes. She makes herself stop eating for long enough to say, 'Esin. This is so delicious. I've never eaten anything like it.'

Esin beams. 'I am so happy. Your aunt, she loved this too.'

September takes a breath. 'Tell me about her? If you want to.'

'She was a good woman,' Esin says. 'Kind. I – I loved her

like a sister. When I met her I started to be happy, and I had thought after I left my country that I would not have happy times again.'

September eats another dumpling. 'So you knew my grandmother? Mariah?'

'Yes.' Esin looks at her plate.

'I got the impression from Marina that she was – not the easiest person to get along with.'

'I know we must not speak ill of the dead,' Esin says, and looks at her plate again.

September puts down her fork. 'We're talking about the woman who didn't want anything to do with me and my mother. If she was unkind to you, I won't be surprised.'

Esin exhales. 'I would not say she was unkind. She was always very polite. But underneath the politeness I knew she did not like me. I still came to clean, and my dear Lucia and I would sit in the garden afterwards and talk of old times.' Esin looks at the clock. 'The time, the time! Everyone will be here before we know it.'

September had picked up *Rebecca, the book group read*, with the intention of just reading the beginning so she knew something about it. According to the back cover, du Maurier's novel was the story of a young woman who was working as a lady's companion when she met and married handsome widower Maxim de Winter in Monte Carlo; everything changed when they returned to his Cornish home, presided over by the strange Mrs Danvers and the shadow of Maxim's first wife, Rebecca. September had thought it sounded a bit gloomy, but she had found herself hooked, reading well into the night until she finished it. She even looked up Manderley to see if it was a real place. It wasn't, but she learned that Daphne du Maurier set a lot of her books in and around Cornwall, where she lived. The idea that September could go there on holiday hit her out of nowhere. She didn't know if she would want to. But it was wonderful that she could.

September opens the door this time, welcoming everyone and inviting them in. Zain and Dan grin at her as though they have always known her, then disappear to play the piano until everyone else arrives. Kit comes next, a gym bag over her shoulder, her hair damp. She smells of minty shower gel. 'Good workout?' September asks, and Kit looks at her for a moment before saying, 'Oh. Yes.' Johnny kisses September's cheek, and then her other cheek – apparently he thinks this is normal – and says, 'I keep wondering about how you're settling in. Anything you need, ask me. I'll help if I can.'

'Thank you.' September catches a glimpse of herself in the hallway mirror and thinks of how different she looks since the last book club. It's not just her hair. She has four pairs of really good jeans now, all in slightly different fits, and enough tops and blouses that she never has a late-night panic about putting the washing machine on.

'So,' Esin says when they are all settled, 'who would like to begin? What do we think of *Rebecca*? Dan, you chose this one, I think?'

'Yeah,' Dan says. 'Our English teacher said it was good and we should read it to help us think about place and about justice and all that. So we thought we'd give it a go.'

Johnny laughs. 'Two birds with one stone?'

Dan shrugs, a great expanse of teenage charm. 'Me and Zain, we're busy people.'

But once he starts to talk, it's clear that Dan found the

novel as compelling as September did. He talks about how creeped out he was by Mrs Danvers, and how he really didn't see a lot of the twists coming. He and Zain are of the opinion that the main character – September hadn't noticed that she doesn't have a name – deserves everything she gets for being stupid enough to marry a man like that. Kit asks him what other choices he thinks the heroine had, and he says, 'You've got to see the signs, whether you're a man or a woman.' William likes the way du Maurier writes about the landscape. 'The earth and the sky have their power, and you do not ignore it,' he says, in a way that makes everyone fall silent. Johnny also enjoyed it, but he agrees that the main character could do more to take charge of her destiny; when he says this he grins at Kit and adds, 'I know, spoken like a true white man', and Kit shakes her head and smiles. Esin laughs and says, 'I was so busy reading that I forgot to think about what I thought. But I want to read it again. I want to see the clues this time.' Zain says the novel shows that you never know what's going on under the surface of anyone's life. 'People think they know all of what young people are doing and thinking, but nobody ever asks.'

And then September clears her throat. 'I loved this,' she says. 'It's the first thing I've ever read where I felt as though I was in it. I'm in a big house, on my own, and I feel as though I don't really know what's going on. You all knew my aunt, and you all talk about her, and I feel,' she will not cry, she will not, so she takes a sip of tea and looks at her hands, holding the saucer, until she's steady, 'I feel as though everyone knows things I don't. About Lucia. About Harrogate. About each other.'

William, next to her, reaches over and touches her shoulder. 'We did not know that you felt this way,' he says.

September nods. 'I'm not – I'm not complaining. I'm just saying it was,' she's careful to find the word she wants, 'it was comforting to see myself.'

September is making her way up the stairs after everyone has left, when there's a knock at the door. Kit has left a scarf behind, so September assumes it's her; but Esin is standing there. 'I was thinking about what I know about Lucia, that you might not,' she says. 'I would like to show you, please.'

September steps back and follows Esin up the stairs and into the main bedroom. 'I have noticed you do not use this room,' Esin says, 'so you may not have found something that Lucia meant for you.' She opens the door of the bedside table. Inside is a stack of parcels: all book-shaped, all wrapped in brown paper, all with gift tags attached.

'Happy many birthdays,' says Esin with a smile. 'Lucia would be so glad that you are here at last.' She touches September on the shoulder. 'I will let myself out.'

On every label is the same message: 'Happy birthday, September! Love from Auntie L.' There's only one that doesn't have the year on it, so September assumes it was the first year of her absence. She opens it to find she was right; it's a copy of *Burglar Bill* by Janet and Allan Ahlberg. Inside is written 'Happy 2nd Birthday, dear September. This lovely baby made me think of you! Love from Auntie L.'

'Oh,' September says, out loud. She doesn't know how to feel about these years and years of gifts and love. So she reads the book, as carefully as if she was reading it to her two-year-old self. It's about burglars who accidentally steal a baby. She wonders whether this is the sort of book that her adoptive parents would have kept away from her; whether they would have thought stolen babies might be upsetting. Lucia, of course, wouldn't have known. When she has finished reading, she goes down to the library and clears a shelf of notebooks. They can go into the office upstairs. Lucia was making a library for her, and this is where her book belongs.

The next morning, in bed, she opens her third birthday present. It's *Dogger* by Shirley Hughes, a book that seems to be designed to explain to kids that things get lost, but then they get found. In it, Lucia had written, 'Dear September, now you are three! Let's choose a teddy bear together. Love from Auntie L.' September decides not to cry, but it's an effort. She puts the book in the library; on the way back to her bedroom, after breakfast, she picks up one of the notebooks she had cleared from the shelf. Each has a start and end date on the cover: September still gets a thrill from recognising her aunt's handwriting, which she comes across every day somewhere in the house. The notebook seems to be lists. But then September realises, with a tiny shiver of the heart, that she's looking at one of the books William was talking about. It's one of Lucia's books of kindness. She opens it at random:

17 June 1987

My kindnesses:
I cut Dad's toenails after his bath. He said they weren't short enough but I didn't want to nick his skin. Mariah came round, playing holy hell about a parking fine – I bet she

forgot to get a ticket – and I helped her to write a complaint letter. If she'd done it herself she would have started World War Three.

Other kindnesses:
Celeste brought cake into work for everyone. I asked for the recipe and she said she would give it to me but she would make an extra one next time, too. An out-of-print book came in and the borrower was over the moon when I called to let her know. I saw a boy in school uniform helping an elderly man with books on a high shelf.

September flicks on: pages and pages of kindness, given out and gathered in. She sees her mother's name: *April came into the library on her way home to say hello*, or *I helped April to send off for university prospectuses, as Mariah had said she was too busy*. It's as though Lucia comes alive: her own life, her own words. September would sit there and read them all day if she could. But she's meeting Marina for lunch. And anyway – the thought takes her breath – this is as much as she will ever have of Lucia's life. She needs to take it slowly. Because, yes, she can re-read, but once she knows everything in these notebooks, there will be nothing else to learn.

September takes a bath then dries her hair, taking her time; resisting the urge to read all the notebooks, to open all the birthday books. Instead, she focuses on drying her hair the way her hairdresser showed her. She can see now why people spend a lot of money on haircuts and styling products. It really does make all the difference. Her new make-up is a pleasure to use. She dresses in a grey and pink striped dress and denim jacket with roses embroidered on the back: she has discovered that there are websites where you can put in your measurements and preferences and a stylist sends you clothes, and this is one of those outfits. Picking up her handbag and bright white Converse high-tops, September goes barefoot down the stairs. She wonders if a dog would make the house feel more like hers.

Marina emerges from the train station with a smile like sunshine and, unexpectedly but not unpleasantly, embraces September. 'You look better already!' she says.

September says, 'Thank you! I feel it,' though she wonders, when she's said it, if that's true. Then, afterwards, whether she looks better, or just as though she's spent money on herself. (And if those things are different.) But she can't follow any of those thoughts to their conclusions, because Marina is talking: the weather in Leeds, the people on the train, the joys of lunch on Friday and then not going back to the office. Before September knows it, they're in a restaurant with wooden tables and sleek cutlery.

They both order pasta with smoked salmon and capers, which September remembers being on the shelf in the supermarket with the olives and pickles. She has an idea that they're berries. Marina orders wine.

'So,' Marina says, 'how are things?'

'Honestly? Strange.'

'Of course it's strange!' Marina pours September a glass of white wine that smells of lemons. 'It would be strange for anyone to inherit a place that size, let alone out of the blue.'

'I had thirteen pounds to last me to the end of the month

when I came to see you.' How quickly that has become unthinkable.

'I see all sorts of things in my job,' Marina says, 'and a lot of it is the worst of people. Which makes it all the nicer when someone deserves good fortune, and they get it.'

'Yes.' But it doesn't really feel like winning. It feels like long overdue justice.

After their food arrives, Marina says, 'Go on then.'

'What?'

'Talk. Tell me why it's strange. Tell me what you've been doing and what you want to do and –' she waves her fork, 'absolutely anything. I'm all ears.'

September takes a mouthful of food. The capers have a tartness that makes the salmon taste more like salmon. It's perfect. And eating it gives her some time to put her thoughts in order.

'It sounds stupid, but I don't think I've had choices before. And I've never had so much time. I've never thought about what I want to do. My parents said I could go to university if I wanted, but I couldn't wait to leave school as it was. So I just got a job in an office. My parents were great. I couldn't see the point of moving out for the sake of it. I suppose – I suppose if they had lived longer, I would have got to that point.' She takes another mouthful: smoothness, smoke, salt, crunch. And then she says, 'Why did nobody come for me?' It comes out in a rush, as though the words know that if September sees them coming, she will bite them back, swallow them. 'All of those years. My grandparents.'

Marina nods. 'I wish I knew more.'

September shakes her head. 'There are birthday presents for me from Lucia. For every year.'

Marina laughs. 'Are they books?'

'How did you guess?' September thinks about this morning, reading *Dogger* in bed. She had bought a teddy bear on the way to meet Marina. She decides not to tell her about it; it feels faintly silly now.

Marina shakes her head. 'Something I've learned. There is no point in speculating. You'll drive yourself insane.' Then she asks, 'When you were a little girl, what did you want from your life?'

The question throws September. She thinks back: her parents, their little garden, warmth and stability. She can't think of anything she wanted, except—

'A dog.'

Marina smiles. 'Well, I imagine that's doable.' She nods at the waiter who comes to take their plates, and they order tiramisu and coffee. 'I loved the *Little House on the Prairie* books and I wanted to be a schoolteacher in a tiny school with nothing but fields and farmsteads for hundreds of miles around. That's probably best forgotten.' September laughs, trying to imagine Marina with her lunch in a pail. She remembers the TV show.

After a moment, Marina continues, 'Probably the first thing you need to do is make the place feel like your own. If memory serves, one of her book group people was an antiques dealer? It might be worth talking to him. Jack?'

'Johnny.' September thinks of the way he had smiled at her when he left book group, and said, *anything you need, ask me*. Maybe she could ask him about getting rid of some of the gloomy pictures as well as the tables and the lamps.

The waiter clears the coffee cups and tiramisu. Marina takes a folder from her bag. She looks at September, measuring. 'I didn't tell you this when you first came in to the office, because it seemed as though I'd already given you a huge amount of information and you were in a bit of shock. I didn't want to – well, to make it worse, I suppose. But now things have settled down—'

'Yes?' September remembers the overwhelm, that day; the panic that had made her blood fizz with the need to run.

'Well, Lucia brought us some photographs. Of you, and your mother. We kept them on file.'

September feels a pre-emptive ache in her heart. But she wants nothing more than to see her mother, no matter how it hurts. 'Did you bring them with you?'

Marina hands over a manila envelope.

September is aware of Marina telling her that she doesn't need to look at them now, that she hadn't thought that she might not have seen photographs of herself and April. But the loudest sounds in the room are those of the tearing of the envelope's flap, and the beat of blood, fast, at the base of September's throat.

She draws out an envelope, fat and worn. On the front are the words 'April and September photographs' in what she recognises as her great-aunt's hand.

The photographs are paperclipped together. 'They're in order,' Marina says.

The first is a school photo of April, in her Harrogate Grammar School uniform. 'April, 1980' is written on the back in Lucia's hand, and September finds herself looking at the writing because the shock of the photograph is so great. It could be her.

September's parents didn't pay for school photographs

because they said they preferred the ones they had of September when she was 'being herself', but September is pretty sure that a photograph of herself at this age would be strikingly similar to one of her mother. They have the same eyes; the same slight curl to their hair; the same nose, which Shaun used to tease her looked like a ski slope. April's teeth are straighter – September realises that she is never going to know whether she had worn braces or not – and her forehead is a little broader and higher.

The next photograph is stuck to a card, which is decorated with what look like hand-drawn flowers and leaves. Inside, the card says, 'You're the best, Auntie L', and is signed by April. September puts her hand on it. Her mother's writing. Her hand is touching her mother's name, which was written by her mother. Looking at the photograph on the front is easier. April looks older than in the school photograph, and is wearing her own clothes – jeans, a T-shirt, a waistcoat over the top – and make-up. Lucia looks happier than she does in any of the photos that September has seen of her aunt online. She and April aren't looking at the camera but at each other, their expressions loud with laughter.

'September,' Marina says. 'Do you want to go?'

September glances up; the world lurches back to the present, to the concern on Marina's face. 'I'm fine,' she says, and Marina seems to believe her, because as she looks back down at the photographs she hears Marina ordering another two coffees, and the sound of notifications as she switches on her phone.

There are more images of April, who must have been an often-photographed child, because these aren't special occasion photographs: April standing on grass in a swimsuit, laughing at someone out of shot; April sticking out her tongue while wearing a bridesmaid's dress; April looking down from a tree. The tree. September's tree. September wants to hold that photograph to her heart, but instead she puts it on the table with the others.

The next photographs are Polaroids. Marina leans over, before September has a chance to examine them. 'Lucia told me she bought April her Polaroid camera, for her eighteenth birthday,' she says.

September looks at the first of the photos. The image is faded; it's hard to make out. But when she looks closer she sees that it's April, sitting up in bed, and in her arms is a bundle of something. Something with a just-discernible nose and forehead. Even given the pale colours and the poor focus, it's clear that April is smiling as widely as her face will allow; that the baby in her arms is more precious to her than anything else has ever been or will be. September feels an ache start just behind her heart, and bloom like blood dropped in water: it spreads to her gut, her throat, her jaw. She feels it move forward into, through, her heart, her lungs. It must leave her body, because Marina seems to feel it. She looks up at September, puts down her phone, and comes to hold her. September is crying, or rather, tears are running soundlessly down her face, off her chin, on to the top of her chest. She holds out the photograph to Marina. 'Look,' she gets out. 'Look how much she loved me.'

When September arrives back at the house, she lays out the Polaroids across the top of the piano. There are a dozen. After the one of April and September a few days after her birth comes one labelled '6 weeks!' in which September is held in the arms of a man, although only his chest and arms, in a pale shirt with a wide pink tie, are visible. It has to be her father. Surely. September tries to find some feelings about him, but it doesn't seem possible. He's too abstract a concept; whereas her mother, so young and so clearly full of love for September, shines from the photographs she is in, and the thought of her fills September with both longing and comfort. There are photographs of April and September together, here, in the Harrogate house. There's one of them at the piano. There's one of them next to a Christmas tree; one of them sitting on the floor, surrounded by books; another of them curled up in what might even be the bed that September sleeps in, judging by the shape of the wooden headboard. (Of course, September thinks, that might have been Lucia's room, then.) There's one of Lucia holding September, the two of them laughing.

Marina had been kind, but September doesn't think she can have any concept of what it's like, to discover an unknown mother like this. To be able to see, in these faded seconds of time, that she was loved, and cherished. September's adoptive parents had told her that there was no reason to think she had been poorly treated when she was found. She wasn't malnourished, she was nicely dressed, she seemed to have all the right developmental milestones for a child of the age she appeared to be. She had the gold bracelet with her name engraved on it. September wishes she had asked more questions. Not least because if she had investigated sooner, she and Lucia might have found each other. The thought of it hurts so very much.

She opens her fourth birthday present, and her fifth:

Alice's Adventures in Wonderland and *Through the Looking-Glass* by Lewis Carroll (Lucia has written, 'And your great-grandmother is called Alice, and it's your mama's middle name!') and *Pollyanna* by Eleanor H. Porter (Lucia's message: 'This was one of my favourite books when I was little.'). She reads them in the garden. Of course, she knows the story of Alice in Wonderland. She can't remember how she felt about it as a child. As an adult it unsettles her, especially the way Alice is so horribly treated by almost everyone and everything she encounters: told off by a queen, eating and drinking things that make her grow or shrink, falling down a hole. Pollyanna is maddening in a different way. She's a girl who makes the best of everything and turns the world around her into cheerfulness with something called 'the Glad Game'. September puts the books down and thinks about Rebecca and the second Mrs de Winter again. Maybe she dozes, because the next thing she knows, her skin is goose-bumping in the cooler air.

William has left the hose connected to the outside tap, so September can give the plants a good drenching now that the sunlight is off them. Once that's done, she goes online to see whether she can get her Polaroids restored or enlarged. And then, because being alone feels like too much, she calls Johnny.

Johnny will be happy to help, he says, and arranges to come round in three days' time. In the meantime, September's TV arrives. It had seemed huge when she'd bought it, but in the living room it looks just right. While she waited for the delivery, and then for Johnny, she read her sixth, seventh, eighth, ninth and tenth birthday books. *The Wind in the Willows* she remembers her adoptive parents reading to her; her mother was very good at doing the voices of Ratty and Mole in particular, and she and her father had gone to the library to find books about river wildlife. It's a lovely moment, especially when she reads Lucia's message: 'Happy 6th birthday, September. Let's go messing about in a boat one day.' *The Borrowers* by Mary Norton she remembers from the TV series, which she had on video and watched over and over: the idea of tiny people living under the floorboards, using scraps and leftovers to make their homes, had charmed her. Lucia wrote, 'Happy Birthday! Now, have you seen my thimble?' September thinks the book might be better than the TV series was, and then she feels a sort of disloyalty, though she's not sure whether it's to the characters in the book, the TV actors, her adoptive parents, or Lucia. *A Little Princess* by Frances Hodgson Burnett is the reverse of September's own life. Well, not really: no one ever made her live in a cold, horrible attic. But when the wealthy, privileged little girl in the story is starved and overworked, September has to remind herself that this is a children's story, that it will be all right in the end. Lucia wrote: 'Dear September, Happy Birthday. Do you think we could make friends with a mouse?' When she was nine, she would have unwrapped a copy of *Black Beauty* by Anna Sewell. Once she gets over the surprise of reading a book that's narrated by a horse, she practically inhales it; she reads it in the garden and when she turns the last page she finds that she cannot feel the leg that's been tucked under her. She does wonder, though, whether she is ever going to get on to anything modern. Her tenth birthday book is more recent: *Matilda* by Roald Dahl. In it

Lucia wrote: 'Here's a book about a girl who loves books!' September imagines Lucia's hand hovering across the page, ready to add 'for a girl who loves books' and then realising she didn't know anything about her niece. When she starts to read, September wonders whether Lucia was sending her a message about how awful her birth family was, that she was better off elsewhere. Matilda's parents are cartoonishly horrible, thoughtless and cruel. September stops reading. She can watch the film on her new TV, if she feels like it. She goes to read some of the books of kindness, instead. She has taken to opening a page at random, whenever she feels as though she wants to connect to Lucia.

17 March 1970

My kindnesses:
Collected April from nursery and walked her home over the Stray. We talked to a lot of dogs. April is so fearless: some of them tower over her, but she's not afraid. She has to be stopped from pulling on their ears.

I bit my tongue when Mariah told me off for bringing her home 'grubby'. I suggested we go shopping, though that was the last thing I wanted, really; I'd much rather push April on a swing. I helped Mariah to find something to wear for a 'do' she and Richard are going to. She's obsessed with 'baby weight', though she looks fine to me, and still fits into most things. She says I wouldn't understand. I bit my tongue, again. April slept in her pram the whole time. Third tongue-biting (it's a good job they are only metaphorical) when Mariah told me off for 'doting'.

Other kindnesses:

Mariah took me to the make-up counter in Busby's because she has read about a lipstick colour that she thought would suit me. It's called 'chocolate kiss' and she was right. She insisted on 'treating me'. This is how she is kind, so I let her.

When I got home Mum noticed I looked tired and said we should have supper on trays in front of the television. Such a relief not to have to chat.

Johnny arrives half an hour late. He doesn't seem to have noticed. 'September!' he says, when she opens the door. 'What a beautiful day to be alive!' He is wearing black trousers, a grey T-shirt and a denim jacket with a hole in the elbow that somehow still looks very expensive.

'Hello!' she says, trying to sound like someone who is, also, glad to be alive. She isn't not. 'Thank you. For doing this.' She has stacked five spindly little tables, all of which are different (and surprisingly heavy) in the hallway. Three lamps, their bases in the shape of a zebra, a parrot and some kind of bear – also surprisingly heavy – are in a box next to them.

'Anything else to go?'

September thinks of all the dismal pictures of hills and clouds. 'I wondered about some of the paintings? They're all so . . . brown.'

'Sure,' Johnny says. 'Let's have a look.'

In the end, they load thirty pictures into the back of Johnny's van, all landscapes of various sizes. He wraps and secures each one as though they are the most valuable things he has ever touched. The tables he wraps in blankets, and the lamps, also wrapped, go into a crate.

September watches as he locks the van doors. She checks herself for feelings of doing the wrong thing, but there aren't any.

'Are you going to come?' Johnny looks at his watch. 'I'll give Marco a ring to let him know we're on our way. We can see what he thinks of this lot, then get some lunch?'

'Sure,' September says. 'Just give me a minute to change.'

Johnny looks her up and down in a way that manages to be both flattering and uncreepy. 'You look great to me.'

'I haven't even straightened my hair.'

September has no idea how to dress for going to sell some paintings and then out for lunch. She opts for what she wore for lunch with Marina. It's nice to have outfits, not just clothes.

The business is transacted swiftly and smoothly. Marco pays her by bank transfer on the spot. Somehow, there's something more dizzily confusing about this sudden chunk of money than there is about inheriting a house and a trust fund of hundreds of thousands of pounds, and September can barely hold back her tears. If Johnny notices she's upset, he doesn't say anything. Instead, he holds the passenger door of the van open and she steps in; his hand on the small of her back feels like something she wants to lean into.

Johnny turns the key in the ignition. 'Lunch? Or is there anything else you want to do?'

September shakes her head. 'You must have work. Or something.'

Johnny says, 'I have a ton of rewiring to do that's been waiting for two months for me to get around to it. And I have a van with a lonely woman in it. If you're self-employed you have to learn to prioritise.'

September thinks she's misheard. He must have said 'lovely'. But that 'lonely' touches a chord. 'I've been thinking about getting a dog,' she says.

Of course, Johnny also knows the woman who runs the dog shelter on the outskirts of Harrogate. Her name is Penny and she looks at September's pristine trainers – she wipes them with a cloth after every wear – as though they have come to life and slapped her. 'Have you had a dog before?' she asks.

'No,' September says, 'but I worked full-time until recently. I didn't want to get a dog when I couldn't be there for it.'

Penny nods. 'I wish everyone thought like you.' She asks September a lot of questions about what kind of dog she would like. September doesn't feel 'one with a waggy tail' or 'one that needs me' are the correct answers, but they're the only ones she's got, so she makes 'I'm not sure' noises until Johnny saves her: 'Come on, Penny. Let us meet some dogs and we can go from there.'

Penny looks doubtfully at September's shoes. 'It doesn't matter if they get ruined,' September says, and feels a little bit sick when she realises it's true.

They walk around the pens, with Penny providing a commentary as they go. There are a lot of 'pandemic pups', acquired when the owners were at home and too much to manage when life returned to normal. There are dogs brought to food banks because the owners cannot afford to feed them, even with help. September listens, and looks; some of the dogs bounce up to the wire, ready to be loved, others doze in the sun. There's a lot of excited barking.

September doesn't know a lot about dogs, but it seems as though these are all well cared for. Happy, even. September is, today and always, so glad that she has no memory of being in foster care. It wasn't for long, and she was sure she was well looked after. But she was still in a place for children who were unsafe or unwanted.

She follows Penny, half-listening to the dogs' biographies and hoping for magic, even though she knows it's ridiculous. Life isn't a film. A scrappy little pup with a black patch of fur around one eye isn't going to rush up and lick her hand while Penny gasps and says, 'She hasn't shown any interest in anyone in the three years she's been here!'

Except sometimes, life is a bit like a film, after all.

They are at the last pen, and September is thinking about the funny little Jack Russell cross who jumped up and down on the spot, and the Collie who looked at her with unblinking brown eyes. But then she sees – well, she sees her dog. It's lying with its head between its paws, and though it doesn't get up, its gaze follows September. There's something clever about its face, somehow; as though it's thinking empathetic thoughts, or trying to do complicated long division. 'She's a Scottish Deerhound,' Penny says. 'Her owners brought her in when she killed their neighbour's cat. It's a breed with a very strong prey drive. Definitely not for beginners.'

September holds out a hand and the dog gets to her feet. She's gangly, all legs, and when she shakes herself the movement ripples down her body, so even when her head is still again her tail is still moving. 'Is she malnourished?' September asks. Penny has said a lot of the dogs are when they come in.

'No,' Penny says, 'that's just the breed. She was very well cared for at home, and she has been here. Like I say—'

The dog pushes her nose against September's hand. September scratches her behind her ears and the dog moves her head, almost cat-like, leaning in. 'Hello,' she says, then, to Penny, 'What's her name?'

'Figgy. But she needs a lot of care and a lot of space. We'd have to do a home visit before we could even think about—'

September glances at Johnny, who laughs. 'Let's book a home visit in,' she says.

Penny sends September links to web pages about Scottish Deerhounds, food suppliers, and a list of equipment that a new dog owner needs. September asks about payment and Penny says that, once the home visit is concluded, she can donate to the dog's home if she decides to adopt Figgy. Johnny says, 'I don't think that's a question,' and Penny says, 'You were always trouble,' and then Johnny and September are back in the van and driving away. September is a fizz of excitement and delight. She is going to have a dog of her own. She says this to Johnny, only just managing to leave out the word 'very': I'm going to have a dog of my very own.

He smiles. 'Are you going to change her name?'

September shakes her head. She knows what it is to go to a new place with your name being the only thing that's yours. 'I like it. I wonder why they chose it.'

Johnny shrugs. 'I knew a dog called Clive once. There's no point looking for sense in dog-naming decisions.'

'Maybe they got her for Christmas. Figgy pudding.'

Johnny nods. 'Could be.'

'I've never eaten a fig,' September says. It's not a complaint;

just a thought. There's something about Johnny that makes her thoughts come out of her mouth. William and Esin, too.

'In that case,' Johnny says, 'I know just where to take you for lunch.'

It's a tatty sort of a place: mismatched chairs and thick, clouded glasses that look as though they've been through the dishwasher too often. The menu is a one-page printout on A4 paper; there are hardly any choices. But one of them is grilled fig with whipped goat's cheese, local honey and candied walnuts. 'Yes?' Johnny asks.

'Yes.' They order sparkling water to go with it, though September has yet to decide whether she likes it, and bread and olives for while they wait. September itches to take out her phone and scroll through the photos she's taken of Figgy. She tears her mind away.

'I found all these notebooks that were my aunt's. William told me about them. Books of kindness. They remind me of when I was a kid. My mum used to run the Brownies and you had to write down your good deed for the day every day.'

Johnny's smile broadens. 'I was wondering if you would find them.'

'I did.' September smiles back.

'I was going to mention them but then I thought if Lucia had got rid of them I would be telling you about something you couldn't have. And it feels as though you've had enough of that.'

September finds she cannot speak. She touches the back of Johnny's hand, nods. He nods back.

'She told me about it once, when I was,' Johnny takes a deep breath, 'I was really struggling. She said to me, when things hurt, writing down kindness helps. It shows you that you matter and that you can matter. And it shows you that not everyone's world is as difficult as yours is, and that therefore yours will get better.'

September thinks about the delivery men who brought the TV, how she gave them £40 for unpacking it, plugging it in, and taking the packaging away. Would that count as kindness? Maybe she should try this. 'Do you keep one?'

Johnny, who is taking a drink of water, almost chokes. 'Me? When I need to do my tax return I have to consolidate the contents of all my coat pockets. There's no way I would be that organised.' His face becomes serious. 'I do think about it, though. Kindness. I – Lucia made me notice it more.'

September is on the point of saying something really ill-advised, like *am I a kindness or something else*, when the food arrives, and saves her.

She was not prepared for how beautiful it would look. There are three figs, forming a triangle in the centre of a large, flat, white plate. Each fig is quartered and pulled apart, the purple blush of skin just visible at the edges of the flesh, which is full of tiny seeds that seem to glow golden. The walnuts are placed at regular intervals around the edge of the fig triangle; the honey swoops in overlapping ovals around them, and in the middle of the plate is the goat cheese, which shines whiter against the white of the plate.

'It seems too pretty to eat,' September says. Something else about having money: everything is made to look nicer.

But she does eat it, and oh, it's perfect. The figs taste of the most delicious earth, the cheese is sharp and twitching with sourness; the walnuts both crunch and melt and the honey, rather than making everything sweet, makes it all taste more like itself. It's bliss.

'Good?' Johnny asks.

September realises that she hasn't so much as looked at him, let alone spoken while she's been eating. She almost apologises. 'Perfect,' she says.

'Good. Would you like anything else? If they have their peanut-chocolate tart on today, it's worth it.'

'No, thank you.' September thinks this might be the best thing she has ever eaten. She wants to hold on to the taste of it for as long as she can.

Lucia, 1987

Lucia can hardly believe that her niece is almost eighteen. Or that she herself is almost forty-five. Forty-five and still living at home. Sometimes she still thinks about Billy and wonders if he was right; that she wouldn't have been able to cope with the hard parts of life that would necessarily come with marrying a Black man in Harrogate in 1969. The woman who was equal to that challenge would not still be living at home, still be working in the same place.

But at first, Lucia didn't have the heart to look for somewhere of her own: even her parents' company had been something to keep the sadness away. And then, she got to like having money to spend, on herself and on other people: she bought herself a treat every Friday, at lunchtime, a skirt or a pair of shoes or a lipstick. She bought books whenever she wanted to. And she spent money on April: books, of course, but day trips and museums and cinemas, days in London, even a weekend in Paris when she was fifteen to see the Louvre. She didn't go to church any more, but she decided to tithe ten percent of her earnings to charities. And somehow, the years passed, and Lucia lives with her parents, still. She supposes that if she had ever dated someone she really liked, or had ever been constrained by things at home, then it might have been different. But here she is. Her days are, for the most part, good ones, even if her twenty-five-year-old self would be horrified at the thought of her life as it is now.

The days when April comes are always Lucia's favourite days. Her niece is the light of her life: she's bright, she's funny, and she has ambition to burn. She wants to be an artist, or maybe a designer. Lucia thinks April is a wonder. Yet all Mariah seems to do is complain about her daughter. The previous Sunday had been a case in point. Mariah and Richard had come for lunch; April had cried off, on the grounds that she had homework to do.

Lucia, going between the kitchen and the dining room with dishes of vegetables and two different jugs of gravy, one made with giblets for her father and one made with sherry for her mother, misses most of the conversation. But she slides into her seat in time to hear Richard declare, 'The latest is, April and her friends want to go travelling for a year before they go to university. And one of them has had her nose pierced.'

He pauses, long enough for Mariah to murmur, 'I don't know what her parents were thinking.' Richard adds, 'She has no thought for what it will cost. The money from this Saturday job of hers isn't going to get her as far as London! I've told her, if she wants to go traipsing round the world like a nomad, she can do it, but she can forget about university.'

'Travelling!' Jacob chimes, as though Richard has made a joke.

Lucia cannot help herself. She says, trying to make herself

sound cheerful and enquiring, 'But surely you want April to have a good education? Don't you want her to get on in the world?'

Richard snorts. 'We want her to be home before ten and dress decently, not be raking around pubs with her friends until all hours.'

Lucia is generally home before ten if she goes out at all, and certainly dresses decently. It's not a full-time job. She should know: she has one of those too. 'Last time I saw April she seemed to be working hard. And very keen about her studies. She could go far, and I think travelling is something young people do now. It's good for them, to expand their horizons.'

Her mother sniffs. 'You never could see past April, Lucia.'

Mariah adds, 'It's a lot harder being a mother, with all of the disciplining and,' she hesitates, searching for the word, 'and managing, than it is being an auntie who just says yes to everything. No wonder she loves you.'

Lucia takes a breath and decides to eat a potato rather than tell Mariah what she thinks of her parenting. She has watched her sister carp and complain almost since April was born. She has never seen Mariah do anything that April wanted to do; instead, she has expected April to conform to what she, Mariah, expected of a daughter. Lucia rarely thinks now about how much she would have liked to have a child of her own – two, three, four – if only Billy had thought her brave enough. Well, she's going to help April to be brave.

'Let's talk about something else,' Richard says, and they all dutifully start discussing the refurbishment of the church hall and the weekend prayer retreat to Lindisfarne that their sparky new vicar has proposed. Lucia speaks only to point out that perhaps the money would be better spent on outreach or doing something for the community. She is ignored. She breaks a plate while she is washing up, and puts it in the bin before her mother can try to glue it together again.

Wednesday afternoons are still Lucia and April's time. April is the model of politeness with her grandparents when she arrives. She asks her grandfather about the garden, and tells her grandmother about something she heard on the radio about people going on holiday to Greece. Lucia heard the same piece, and knows for a fact that April will have listened to it while being driven to school, having missed the bus again. She swallows a smile and it warms her all the way down. 'Anyway,' April says, 'Aunt Lucia has said she'll help me with some art homework, and I really want to do well in my exams. My teachers say I should be able to get into a really good university if I work hard.'

'Oxbridge, I hope,' her grandfather says. Lucia catches his eye just long enough to convey *I haven't forgotten what you said on Sunday*, and then she and April leave the room.

April has brought a bag containing a sheet, a stapler and a pair of pinking shears. 'I want to work out how to make a toga,' she says, 'and I'm going to paint all the things that all those wise old Greeks and Romans said on it, and then I'm going to put it on a female mannequin who's covered in blood and has her eyes gouged out. It's a comment on how damaging the patriarchy is, even when it's perceived to be benign.'

Lucia nods. She loves her niece's audaciousness, her imagination. Her throat hurts with it. 'Do you want me to be the model?' Lucia asks, and when April nods, she strips down to her underwear and waits to be swathed. April approaches her with the sheet and puts the bulk of it over one of her aunt's shoulders. Then a smile sneaks on to her face and Lucia braces herself, because she knows what her niece is about to do. 'Boop! Boop! Boop!' April says, and pokes each of the three moles that sit side-by-side on the skin just above Lucia's belly button. 'Boop, boop, BOOP!' She can't complain: April has the same moles in the same places, and Lucia started it, when April was a baby.

April has a Saturday job in Harrogate while she is in the sixth form, working in a shop that makes Lucia feel old every time she walks through the doors: the music is too loud, the clothes strange, the clientele all younger than her by at least twenty years. But she is proud of April for getting a job. At first, Mariah and Richard had disapproved, saying April should focus on her studies, but April had insisted, making the case for learning about the world and taking responsibility for herself. As one of the frequent conversational topics at family Sunday lunches, led by Mariah and Lucia's father, with their mother and Richard joining in the chorus, was Young People Today Don't Know They Are Born (Bring Back National Service), April won the day. And Lucia was also proud of her niece for wanting some independence. 'You know what they're like, Auntie L,' April had said afterwards. 'When I go away to uni they've said they'll give me money to get started and then I can just ring them for a top-up whenever I need. But that means I'll have to keep phoning home and saying I need tights and tampons, because they aren't going to fork out for nights out, are they?'

Lucia meets her niece after work. Sometimes they go to the cinema, sometimes for a meal. Occasionally, they have a quick coffee before April goes to meet her friends or go to a party, but April was like her aunt in that she'd rather have a full-on conversation with two or three people than spend time in a big group. Lucia is careful to avoid making plans for Saturday nights. She knows her days with her niece are numbered; and anyway, she would rather laugh with April than do almost anything else. There will be time enough for concerts and weekends away to visit distant museums when April is settled at university, though April has already made her aunt promise that she will come and stay. April is determined to go to art college in London, something Mariah and Richard obviously think is ridiculous, but seem to have realised is a battle that they won't win.

On the day things change, Lucia meets April at five as usual. April has a strange look to her, the one she often has when she is tired or has argued with her parents: too-bright eyes and picked skin around her fingernails. But, rather than immediately launching into a tirade about Mariah and Richard or telling Lucia, again, about how impossible A-levels are, she is quiet. Silent, almost.

As soon as they have settled with their coffees, April says, without preamble, 'Something's happened and I need your help.'

'Okay.' Lucia flounders through some possibilities. April can't be pregnant; she would have told Lucia if she was seeing someone, and just a couple of weeks ago April had been wondering out loud about what it would be like to lose her virginity. Lucia had thought of Billy, and even though they had never got that far, she had felt confident in saying, 'So long as you want it to happen, and you're kind to each other, it should be . . . nice. Though like anything it will get better with practice.' April can't have fallen out with Mariah and Richard again, because Mariah would have been on the phone to their mother like a shot.

April takes a deep breath, looks Lucia straight in the face, and says, 'I'm in love.'

'Oh. Well . . .' Mariah and Richard might not be, in Lucia's view, the best of parents, but surely they will be at least slightly prepared for the fact that their seventeen-year-old might have a boyfriend. 'That's lovely, I didn't know you'd met someone.' Sadness writhes, scaly and alive, deep in Lucia. Looking back, later, she would see that this was the point where her relationship with her niece lost its essential honesty, its purity. She could never tell April about the way her own heart was broken, by a combination of her own cowardice and her parents' prejudice – no, actually, it had just been her own cowardice. She could have fought harder for Billy. She should have.

April looks down at her hands. 'It's been very sudden. You know when I went into Leeds last week?' Lucia nods. There had been a sixth-form art trip to look at some of the industrial architecture. 'We had some free time and everyone else wanted to shop, but I wanted to work on my sketches. So I went to a coffee shop. It had those little round tables, like they have in France?'

It seems to be a question, so Lucia nods. 'Iron legs?'

April smiles, as though this is confirmation that she should trust her aunt. 'Exactly! And I was just working away and then this voice said, "You're really good, aren't you?" And I said "Yes" and looked up at him and – that was it.'

'Love at first sight?' Lucia smiles. She cannot help it. She doesn't know if she's smiling at April or at her own younger self, standing at the desk at the library and finding herself looking at, as it turned out, the most beautiful man she would ever know.

'I knew you'd understand,' April says. The colour is coming back into her face. Lucia realises that her niece was worried about telling her this. And the smallest of forebodings blooms in her gut.

'So, tell me about him,' she says.

April shakes her head. 'I will. But I need to ask you something.'

'Anything.'

'I want to spend some time with him before I say anything to Mum and Dad. You know what they're like. So I wondered if – could I say that I'm with you tonight, but go and see him?'

'I don't like to lie,' Lucia says. And then, she thinks, but you did lie. You let everyone think that you'd been the one to call things off with Billy, to save yourself from their pity. She gives herself a shake. She could make life easier for her niece. 'But I also know what your mother's like. So, of course.'

April squeezes Lucia's hands across the table. 'Thank you! Thank you! What shall we say we did?'

Lucia has brought a newspaper with her, so they look at the listings and decide on the film. Then April heads off – 'he's picking me up at the station at quarter past six' – and Lucia goes to the cinema on her own. Halfway through, she realises she knows nothing of where April was going or who she was seeing. It feels as though she is holding her breath right up to the time that Mariah, Richard and April arrive for lunch, the next day.

And so it continues. Lucia meets April from work; they have a coffee; then April goes off to meet Rex and Lucia goes to the cinema, or sometimes, for a meal, though if she does she chooses somewhere inconspicuous and sits with a book. She's always trying to find new, interesting reads for the reading group she runs at the library, and the last thing she needs is to be seen by one of her father's Rotary colleagues or her mother's flower rota or WI friends. But Saturday nights prove to be safe enough. Either that, or a woman approaching her forty-fifth birthday is genuinely invisible. Gradually, Lucia learns more about Rex from April. He works in sales; he's from London originally; he makes her laugh and laugh; he has the bluest eyes you've ever seen. After a few weeks, April shows Lucia a strip of photo-booth images of her and Rex, faces squashed together, laughing, kissing. It makes April's heart hurt. She has no photographs of her and Billy.

'How old is Rex?' she asks one week, after hearing about the walk the two of them had taken alongside the canals in Leeds, the way that kissing him felt 'electric'.

April's eyes take on the ready-for-a-fight look that Lucia knows calls out an answering spark in Mariah: her sister has never been able to see that all the things she criticises her daughter for are the things that run strongly in herself. 'He's twenty-six. But everyone says I'm a very mature seventeen.' Then, before Lucia has a chance to react, she leans forward and whispers, 'I want to have sex with him.

I know he's the only man I will ever love. You have to help me have a night away.'

Of course, Lucia says no. The idea of April – who is still a child, really – with a man so much older than she is makes her uncomfortable. April looks upset, but she agrees that Lucia must do what she thinks is right, and Lucia immediately thinks how mature her niece is: as mature as a twenty-year-old, at least. At times, more mature than her own mother.

Lying in bed that night, she thinks of the people who looked at her and Billy and saw, not love, but difficulty, a mismatch. Something that went against the rules. So she tells April that she has changed her mind. But that she wants to meet Rex before she agrees for certain.

And so he walks into their Saturday cafe. He and April have been seeing each other for six months. He seems small to Lucia. Not only physically – she realises she had assumed April would fall for someone who was as tall and handsome as she was slight and beautiful – but in himself.

She tries to see what April might see in him. She notices that he has excellent manners; he shakes Lucia's hand, asks her about her day, and seems to make a point of being on the very edge of the conversation, so that April and Lucia are able to have their usual time together. He brings their coffees, and a plate of cakes, because, he tells April, 'I know you don't eat properly when you're at work.' When April talks, he listens. He's read a book she recommended, and he's brought a magazine with an article about the photographer Nan Goldin with him, because he thinks April might be interested in it. Lucia watches them together, and she realises: her bold and fiery niece is completely herself, completely at ease, with someone who seems to be an utterly ordinary man. But then she remembers her failed attempts to get her family to accept Billy, and the way her mother curled her lip and said, 'But why him, Lucia? Of all the men in the world, why does it have to be him?' She had tried to explain how Billy was the only person she had ever known who had seemed to see into every part of her and accept everything that he saw. She thinks of that now. She thinks of Billy telling Mariah that she, Lucia, was the best person he knew. If this is how April and Rex make each other feel, then she won't be the one to get in the way.

When April goes to do her make-up – although Rex tells her that she is perfect as she is – she asks him, 'How old are you?'

'I'm twenty-six,' he says. At least he's honest: Lucia had been interested to see if he would lie to her. Then, with a spark that makes Lucia like him, he adds, 'I don't think it matters.'

She shakes her head. 'I'm forty-four, and if I had a relationship with a man nine years older than I was, I don't expect anyone would raise an eyebrow.' She almost laughs as she thinks of how, on the contrary, her parents would be hugely relieved at having her taken off their hands, as they would see it. Though now they are getting older, their desire to introduce her to what they consider to be suitable men from church or the Rotary seems to be waning. ('Suitable', she has realised, means 'available'. Her parents seem especially keen on widowers, as though Lucia is more of a useful replacement than a person in her own right. She can imagine them talking to one of these men, explaining how good she is at carrying trays up and down stairs, and cleaning the high places.)

'Exactly,' Rex says. 'Age is just a number.'

Lucia smiles, but she doesn't mean it. How wrong he is, thinking he can charm her like this. 'But April is barely eighteen. Some people would say, almost a child.' She tamps down her usual desire to Make Things Nice, and waits.

Rex clears his throat. Somehow, Lucia knows that this is not a good sign. 'I know it's not ideal,' he says, 'none of this is. But I do love April. I love her very much.'

And then April returns, all smiles and cherry-blossom perfume, and Lucia doesn't get to hear what it is that Rex was going to say. Though she guesses soon enough.

In the run-up to April's exams, Lucia does all she can to support her niece. She helps her to revise, asking questions and making up mnemonics to help her to remember details of history. She does proofreading, unimportant bits of sticking and sorting, tidying up. When she goes to the sixth-form art show, she is so proud of her niece that she could die, and furious with Mariah and Richard, and with her own parents, who tut at nudity and proclaim that art didn't look like this when they were young. When April gets As for everything, Lucia is not surprised. Her niece accepts a place at Goldsmiths College in London, and Lucia waves her off with a certain knowledge that her own life will be lonelier for April's absence.

June 2024

Having passed Penny's stern home visit, September has been buying dog beds and bowls, blankets and toys and food, ready for Figgy's arrival at the weekend. But first, there's book group.

September welcomes everyone with more confidence this time. The library feels a bit more like her own room now. She's found a bird book, with pencil ticks next to some of the birds, but it hasn't been a lot of help, as she only manages to get a sense of song and brown-ness before the finch or sparrow or whatever it might be has flown off. Because the library is pretty much all shelves, there's no room for (dismal) pictures. September has arranged a weekly flower delivery and follows the instructions on the lid of the box the blooms come in, arranging them in a huge, heavy crystal vase she found in one of the kitchen cupboards. She likes the mirror above the mantelpiece, which is the width of the fireplace and framed by the same dark wood of the bookshelves, and reflects the light from the window into the corners of the room. Her little shelf of birthday books is growing. Every time she opens another of the parcels and reads Lucia's message to her, she feels warm from the touch of love down the years. But she has struggled a bit with the gifts for the eleventh, twelfth, thirteenth and fourteenth birthdays.

She had been thrilled to unwrap her eleventh birthday present, *Little Women* by Louisa May Alcott. She remembered enjoying the film; and in the front, Lucia had written, 'This was my favourite book when I was eleven. I wished for sisters like these.' But she had found it preachy and dull, and a lot of it seemed to be about teaching women to know their place and make the best of having nothing. *To Kill a Mockingbird* by Harper Lee, her twelfth birthday present, she remembers from school; she can't get into it without the shadow of bored and boring classroom days discussing racism and inequality. Lucia's message that 'This is so important and I can't wait to talk about it with you!' doesn't make her feel any better. *Jane Eyre* by Charlotte Brontë – 'I cannot believe that you are thirteen years old, darling September' – is the worst. September perseveres until three-quarters of the way through, and then puts it aside. She doesn't know why it makes her feel like throwing it out of the window, but it does. After that, *Noughts and Crosses* by Malorie Blackman is a relief, and she races through it. 'I couldn't put this down', Lucia has written, and September feels the same way, and then gets an extra bump of love to think she is sharing an experience with her aunt. The book is set in a segregated alternative world where 'crosses' (Black people) have power over 'noughts' (white people), and it makes September think more, and feel more uncomfortable, about racism than *To Kill a Mockingbird* did at school. After it, the book group book, *Silas Marner* by George Eliot, which from the back cover looked as though it was going to be slow and depressing, had been something of a relief. She can't wait to talk about it with the others.

Maybe if she and Lucia had known each other, they would have chosen books together.

Dan and Zain arrive first; they both high-five September and then start to play the piano, squashed together on the stool, Dan using one hand on the keys and beating a rhythm on the top with the other. Then William arrives. September saw him yesterday, when they talked about William's travels with his RAF squadron as they pulled up weeds. ('We must get these out before they flower,' William had said, 'or we'll be in trouble later.') This morning, September harvested the first of the strawberries and gooseberries; she shows him the bowls of washed fruit in the kitchen. She and Esin are going to make jam. William shakes his head and smiles at September. 'Every time I lay my eyes on you, I think how you are like Lucia's mirror,' he says. This is a kindness William is doing for her, on top of everything he is teaching her in the garden.

She will add it to the book of kindness she has started, tentatively, to keep. It's making her wonder whether she was kinder before she could just give money to everyone: most of her kindnesses seem to be tips and donations.

William stays talking to Esin in the kitchen. Johnny helps September to move the chairs into place, after kissing her on both cheeks. It feels more natural this time. Johnny smells of the wool of his sweater and the bitter musk of his aftershave. 'I've spoken to my decorator mate,' he says, 'they'll call you. Their name's Jojo.'

'Good,' September says. She buys home decor magazines now, but the array of possibilities and the vocabulary – colour-washing and feature walls – feel overwhelming. Hopefully Jojo will know what to do. 'Thank you, Johnny.'

He shrugs her thanks away. 'No worries.'

Kit is the last to arrive. September can tell she's tired. 'Long day?' she asks.

'Aren't they all,' Kit responds. She seems so young; she reminds September of herself in her mid-twenties, desperately trying to be a grown-up, wishing she was still a child. September asks her where she works and Kit tells her, shortly, 'Bettys'. It takes September a moment to realise she means the famous Bettys Tea Room, in the middle of Harrogate. 'I've never been there,' she says, and Johnny says, 'Noted'. September turns back to Kit with another question but, remembering the sheer drain of having to chat to people all day when you work in the customer service world, she leaves Kit be and goes to help Esin with biscuits and cups.

September takes her seat in the circle of chairs and feels herself relax. This week, Zain introduces *Silas Marner*, his pick. 'I chose this because my mum says it's her favourite book. She's like Lucia used to be, always reading, always helping people.' He looks around the group, smiles a smile that says, 'There's more to me than meets the eye.' 'I really liked it,' he says. 'To begin with, I thought, man, this is going to be a slog. Poor people getting screwed over, I see that around me already. But it was good.'

September had had a similar thought. In the opening pages, Silas is accused of theft and loses everything, going to live in a new place where he shuns company, works hard, and is robbed again. It's only when he finds an orphan in the snow, and adopts her, that his life starts to change for the better.

William nods. 'That child saved him.'

September feels tears in her throat, and she asks the question that has been bothering her since she came here, since she started to read. 'Does anyone know why there are so many orphans in books? I never read much before. But since I've been here, everything I pick up seems to have orphans. Even when it's not about being poor.' She thinks of Teddy in *Little Women*, the second Mrs de Winter, as well as Oliver Twist in the next book club book, which she's just started to read. Jane Eyre, the orphan that she just could not get on with. The little princess, forced to live in a cold attic.

Esin says, 'I think when you put an orphan in a book, anything can happen to them. Because they have no one whose job it is to love them best of all the people, and to protect them from harm.'

Zain nods. 'Because your parents are always stopping you from doing stupid shit, innit?'

Dan laughs. 'Trying to, in your case, my brother.'

Esin shakes her head. 'That poor mother. Dying in the snow and not knowing if her child will be well.'

September closes her fists, tight. She hopes that April didn't worry about her as she was dying; and at the same time, knows that she did. She must have. She thinks of that first Polaroid. Her mother loved her so much. When she looks up, Johnny is watching her, carefully, as if he knows that this is not easy.

William smiles. 'But anything can happen to an orphan

in a good way. They can find a place. Their parents have not left them on purpose. If they can learn that then they can be themselves.'

'Not all books have orphans,' Johnny adds.

'But parents die in books,' September says. 'A lot.'

'People die in real life,' Johnny says, and when September looks at him she realises that busy, chatty Johnny with his fingers-in-pies and his I-know-everyone is not quite the carefree soul he portrays himself to be. She feels things veering away from her.

'Has anyone read any other George Eliot?' Kit asks. 'I really loved *The Mill on the Floss*.' September glances at her, wondering if she, too, has picked up on Johnny's discomfort. But Kit's face looks as closed-off as it usually does.

When everyone leaves, September takes her own book of kindness. She thinks for a long time before she writes in it:

Johnny helped with the decorator and the chairs
Everyone treated me like one of them at book group
My mother loved me

And on the other side:

I gave Dan and Zain the leftover biscuits
I hosted book group
I put out the veg and some berries for book group people to take and they did

She feels, not exactly better, but as though she is attached, a little bit, to this new life. She takes one of Lucia's books of kindness from the shelf and turns to a page at random. She has tried reading them chronologically, but they make such an ache in her as she traces her great-aunt's life without her.

She happens on a page where her mother is mentioned.

7 August 1987

Kindnesses out:

I took April shopping for things for university. Mariah and Richard have given her money to choose her own practical things, bedding and towels and shoes, and she insists she's saved enough for her art materials. But I want her to be so – free – when she gets to London. We went to Leeds and went round the markets and the arcades. April saw a handbag she liked, with fringing, but she wouldn't buy it for herself so I did. She wasn't sure about paintbrushes so I said 'better safe than sorry' and bought them all. We went to a haberdasher's for proper scissors for her dressmaking module. I don't know if I was being kind or whether I was just doing the things I wished Mariah would do. Maybe they're the same.

While we were in Leeds I bought a single ticket for the opera next weekend, and a hotel room. I'll let Mariah think we're both going.

When we got back I went home with April so I could make sure she enjoyed showing Richard and Mariah what she'd bought. I let them tell me off about the handbag. They have no idea what paintbrushes or proper scissors cost so didn't say anything . . .!

I don't know if any of this is kind because I would do anything for April. And it's only money. But today is a day that

April and I will always remember, I think. Her life is so full of possibility.

Mum asked me to go with her to the Women's Institute meeting on Thursday evening and I said I would, even though I've no desire to go to a talk on keeping chickens.

Kindnesses seen:
  April holding doors open for everyone and anyone, and chattering away to a woman on the train who afterwards she said she thought looked lonely.

April putting change in a collection tin at the till of the cafe.

Richard drove me home because he could see I was tired.

The next day, Penny delivers Figgy as promised. When the van pulls up outside the gate, September, watching from the kitchen window, feels a lurch of happiness that she associates with long-ago Christmas mornings. She is at the gate before Penny has opened the back doors of the van.

'Here you are, Figgy, your new home!' Penny says, then, to September, 'Is Johnny here?'

'No,' September says, and then Figgy is pushing her nose into September's hand for the dog treat she's holding, and September kneels to rub her ears. 'Hello, Figgy,' she says. 'This is your home now. I'm going to take good care of you.'

'I can tell you are,' Penny says, then, abruptly, 'Johnny obviously thinks a lot of you. He isn't as tough as he looks.'

'I don't think any of us are,' September says, though this may not, she realises after she's spoken, be true of Penny herself, who is giving off a sort of alligator-wrestling energy which seems completely authentic. She gets up and takes Figgy's lead from Penny; the leather is cracked and scratchy and September thinks, with a tiny rush of pleasure, I'll just get a new one. She's been surprised by how quickly she has got used to the fact that she owns a huge house; that she is, by anyone's standards, a wealthy woman. Having, owning, is becoming her normal, and the September who worked in a supermarket is someone she wants to hug, rather than a past version of herself.

But now the arrival of Figgy, the ease with which she thinks of buying a new lead, give her a spike of unbelief. 'Do you want a coffee?' she asks Penny. She's not sure how long the handover is going to take, and her former self dealt with enough stroppy people to realise that the best thing to do is to present an unruffled front.

Penny shakes her head. 'I've just had one. I'll stay for a bit just to check that she settles.'

September nods. 'Of course.' Next to her, Figgy stands, nose in the air, sniffing and looking. September thinks, yes, this was me, when I first came here. She takes a cautious step; Figgy follows. Then she slips Figgy's lead off and watches as her dog – her actual dog – walks cautiously across the grass, nose to the ground, as though she's looking for something that she dropped. Then, all of a sudden, Figgy stands up, legs taut, and, without warning, starts to run around the garden, skirting the tree and leaping over the taller plants. September and Penny both laugh with the delight of it. Figgy runs two circuits, three, four, before coming to a standstill next to Penny, who puts a hand on her shoulder and says, 'You enjoyed that, didn't you? I think you're going to like it here.'

September shows Penny the bed in the kitchen, the bowls, the food she has bought. Penny seems to unbend a little and tells September some useful things: if you don't want her on the sofa, never let her on the sofa, not even once; try to feed her at the same time each day; make her bed a place in which she is never disturbed. Figgy seems unbothered when Penny leaves; she even leans on September, weight all the way up to her thigh, and September thinks, *Yes*. Penny winds down the window and calls, 'Be careful with Johnny.' September realises it isn't advice to guard her own heart, but a warning. As though she would ever have the power, or the will, to hurt Johnny.

It seems that Lucia made a good life of living here, alone. September will do the same. Being on her own is something she has learnt how to do, surprisingly quickly. Or perhaps it's truer to say that she was on her own even when she was with Shaun.

Figgy seems uninterested in September's sandwich and lies next to her as she eats it in the garden. Afterwards, September fetches her book, and Figgy sleeps beside her. September soon gives up her pretence of reading and watches Figgy – herdogherdogherdog! – whose paws twitch as she dreams of ... whatever dogs dream of. September reaches for her phone and googles dog behaviour, and then leads and collars. She buys a bright red house collar, which Figgy will wear all the time, and a matching, thicker martingale collar for when she's being walked along with a leather lead. She almost shivers at the pleasure of it and, just for a moment, wonders whether she should send Shaun something. Some decent pans, maybe. But instead, she closes her eyes, and drifts into sleep in the sunshine.

'Well! It's all right for some!'

September isn't sure whether it's the voice that wakes her, or the low thrum of a gathering growl that's coming from Figgy. She starts to alertness to find a woman standing not-quite-over her 'All right for some!' she repeats, and laughs. September gets to her feet; one of her legs is asleep and she stumbles slightly, reaches behind her for the arm of the bench. Figgy stands too, and September puts her hand on her dog's neck, curling her fingers round the collar. Figgy is a gentle soul, September is sure. She's equally sure that, if Figgy decided to move, September couldn't hold her. But she seems relaxed now, regarding their visitor with a cool curiosity.

'Can I help you?'

The woman is short and round; she's carrying the sort of wicker shopping basket that would demand its own seat on the bus, though this woman probably drives everywhere. 'I'm your neighbour, on the other side from your vegetable garden. I thought I'd come and say hello.'

'Hello. I'm September.'

'Cassie. Pleased to meet you.'

'Would you like a cup of tea?' September really doesn't want to ask, but Cassie clearly isn't going anywhere.

'If you have time!' Another laugh. 'Your dog isn't going to attack me, is it?'

'She,' September says, and regrets the tea invitation even more. 'I don't know, she's only just arrived. She hasn't attacked anyone yet, though.'

Cassie has lived in the house next door for fifteen years. Her husband is a banker and they have four children aged between twelve and six. Cassie doesn't like dogs but would have a cat, except that her oldest, Jude, is allergic, so they have to make do with rabbits. Her second child, Petra, is lactose intolerant. The twins, Tessa and Rachael, are no trouble except that there are two of them. Cassie dislikes bergamot intensely, but will drink any tea except Earl Grey, and thinks Bettys Tea Room would do a lot better if they weren't so snobbish about coffee. September learns all of these things before she has finished making the tea, and before Cassie has asked her a single question about herself. She doesn't really mind; she just keeps an eye on Figgy, who has settled in her bed and closed her eyes. September wonders if her dog is pretending to be asleep. She puts half a packet of chocolate digestives on to a plate.

'What a treat!' Cassie says. 'I bake everything from scratch and you forget how different shop-bought is. I should buy biscuits more often, then I might have a bit more time to spend on more important things!'

'Yes,' September says – she used to bake with her grandma, but can't say she has any desire to start again – and, from Cassie's face, realises that she was supposed to say something about how she is sure Cassie's home-made biscuits are delicious.

'What about your family?'

'Oh, there's just me,' September says, lightly, although the words sting the backs of her eyes on the way out.

'It's a big house for just you.'

September would like to have the courage to say, yes, and nothing else. But she gives a sanitised version of how she came to be here: her part of the family had lost touch with Lucia's, and it was only after Lucia's death that the solicitor made contact. Cassie puts her head on one side. 'You have a look of Lucia, now I think of it,' she says. 'Same eyes.'

September feels the breath go out of her. Being told she looks like Lucia gets her every time. She warms to Cassie the way she always warmed to supermarket customers who came back to apologise when they had been rude.

'Did you know her well?'

'Lucia? No.' Cassie's mouth makes a shape that makes September want to retract her previous good feeling. 'We always invited her to things, of course – community things – but she rarely came. I'd have thought she would be interested, given all of her,' Cassie pauses, 'activities. But Neighbourhood Watch and the group to oppose the social housing development weren't her cup of tea. She seemed to prefer the company of miscreants and ne'er-do-wells to her neighbours.'

'Miscreants?'

'Well,' Cassie sighs, as though putting down a burden, 'I know she meant well, but she did seem to spend a lot of time with people who –' she lowers her voice, '– weren't like us. There were plenty of things she could have got involved in, through Neighbourhood Watch and with the Rotary and so on, putting money into the community via charities so that the people who needed help got help that way. Her father was President of the Rotary, you know, and her mother was President of the Inner Wheel. Before my time, of course, but older members still talk about them. But Lucia very much preferred to be hands on.'

September thinks of Dan and Zain, of Esin and William. She wants to ask, is it only the people who are not white that you think she should have kept away from, or would you have objected to me, too, when I was poor? Instead she says, 'I'm still finding out about my great-aunt. But I admire her. A lot.'

'Of course!' Cassie beams. 'She was marvellous, of course, I didn't mean to suggest otherwise. But it was something of a relief when the house was empty and there wasn't so much coming and going.'

The questions and retorts line up in September's brain, ready to march out. How much coming and going does your family do? Would you rather you were able to form a committee and decide yourselves who could move in?

But she doesn't say anything, except, 'Well, as I say, I'm still settling in.'

'So you're staying?'

'Yes,' September says firmly, 'I'm staying.'

'That's such good news,' Cassie beams. 'We were afraid that Lucia would have left the place to a charity that would make it into some sort of halfway house for waifs and strays.'

Figgy, presumably dreaming, makes another of her low growls. Cassie glances at her, and then at September. September says, 'Figgy's just arrived. I don't know what her noises mean yet. But I think a growl might be a warning?'

Cassie half-laughs. 'Oh!' she says, then, 'I brought you something.' She brings a tin from her basket and puts it on the kitchen table with a clunk. 'It's my prizewinning fruit cake.'

'Thank you.' September feels genuinely touched. However – let's call it strange – Cassie is, she's bothered to make a cake.

'A pleasure,' Cassie says. 'It won first prize two years running at the Women's Institute annual competition,'

September realises she was supposed to ask about the prize, 'and the following year, the organisers asked me not to enter so I could give everyone else a chance!'

'It must be delicious,' September says, and then asks, 'how long will it keep?'

'There's so much booze in it that it will keep until Christmas!'

'Great,' September says. 'In that case I'll keep it and share it with book group. That's three weeks.'

'Oh, you're keeping on with the book group? I assumed you would put a stop to it. It seemed very odd, that they kept meeting after Lucia died, although her solicitor assured me that it was all above board.'

'It was, and it is,' September says. 'Would you like to come? We're reading *Oliver Twist* for next time.'

The expression on Cassie's face is a fight between politeness and horror. September suspects that the road which led to Marina assuring Cassie that the book group was entitled to meet was somewhat more unpleasant than Cassie has suggested.

'Oh,' Cassie says, 'I belong to a book group already. We're reading underrepresented women in translation this year.'

September nods. 'That's a shame. I'm sure everyone here will enjoy the cake, though. Thank you for bringing it.'

'You're very welcome,' Cassie says.

September deploys her customer-service smile and waits for Cassie to finish her tea.

'Have you been baking?' Johnny asks, when he arrives the next day. They are going to Bettys Tea Room for afternoon tea.

'What? No,' September says, and then, realising he is looking at the cake tin on the table, 'Oh, that! My neighbour came. She brought a fruit cake.'

'Cassie?' Johnny says. 'She was a pain in Lucia's neck, always complaining about everything. And after your aunt died she tried to stop the book group from meeting here.'

'That's because you're miscreants and ne'er-do-wells,' September says. She takes the lid off the cake tin. 'Though to be fair, this looks like a good cake.'

Johnny claps his hands. 'Right! let's get this show on the road. I still cannot believe you haven't been to Bettys.'

'I used to be poor, Johnny,' September says. 'And even before I was poor, I had parents who believed in saving and giving to others rather than spending on themselves. Afternoon tea wasn't really something we did. Not out, anyway.' She isn't annoyed, but she hears a weariness in her own voice.

Johnny looks at her, uncertain. 'I thought you wanted to go.'

It's such a strange thing, to see him discomfited. Johnny is one of the most naturally confident people September has ever met, easy in every conversation, happy in his skin. Or that is what she has thought. Now she looks at him again. She thinks of how she must seem, these days, with her pricey clothes and her hair and nails always done. Appearances can be deceptive. Hers certainly is. Maybe that's what makes her say, 'Why did Penny warn me about being careful with you?'

The light seems to go out of Johnny; he bends to Figgy, who is happily devouring the pig's ear he brought for her. September buys high-protein, grain-free raw food meals for Figgy, which she always eats, but she does seem to prefer any old animal offcut. Clearly this is how you make friends with a hound. 'What did Penny say?'

September shrugs. Maybe she shouldn't have said anything. 'Nothing, really. She just gave me the impression that if I did anything to hurt you, she and all the dogs she could find would be round to sort me out. I thought she must be your ex. Or something.' Johnny is leaning against the side of the table, looking out of the window, his body still. 'I shouldn't have said anything,' she adds.

Johnny looks up at September then, and the brightness is back in his eyes. 'Of course you should. Penny's just a bit protective. She treats her friends like she treats her rescue dogs.'

They both look at Figgy. This is the first time September has left her alone in the house. She puts on the old kitchen radio, which is stuck on a classical music station, for company.

It's another bright day. September has bought something called a tea dress for the occasion. Before, she used to think of clothes as everyday or best. Their categories were simple: jeans, trousers, tops, blouses, dresses. Now, she knows that everything can be subdivided. Tea dresses are a whole category of dress of their own, and they are pretty and a little bit floaty. She's wearing a floral one today, with rose-gold sandals.

September and Johnny walk in silence across the Stray. Then, as they turn the corner of the road that leads to the town centre, Johnny begins to talk. September wonders if it's easier to tell someone things, important things, if you don't have to look at them as you do so. She thinks of Shaun, concentrating on putting documents into piles as he talked about his debts. 'Penny and I have known each other for a long time,' Johnny says. 'We went to school together, and we both went to Lancaster uni, though really by chance. I was doing History and she was doing Geography. I think we both assumed that we'd only stick together until we found our feet, but we ended up in the same crowd most of the time. Her best friend was Skye. Skye was my girlfriend.'

'I see,' September says, but realises immediately that she doesn't. If she knew Johnny better she would take his arm.

Johnny shakes his head. 'Skye and I were – we were perfect together. There wasn't a day when I wasn't mad with happiness just to wake up with her. I hated the bits of the holidays when we weren't together. She was just – she was beautiful and clever and funny. She was perfect.'

September doesn't say anything. She's noticed how often he has said 'was'. She wants to stop this story, to close the book before anything bad happens.

They walk in silence as they cross James Street, dodge the tourists around the war memorial. Johnny says, 'We were going to get married straight out of uni, but her parents persuaded us to wait a year. We found a flat to rent and moved in. Then—'

'Johnny—' September says. She feels sick with the thought that she's made him talk about all this awful, awful history, based on her mild dislike of Penny and the idea that, if she were ever to have a relationship again – and she certainly isn't ready, isn't thinking about it at all, really – then someone like Johnny would be the sort of man she would like to be with. Someone kind and warm and a bit silly, who asked her what she wanted to do, who listened when she talked.

Someone who is walking beside her with his head tilted slightly away, so he can pretend that he isn't crying. September puts her hand on his arm and wishes she could unask her question.

'It's fine,' he says. 'You'd find out sooner or later. It's part of me.' He takes a breath that gutters in his throat. 'A drunk driver hit her car three weeks before our wedding. She died instantly.'

'Johnny, I'm so sorry,' September says. She slows her steps, but Johnny is still walking, so she addresses the air beside him. 'I'm really sorry for what happened to Skye, and you, and for bringing it up.'

Johnny shakes his head. 'I'd have wanted you to know,' he says.

And then they are at Bettys. As they wait to be shown to their table they stand in a silence that September judges to be not uncomfortable, though she's not sure she really knows Johnny well enough to be able to tell.

The Imperial Room, upstairs at Bettys, is where a full afternoon tea is served: if you want something different, or less substantial, then you sit in the cafe downstairs. The tea room is grand and beautiful. The ceilings are high and hung with chandeliers. There's a piano in the corner; it takes a moment for September to realise the pianist is playing 'Somewhere Over the Rainbow', with many tinkly extra bits. They are shown to their table, which overlooks the gardens; once they are settled, September takes her time to look around. At first, she thought that having money meant that you didn't have to worry. Then she thought it meant you could have what you like: a dog, a haircut, a pair of trainers even though you already have a pair of trainers. Now she's beginning to realise that money means that everything can be beautiful. 'What do you call the—' she asks Johnny. 'The white bits on the walls.'

He looks around, puzzled, and then says, 'Mouldings. The Georgians were very fond of general –' he indicates the curtains '– swaggers.'

'Is that a word?'

'It is now.' Johnny laughs. September hadn't got around to looking at the curtains yet. They are thick and embroidered with flowers, over a striped blind.

The table is laid with white linen and there's a plate, cup and saucer with a pattern of pale green leaves around the edges; when September lifts the cup, the word 'Bettys' is in the middle of the saucer.

Their waitress arrives. 'Welcome to Bettys,' she says, then, 'Oh.'

'Kit!' Johnny says. 'Good to see you.'

'Hey.' Without her rows of chunky earrings and her cat-eye eyeliner, with her hair slicked rather than ruffled, Kit is almost unrecognisable. She looks younger. She's wearing a white lacy blouse and black trousers; there's a brooch with a 'B' at her collar.

'Hello, Kit.' September thinks of how weird it used to be to meet people she knew in real life when she was at work. 'I forgot you worked here.'

'Yup,' she says, and then, as though a door has closed, she says, 'I'll take your order for tea whenever you're ready. You can try as many different teas as you'd like; just let me know when you've finished your first one and tell me whether you'd like the same again or something else from the tea menu. Are there any allergies I need to be aware of?'

Johnny shakes his head; September does too. They order the house blend of tea.

When Kit has gone, Johnny says, 'She used to work at York uni.'

September says, 'I used to work in a supermarket.' What she means is: I know what it's like, to wear a uniform in a place that isn't the place you would have chosen to be.

Johnny laughs. 'You may have mentioned that, September.'

Afternoon tea comes on a three-tier stand with something that may be an acorn, an upside-down pineapple or an artichoke on the top. September has to take Johnny's word for the last one; she only knows artichokes as things that come in jars of oil and live near the capers on a shelf. There are sandwiches on the bottom tier, scones with pots of cream and jam beside them on the middle tier, and six tiny cakes on the top, three of each kind. The cherry tarts have a shard of white chocolate sticking out of them, like a stalk. September thinks: *It's someone's job to think of that. It's someone else's job to put the pieces of white chocolate in.*

Everything is small and dainty, which is to say, September feels clumsy and overwhelmed as she tries to work out how to eat a sandwich which is stacked with smoked salmon, some sort of soft cheese, and has a little piece of something pink and pickled on top. 'I bet you can't get it in in one go,' Johnny says, as he does; she laughs and does the same. The roast beef sandwich is two bites of deliciousness; the egg sandwich spurts, a bit, but the bits land on the tiny plate and September scoops them up with the tiny fork. The tea comes in silver teapots which have a strainer with them;

there's an extra pot of hot water, which gives September a stab of remembering her grandmother, who believed in tea leaves and strainers and topping up with hot water, too.

When Kit comes back, she seems a bit more relaxed. 'I wasn't expecting to see you,' she says.

'It must be lovely working here,' September says, and then feels patronising. Kit doesn't respond, except to ask if they would like more sandwiches. Johnny says, 'Absolutely, we would,' and while they wait, September notices that the painting on the wall just across from them is yet another gloomy landscape.

'So, what are you planning to do?' Johnny asks, once they have started on the scones.

'Do?'

He shrugs. 'You don't seem the sort of person who –' he laughs, a sound loud and wide, '– whose life is only about going out for afternoon tea.'

September springs to her own defence. 'I help William with the garden, and Dan and Zain come and play the piano, and I'm really still getting used to everything. And I've got Figgy now.' The thought of their walks through the park and the quiet, early streets warms her. Figgy has only run away once, and that was after a rabbit, which September thinks is probably okay. A dog is a dog, after all, and Figgy came back when the rabbit disappeared into a bush.

Johnny shakes his head. 'I'm terrible at this,' he says.

'At what?'

That laugh again. 'Talking. Saying what I mean. Basic human interaction.'

September thinks about the way Johnny talked to Marco

and Penny, and how he always has something to say at book group. 'I don't think that's true.' She looks at him seriously, so he knows she isn't flirting.

'I was trying to ask a question that came out wrong, and I offended you.'

'I'm really not offended,' September says. 'Give it another go.'

'Right-oh.' Johnny closes his eyes – switches off that cool grey gaze – and seconds pass. September takes her second scone, cuts it, spreads the cream and jam while she waits. Johnny opens his eyes and says, 'You've inherited more than a house and money. You've inherited a new life. You seem to me to be someone who might want to do something with it, once you've found your feet. My question was something about that, but I'm not sure I can tell you exactly what.'

'Of course,' she says, 'I'd like to be helpful. But I don't know how. I don't want to be . . .' She thinks of Cassie, who followed up her visit with a note through the door, which includes an invitation to the Inner Wheel and a request to donate bric-a-brac for a church fundraiser. 'I want to be a good person, of course I do. But at the moment I can't think much beyond things like getting the house decorated.' She almost adds, *I owe myself kindness, because there hasn't been a lot of it in my life lately.* Instead, she goes with, 'I'm keeping a book of kindness now.'

Johnny nods. 'When Skye died I ran marathons and wrote articles about being bereaved, to raise money and to raise awareness, but I realised that I was getting something from it. There's something comforting about everyone feeling sorry for you. It validates your own sadness.'

'Yes,' September says, 'when my parents had died I used

to go and see their friends. I thought it was what they would have wanted, and maybe they would, but I think it was really for me.' She trails off. Two dead parents is nothing like as bad as your fiancée dying before your life together has even begun.

But Johnny nods. 'Exactly,' he says.

The toilets are up a flight of wooden stairs. Everything at Bettys seems to be beautiful, including – maybe especially – the loos. The wallpaper is covered with a cherry blossom pattern, and there's a white orchid, vast and beautiful, in a ceramic pot next to the sink.

September imagines one in the living room, on one of the tables she has kept. She wonders how easy they are to keep alive: she only knows about outdoor plants. Still, if they die she could always replace them. She checks her make-up and puts on a fresh coat of lipstick, looking in the mirror. She thinks of that first day in Lucia's house: the hallway, the sideboard, the mirror. She has more lipsticks now. She remembers how lost she was, then: how frightened, although she didn't know it. She had only just learned her mother's name.

They don't quite eat everything. September says 'yes' to taking the leftovers home. Johnny walks back with her, and the sun is shining. September left a twenty-pound note folded under her plate, for Kit. Life feels good. 'Do you want some more tea?' she asks, with a laugh, when they get back to her gate. Johnny rolls his eyes. 'No, but I really need to pee,' he says.

When September opens the door Figgy is not waiting

to greet her, tail wagging, the way September thought she might be. Johnny goes to the loo and September goes into the kitchen, where she is hit by a smell of acid and bile. Figgy is lying in her bed, panting, and there are little piles of vomit and trails of diarrhoea all over the kitchen.

'Figgy!' But when she gets close, Figgy growls and bares her teeth. She tries again; the growling becomes snarling.

Part of September wants to cry – her precious dog, unhappy and unwell – but the bigger part needs to act. 'I'm going to ring the vet,' she tells Johnny, and as she waits for someone to pick up, Johnny says, 'September.' He's holding the tin that the fruit cake came in. 'This was on the floor.'

'Oh.' September hangs up the call. 'What a relief. So I guess fruit cake doesn't agree with you, hey, Figgy?'

'No,' Johnny says, 'dried fruit is poisonous to dogs. You need to get hold of the vet, now.'

The vet comes. She explains that dogs growl and snarl when they feel weak or vulnerable; they don't want the pack to turn on them. She puts on thick protective gloves then sedates Figgy. September and Johnny help to lift her on to a wheeled trolley. September tries not to think of the phrase 'dead weight'. The vet puts Figgy into her van to drive her to the surgery, a couple of miles away, and Johnny and September follow in Johnny's car. September asks him to leave her at the vet's while she waits for news, but he stays; after an hour's wait, the vet tells them that Figgy needs to stay on a drip overnight, to try to flush her kidneys. But, she says, it's good that she's still alive. Many dogs who eat dried fruit are not so lucky.

Johnny drives September home.

'Are you going to be okay?' he asks when they pull up outside the house.

'Yes,' September says, then 'No.' A big house, she realises, is worse when you're sad. So much space to feel small in. Small and stupid. Penny was right. She shouldn't have got a dog if she couldn't look after it properly. She feels tears in her throat.

Johnny turns off the engine. 'Why don't we take that massive TV of yours for a spin? Let's watch a film?'

So they do. They settle on the chesterfield – September cannot decide whether she likes it or not, so she's keeping it for now – and flick through films. When she says she has never seen *Home Alone*, Johnny puts it on, and it's just the thing: ridiculous and funny. 'Are you up for *Home Alone Two*?' Johnny asks when it finishes, and September says yes, but before they watch it she goes into the kitchen, with its sharp stink of bleach from the cleaning they did while they waited for the vet to arrive. She makes tea, and puts crackers and cheese on a plate; Johnny smiles when she returns to the living room, and when she hands him his tea, he says, 'I thought when we left Bettys we said we were never going to drink tea again.'

September laughs, and then stops. The vet said there wouldn't be any news until morning, but still she checks her phone.

'Hey,' Johnny says. 'She'll be all right.'

'I shouldn't have—' September begins, but the list is so long that the things she shouldn't have done form an inexpressible clump in her throat. She shouldn't have left the fruit cake out. She shouldn't have gone to Bettys. She shouldn't have got a dog if she didn't understand all the things that could poison it. She shouldn't have got a dog – she sees it, suddenly, and feels a fool for not knowing before – she shouldn't have got a dog to assuage her own loneliness, to make her feel better about rattling round in a great big house. The kid in *Home Alone* coped better than she did.

'Hey,' Johnny says again, and puts an arm around September's shoulder, pulls her in. 'You'll be all right, too. I promise.' And September doesn't cry, although she had thought she might. She closes her eyes. There's something about Johnny's warm body, the feel of his breath moving in and out of his chest, slow and calm, that lulls her, and even though she was sure that she wouldn't – couldn't – sleep, the next thing she knows he is nudging her awake and coaxing her to bed. When her phone wakes her at eight in the morning, with an update from the vet, she goes downstairs to find Johnny asleep on the chesterfield.

Kindnesses in:
Johnny stayed
The vet and the vet nurse were so kind even though
   I was an idiot
Figgy has forgiven me
Thanks to Lucia I can have a dog, and pay a vet
Even though Esin is a bit scared of dogs, she was nice
   to Figgy and to me

Kindnesses out:
I donated to an animal charity
I tipped Kit £20

*   *   *

It's two weeks since Figgy ate the fruit cake. Johnny has popped in most days; at first it was to check on Figgy, and then it was to watch more of the *Home Alone* films, then the *Die Hard* series. There's a delightful sort of childishness to it, a simplicity in following the sequence and a restful lack of decision-making. Sometimes, they get a takeaway. One evening, Johnny arrives while she and William are harvesting courgettes, carrots and gooseberries. William stays and watches *The Big Lebowski* with them, as they've moved on to the Coen brothers. September orders pizzas and they open a bottle of wine: William's laugh is a resonant rumble that sets September off even when she doesn't think the film is as funny as he and Johnny seem to. When the two men leave, September gives Johnny a carrier bag full of carrots and courgettes, and he takes half of them out of the bag, puts them back on the kitchen bench, and says, 'As I don't have any donkeys, this should do me.'

William takes a small bag of carrots. 'I also do not have a donkey,' he says, and the sound of laughter lingers after September has closed and locked the front door behind them.

Kindnesses:
The dog groomer said Figgy was her favourite dog of
   the day
The Oxfam lady says Lucia's coats will be useful, and
   she was too kind really – so sympathetic that I didn't
   have the heart to tell her I didn't know her
Johnny

Kind things I did:
Took carrots and potatoes to the food bank. They

wouldn't take them so I left them outside the gate here

Paid Zain and Dan to help William with jobs in the garden at weekends

Tipped the dog groomer £10 and donated £50 at the Oxfam shop

September didn't think she would enjoy *Oliver Twist*. She remembers a film of it that her parents really didn't like; something to do with stereotyping. When she took the book from the shelf in the library, she looked at the small, dense text, and felt certain that reading it would be a slog. But she has found it compelling. It's about so much more than a boy in a poorhouse asking for more. She and Esin talk about it while they make gooseberry jam. Esin has found an old jam pan in the back of a cupboard, and September realises it's exactly the same as the one her parents used to use for plum jam and green tomato chutney from the gluts at the allotment. The kitchen gets hot and sticky, and the smell of the boiling fruit is sharp-sweet. Esin says, 'It is so strange to me that there would be an orphanage. In my country, someone would take you in.' Her eyes widen. 'Oh, September. I am sorry.'

September shakes her head. 'Don't be sorry. Lucia would have taken me in if she had known where I was.'

'Yes,' Esin says.

'Do you miss your family?' September says, before she has thought about what she's asking. 'Esin. I didn't mean – of course you do.'

Esin puts down the jars she's been sorting through; they are going to sterilise them in the oven. She takes September's hand. 'I miss my father, but I know he is gone now. I am sorry I was not with him when it happened. But these sadnesses, they must not stop us from living our lives. My father used to say, even on a mountain, there is still a road.'

September nods. And then she remembers something she has not thought about in years. 'My dad used to say, bloom where you are planted.'

William arrives first, and admires the ranks of labelled jam jars. 'Soon,' he says, 'we will all wish we had never seen a gooseberry. My wife, though, she would have more jam than bread.'

September smiles. 'I like the sound of that,' she says.

Johnny is next through the door. 'You look nice. As does Princess Figgy.'

September laughs, and decides to ignore what he's said about her. It's easier. 'She's been groomed. I don't think she liked it much.'

'She is always beautiful,' Esin says.

'I had a quick shower after we made the jam,' she says, just to cover her embarrassment. Johnny isn't complimenting her on her cleanliness.

Fortunately, the doorbell rings again before anyone can say anything else. She goes to let in Dan and Zain, who are soon followed by Kit.

September now buys Coke and Fanta for book group (and herself), as an alternative to tea, coffee or water. It seems to her, sometimes, that Lucia's habits solidified somewhere in the mid-1970s, and although she respects that, she wants Dan and Zain to have things they might not get at home, and Kit to have a change from tea and coffee. She puts out crystal glasses, though, in the hope of appeasing Lucia's ghost.

It's William's turn to start: he chose *Oliver Twist* for them. 'I had this book as a boy,' he said, 'and I read it like an adventure. It is full of escapes and good things happening if you wait long enough.'

Kit presses her lips together. September knows she is thinking about Nancy, who is abused by Bill Sikes.

William continues, 'But when I read it again when I was older, I saw so much darkness. And I have read it once more, just now, and found that things are not so very different as they were then.' He shakes his head. 'Maybe I should have chosen something else.'

'Not a lot of brown people in this one for sure,' Dan says. 'It's like we didn't exist.'

William nods. 'Very true.'

Esin nods. 'It is certainly a classic. I think everyone must know about it.'

'Classic don't mean white,' Zain says.

Esin's hand goes to her mouth. 'Oh, no, no!' she says. 'I know that. But in the days before, so many white writers, and they see what they see.'

Kit says, 'So many male writers, and they see what they see, too.'

'It is pretty unkind to Jews, as well,' William says. 'Those people had enough to put up with.'

September starts to feel a squirming discomfort. She didn't think of any of these things. She thought about Nancy, and her violent boyfriend, and she thought about what it is to be poor. There's a moment of quiet; then Johnny speaks.

'This isn't a defence of anti-semitism. But Dickens writing about poverty like this was pretty revolutionary.'

'But what he shows,' Esin says, 'is that the poor do not matter. Oliver only starts to matter when he is a rich man. If he had not become rich, what is the story?'

'He matters to Dickens,' Johnny says, with a smile.

September finds her voice. 'I wasn't much of a reader until I came here. And I've liked most of what we've read.' She thinks of the birthday gifts she's unwrapped, the way she's felt when she's read about all the orphans. They have felt, sometimes, like messages from Lucia. 'But there was something about this. I felt as though – as though I could really relate to it.' As she says this, she feels ridiculous. She imagines Shaun, laughing at her for 'relating to' – she can see him, making quote marks with his fingers – a fictional small boy from a couple of hundred years ago.

But Shaun isn't in her life any more. These people, her friends, are watching her, waiting. 'I mean – being poor is horrible and it grinds at you, so it's all you can think about. I thought that came over really well. If you're hungry, you're hungry.'

'This is true,' Esin says. 'When your life is struggle then all you think of is struggle.'

Kit, who hasn't said anything yet, makes a noise in her throat.

'Kit?' William asks.

Kit shakes her head. 'Nothing,' she says.

'Please,' September says. She thinks of Kit-at-work, her make-up muted and her slight air of embarrassment.

Kit exhales, and looks at September. 'Did you ever live in a poorhouse? Did you ever live on the street? I don't think you can live here and talk about poverty.' She casts an arm around, managing with her gesture to take in not only the house and the garden, but all of September's frivolity; the fact that she's signed up to every streaming service, the amount of takeaways she eats, Figgy's selection of beds and leashes. 'You struggled before you got this massive inheritance. We get it. That doesn't make you Oliver Twist.'

There's a moment of silence. September realises she needs to be the one to break it. She feels a surge inside her: it takes her a moment to realise that it's power. She has power. She could ask Kit to leave, ask them all to leave, cancel book group for ever. She could demand an apology. Anything she asked for right now would be done.

She imagines the notebook beside her bed; writing in it tonight, 'I was kind to Kit.' She takes a breath. 'I know how lucky I am,' she says quietly. 'I just meant I've never related to a book in this way before. That was all.'

The room exhales. Kit nods, but she doesn't say anything. William talks about how easy it was for people to drop through the holes in society, how it seems to be becoming like that again. September thinks of how, somehow, a hole opened up beneath her when she was a child, and no one was able to pull her out of it.

Book group fizzles out pretty quickly after Kit's challenge. Dan and Zain play the piano; Johnny makes more tea. But the group parts early and without the usual cheerfulness, and September finds that even the slow deliberateness of washing the crystal glasses by hand, and then the rhythm of brushing Figgy before bed, can't relax her.

She wonders whether Lucia had been seen as – whatever Kit sees her as. Penny too, perhaps. Selfish? Ignorant?

Playing at life because she doesn't have to work at it any more? The unfairness of it stings at the corners of her eyes, hurts her throat. None of them know what her life was like. She should have asked Kit whether her parents are still alive, whether she has ever had a boyfriend who stole from her, if she knows how cold it is in the storeroom at the back of a supermarket but it doesn't matter if you get through the first hour because after that you can't feel your feet at all.

September runs a bath but finds that she cannot enjoy it. She thinks about the cost of the hot water. The bath bomb had seemed such a fun thing to buy but cost more than she once would have spent on a six-pack of soap that would have lasted her for months. When she gets out, hot and discontented, she wraps herself in a towel that belonged to Lucia and is probably older than September herself is, but it's thick and warm and has at least a dozen identical companions in the airing cupboard. September's moisturiser cost £10, which Marina said was 'cheap as chips', and she has a separate body butter that was twice the price. By the time she puts on her pyjamas – new, too, and the fact that she bought them because she used to sleep in Shaun's band T-shirts doesn't feel important any more – she's crying. Figgy comes to her where she's sitting on the bed, and pushes her nose into her side; September pulls herself together. Her phone buzzes: it's Johnny. Sorry I had to dash. Are you ok? She almost says no, but what would Kit think of that? Crying because someone said she wasn't as badly off as she thought she was, to a man whose fiancée died? Fine! she types, and then takes the exclamation mark off. Fine. Just going to bed. Thanks for checking.

In her book of kindness, September writes:

Kindnesses to me:
Esin and the jam. I never would have tried on my own. And she's going to bring some saffron from home so she can teach me to make the crispy rice dish (I think she said tahdig) we had before book group
William showed me how to check for slugs when he would have been quicker doing it on his own
Marina wants to take me out for lunch again
Johnny messaged to check in

My kindnesses:
Putting the extra veg outside the gate for people to take
I was kind to Kit
I hosted book group

She looks down at the list; then she flicks back through the pages. She sees how people have gone out of their way to help her – not just Johnny, but Esin and William and even Dan and Zain with their WhatsApped videos of their music. In return, her efforts feel minimal. 'Giving away what she doesn't want or has too much of' would sum it up. That's not kindness, not really. She thinks of all the things Lucia gave and hosted and organised and donated, listed in those books of kindness that she filled in so conscientiously. September chooses another page at random.

4 January 1993

Kindnesses in:
I can hardly write this down for crying. Celeste came to find me in the staffroom at lunchtime and asked me about Christmas. I thought it was going to be the usual 'lovely, how was yours', but when I started to talk about taking my parents to church she put her hand on my arm and said she didn't mean that, she meant she knew it was a year since I had last seen my niece and she thought it might have been hard. I couldn't even speak. Everything I've been holding in over Christmas just built up and built up and came out. When I'd cried my eyes out I saw that Peter was eating his sandwiches in the corridor so he didn't disturb us. Celeste talked more about April and September than my whole family did over the holidays. It was as though they had never existed. Sometimes I don't know what I did to deserve them.

Lucia hasn't written any kindness she performed that day. September thinks of how much of Lucia's life, after April left, was one great effort of kindness and tolerance to a family that seemed to ignore anything that was difficult; and, in doing so, made Lucia's life so thankless. September wishes she could thank her now.

And then she thinks, *I can*. Out loud, she says, 'Dear Aunt Lucia, thank you for the books. Thank you for the house. Thank you for trying to find me.'

It's not enough.

She thinks about Marina asking her what her plans are, Johnny questioning her, over tea at Bettys, to try to find out what she was going to do. They are both right: she needs to do something. She can be truly useful, if she tries. She can repay Lucia's kindness with true kindness of her own. Giving money away doesn't really mean anything when she has more than she could ever spend.

First things first. Kit's number is in the book group WhatsApp. September messages her: You were right in what you said. Would you like to talk more? I could meet you any time. She's not sure that she'll get a response: she suspects that Kit has been quietly seething at her since the first time she mentioned how hard her previous life has been. But she gets an immediate reply: Thank you. I'm sorry I made it about you. 12 tomorrow outside Bettys?

Before she goes to sleep, September adds another entry to her 'Kindnesses to me' list for the day: 'Kit replied.'

September takes Figgy with her to meet Kit. She's worried that, left to herself, Figgy will manage to eat something poisonous again, or injure herself in a way that September has not foreseen. She's bought a book about Scottish Deerhounds now, and it mainly confirms what Penny said, that they are not a starter dog. So September is determined to be the owner Figgy deserves from now on. She's texted Penny to ask if she can recommend a trainer, adding that she knows that it's she who needs the trainer, not Figgy.

They walk into town and find a bench in the park opposite Bettys. September takes *Fingersmith* – her fifteenth birthday present from Lucia – from her bag. She feels as though she is gobbling it, rather than reading: there's a visceral need to find out what's going on in this strange historical mystery. She wishes she could talk to Lucia about why she chose the books she did for her. Though the dedications in the books are a clue: in *Fingersmith* Lucia wrote, 'So many people are talking about this, and I think they are right. I want to give it to everyone I know, and the first person I'm giving it to is you.' Her sixteenth birthday gift was *Northanger Abbey* by Jane Austen, the story of Catherine Morland, unmarried and passed around her relatives, who lets her imagination run away with her and causes problems for herself and hurt for others as a result. Overall, it made September feel loved, as did Lucia's note: 'Dear September, Now you are sixteen, and I love you more than I did on the day I first met you, even though then I thought I could never love anyone more.' *Behind the Scenes at the Museum*, by Kate Atkinson, September thinks she liked, but she was so unsettled by the way the worlds bled one into another that she felt as though the earth wasn't steady under her feet. 'Dear September, Happy 17th Birthday! When we see each other again we'll have so much to catch up on. This book made the breath go out of me at the end.' Her eighteenth birthday gift, *The Yellow Wallpaper* by Charlotte Perkins Gilman, unsettled her too, and makes September wonder about what Lucia's life was like in 2009. It seems she was sad: 'Dear September, when I try to imagine you now I can only think of your mother. She and I read this when she was doing her A-levels.'

Kit emerges shortly after noon; September is so absorbed in the world of Susan and Maud that she jumps when Kit touches her on the shoulder. '*Fingersmith* is brilliant, isn't it?' Kit says. 'It might be my favourite book.'

September nods, and puts her bookmark in place. Kit sits next to her on the bench. She has put a denim jacket on over her white blouse. September thinks of the unpleasant crispness of her old uniform, the way she would always put something on over it, even on the warmest days. She had never been ashamed of her job – she worked hard, and she did well, and if the pandemic had showed them anything it was that supermarket workers mattered – but when she was away from the shop, she didn't want her uniform to define her. In other circumstances, she would have said so to Kit. Instead, she says, 'I almost bought sandwiches on the way, but then I thought you probably get to eat at work.'

Kit makes a noncommittal motion with her head that makes something in September pay attention. She notices the thinness of Kit's wrists, the way her rings are loose.

She should have brought sandwiches.

She should have seen this sooner.

'I shouldn't have talked to you like that,' Kit says.

'Yes, you should. People should say what they think, and anyway, you were right.'

Kit turns her head; September sees surprise in her eyes. 'It wasn't really about the book, though.'

September laughs. 'Okay. You didn't obey the rules of book group. I accept your apology.'

Next to her, she feels Kit relax. 'Thanks.'

'How long have you worked at Bettys?'

'Eight months.' She says it in a way that tells September every day has been a grind.

'And before that?'

'I was a course administrator at York uni. I loved it. Everybody was great and there was always such a lot to do. But not boring, you know? Every day was different. Then the course was cancelled and so I was made redundant.'

'I'm sorry. That's rough.'

'Yeah.' Kit side-eyes September: a look that says, like you'd know.

September takes a breath. 'I've never been made redundant. But I had a job with an advertising agency that I loved. They closed down and I couldn't afford my flat any more. That's when I moved in with my terrible boyfriend. I only found out he had been stealing from me when I inherited.' She realises how she might have sounded: here, in the daylight, it seems clear that Kit's combativeness came from fragility, from fear. 'I'm sorry. I wasn't trying to—' she stops, before adding, 'I wasn't trying to win.'

Kit interrupts. 'I couldn't afford my flat. So I live in my car.' She looks down at her hands. 'Nobody knows.'

With those words, September is straight back to her just-two-slices-of-bread-but-looks-like-a-sandwich in the supermarket staffroom, back to pretending she was busy and couldn't go out with people from work; and, at the other end of her own past life, making out she was absolutely fine with Shaun's refusal to 'work like a wage slave' when that was what *she* had to do. And that was before she knew he was living off her. 'Could I give you a hug?' she asks. Kit shakes her head, but then puts her hand in September's. It sits against her palm, so pliant as to feel boneless; September doesn't squeeze. Something in her tells her not to talk any more, so she doesn't. She waits; but already she is thinking of all the empty rooms in her warm house.

Kit nods, not looking at September, not moving her hand. 'It's better now. The winter was bad. And I only really sleep in the car.' She laughs. 'Before I lost my job I had a gym membership, so I've kept that going, and I go there and shower. I can hang around in the staffroom at work before my shift, and the library is great for reading and being left alone. And I'm actually saving quite a lot. It won't be for ever.' Kit's voice trails away.

September takes a deep breath. She mustn't make things worse.

'I think you were right, what you said last night, about how I have no right to talk about being poor,' she says, 'but I do know what it's like to think about money every single minute of every single day. And to be always looking forward to when it will be better, but having no idea how to get there.'

Kit nods; the vigour of her movement tells September she's said the right thing.

'Even when I've saved enough for a deposit and the rent,' she says, 'I won't have references from a landlord. And I use my old address for the doctor's, but they'll find out sooner or later.'

'Are you ill?'

The nod turns to a shake. 'No. But the car gets damp and there's mould, and in the winter I had a cough for about four months.'

September wants to cry. Kit must be in her mid-twenties, but right now she looks younger than Dan and Zain; her confession seems to have stripped her bravado from her. 'Your family?' she asks gently, though she knows the answer won't be a good one.

Kit sighs. 'I came out to them as gay when I was fifteen. They said it was a phase. By the time I was eighteen we were hardly speaking. One of the neighbours saw me with my girlfriend in the park and my parents said I needed to "stop it" or move out. I moved out. I stayed with my girlfriend for a bit, and then when we split up she let me stay in the flat when she went travelling. She met someone else, they moved in, by then I had my job and the money my parents had saved for me going to college, so I got a little place of my own to rent. Then I lost my job.' Kit's voice has remained even, quiet, but at these last words she raises her hands, palm-up, open-fingered, and looks at them as though she can see the grains of her old life falling through them.

'I'm sorry,' September says again.

'Yes,' Kit says, as though she's empty. 'What time is it?'

'Half past.' Figgy raises her head and yawns, grandly, making them both laugh. September thinks Kit is going to get up, but instead she says, 'I've got ten more minutes of Vitamin D.' She closes her eyes and turns her face to the sun. September looks at her; she wants to gather her up. She also wants to go and have a word with Kit's parents. She thinks of her own mum and dad, and cannot imagine a single thing she could have done to disappoint them. Except – it crashes on her – except, failing to share her good fortune. She thinks of the conversation she had with Johnny, the carrots at the gate, left for wealthy neighbours who probably usually buy organic carrots from the farmer's market without a thought for the cost.

'Kit,' September says, 'I have plenty of room. Come and stay.'

Kit says no, of course. September thinks she probably would have done the same, in the circumstances. It's hard to admit to something you're ashamed of, let alone face the person you've confided in the next day. The only person September had ever talked about her circumstances with, before, was Michelle at work, who was leaving the following week. It had been after one of Shaun and his brother's Big Nights Out, which had come the week after September had had to turn down an invitation to a hen do because she couldn't afford it. All she could see, that day, was struggle. Michelle had asked if she was okay and September had started to cry and could not stop. Michelle had been kind and sympathetic, but September had still avoided her afterwards until she left.

Later, she composes a careful WhatsApp. Dear Kit, I respect your decision. But maybe come and stay for a week and park the car on the drive and let it air? If you like you can help me do some sorting. I need to go up and have a look at what's in the loft. September.

She has no idea what Kit will say, but she goes upstairs and looks at the bedrooms, anyway. Her first thought is to put Kit into Lucia's room, which has an en suite, but when she goes in to open the windows, she realises that there's so much personal stuff – so much stuff, generally – that it would feel like staying in a museum. So she moves her things, and Figgy's bed, out of her own bedroom into her great-aunt's, puts fresh white linen on both beds, and sets to work in her new bedroom.

The built-in furniture is dark and old-fashioned, but it's polished and pristine, and there's enough space in the room for it not to be oppressive when the curtains are open. The curtains, dark brown velvet with pelmets and tiebacks, have no redeeming features. September thinks of something Johnny said, about how if you can't live with it, there's bound to be someone in the world who can, and that's how the antiques business works. And then she brings empty boxes from the fourth bedroom and starts to empty drawers and cupboards, to make space for her own things. Now she knows so much more about Lucia, it doesn't feel so strange. She doesn't feel as though she is snooping any more.

On the opposite side of the room to the built-in wardrobes there's a very grand dressing table, carved with acorns and leaves, with a triple mirror. The top is bare and polished to a bright shine. September sits on the stool – covered in the same brown velvet as the curtains – and investigates the drawers, two on each side. The right-hand drawers hold only an unopened box of handkerchiefs and a tin full of buttons. The top left-hand drawer contains the remnants of the most austere beauty routine September can imagine: a jar of something called 'cold cream' and cotton wool balls in a wooden box. It seems to be a rich people thing that they take everything out of the container it comes in and put it in another one. She has already found a tin of used stamps in the library, and tins for safety pins and bits of ribbon in the kitchen. September throws the cold cream away without opening it; there's something unsettling about a dead person's half-used cosmetics. She laughs at herself. She's living in her dead aunt's house surrounded by all her things, using her cutlery and crockery and sheets, but moisturiser is giving her weird vibes.

September moves across to the drawers. The top drawer contains the most sensible knickers she has ever laid eyes on. There's something strange about them, too. After a moment she realises that they have been ironed. She laughs and puts them in a bin bag, saying, 'Sorry, Aunt Lucia!' to the air and hearing her mother's voice in place in her head where memory and imagination meet: 'You could have cut those up for dusters.'

There's an envelope at the back of the drawer. It's addressed to Lucia, in handwriting that September recognises as April's. She puts her palm over it for a moment.

Inside the envelope, there's something carefully wrapped in tissue paper.

She sits on the bed to unwrap it.

Inside is a ring, small and delicate, with green stones forming a flower, or a star. She imagines her mother, perhaps finding it in a market or a second-hand shop, thinking of her aunt and deciding that she would like it. Wrapping it in tissue, writing a card, which Lucia might have used as a bookmark. Some of the books in the library have postcards and Christmas cards marking pages. She wonders whether Lucia ever wore it. She slides it on to her finger – it's a little loose – and thinks: *I am wearing something my mother chose. Maybe she tried it on, in the shop where she bought it.* September looks at the envelope: she can't make out the postmark. Maybe she was already born, a baby in a pram, when her mother chose this. Maybe she was big enough to be held up to the postbox to slide the letter in.

Lucia, 1988–91

April doesn't come home from university often, and Lucia doesn't blame her. Her home is even less of a happy place than it was before. Mariah and Richard make little effort to hide their increasing dislike of each other. Lucia can see that they are both drinking to excess: or perhaps it's more accurate to say that they seem never to be not drinking. Lucia finds just being around them on Sunday lunchtimes a trial. They complain about April constantly, though without consistency. One week, Mariah is upset because April has 'abandoned them' and never so much as calls; the next, she is complaining that she was almost late for a concert because April called and 'wouldn't stop talking'. About what? Lucia enquired, and Mariah waved her hand, and said, she's worried about her work, in a way that suggested this was a ludicrous thing for April to care about. Richard returns, again and again, to the theme of April's degree – or 'this so-called art degree' as he refers to it – and what use it is going to be to her. 'No money in being an artist,' he says. When April does come home, she usually lasts about three hours before she calls Lucia. 'Auntie L, you have to HELP

ME,' she breathes down the phone, and then the two of them meet in Harrogate, for tea or a film or, now April is a legal adult, drinks. April is fond of Manhattan cocktails, which she makes with great concentration; Lucia could grow to like them, too. They are certainly better than the sherry her parents drink, and most of the wine she buys, by the glass, if she goes out with her colleagues.

April usually comes home because Rex isn't around. He travels a lot, according to April, who seems to miss him a good deal. It's clear to Lucia that his 'travelling' includes spending time with his wife, and she assumes April knows this too, though it's never mentioned. Lucia has been forced to revise her previous opinion of Rex as someone who cannot possibly hold April's attention for long. She seems to adore him the way Lucia once adored Billy. He wants to come and meet her family, she says, because he sees his future with April. But April doesn't want him to see what they are like. 'Except you,' she says. Lucia remembers how her parents and Mariah treated Billy, and when Mariah and Richard complain about not meeting any of April's friends, she jumps to April's defence. She also points out that Mariah and Richard could always go to London to see their daughter. 'Oh,' Mariah says, 'we can't all be like you, Lucia. Footloose and fancy free.'

Lucia goes to stay with April at least once a term. The flat in Notting Hill Gate is small and dark, but April has draped it with sequinned scarves and lamps and mirrors she buys in markets. Her cutlery and crockery are mismatched; her fridge is full of carrots, hummus and yoghurt, and not a lot else. 'I usually eat at college,' she says. Lucia sleeps in April's double bed with her – it practically fills the bedroom – and often lies awake listening to the traffic and the sounds of chatter in the street. During her London weekends, she and April go to art galleries and flower markets; they eat in vegetarian restaurants where everything tastes slightly undercooked, though April laughs and says that's her aunt's northern palate; they lie in bed and do crosswords in the mornings. April smokes, now, leaning out of the bedroom window; Lucia knows she ought to disapprove, but she imagines herself, in a different life, doing the same thing, waiting for Billy to come home. He'd tease her about her freshly cleaned teeth when he came in. She forgets, more and more, that Billy didn't love her enough. The fact that she let people assume she was the one who ended it still gives her a gnaw of shame. She likes to think she would tell the truth, now.

In her first summer at university, April gets a job in a bar at weekends and in a gallery during the day. She hunts down broken dolls from flea markets and second-hand shops, for a project that she's planning for her second year. She comes home for Lucia's birthday, in early October, and horrifies her parents and grandparents with her bleached hair before heading back to London with a spring in her step. She comes back only briefly at Christmas – 23 December to 2 January – pleading work, and although Lucia is sorry to see her go, she can't blame her for spending as little time as she can with her family. Her parents and grandparents seem to make a point of showing no interest in her life in London, talking only of their friends and what's happening in their world. Whenever Lucia's mother says, 'Oh, April, you won't believe who's died', she and Lucia don't dare make eye contact for fear of laughing. 'If it wasn't for you, Auntie

L, I don't think I'd come back at all,' April says when Lucia waves her off at the station.

It's Easter when April comes again. A series of work events for Lucia, and time with Rex for April, means that Lucia hasn't been to London at all that term.

Seeing April again is a shock. She looks wan and dull. She sleeps and cries. Mariah and Richard speculate that she is upset about 'a boy'; but when Lucia asks, quietly, whether there's anything wrong between her and Rex, April says, 'anything but', and bursts into tears again. There's an explanation, but Lucia doesn't ask. April will tell her when she's ready.

The letter comes two weeks after April has returned to London.

Dear Auntie L,

I know I've asked you to keep a lot of secrets, and now I'm going to ask you to keep another one, but not for long. I think you might have guessed though. I wanted to tell you when I was home but I didn't want to make things difficult for you. And I was scared that you would be disappointed in me. But Rex says that there's nothing I could do that could disappoint you, and I think he's right. I'm going to have a baby, in September. It wasn't planned but I'm happy and so is Rex. We think we can manage for me to finish my degree. I've talked to college and they say I can see how I get on and defer my last year if I need to.

The letter goes on: excitement, plans, hopes. Lucia reads it, again and again. She cannot reconcile April's looping handwriting, the memory of her pale face and her tears, with the idea that she's going to have a child. With Rex. Who shows no sign of leaving his wife and making his relationship with April permanent. Not even now. Lucia wonders if he already has children; cannot bring herself to ask.

Lucia writes back: she tells April that the timing might not be ideal but she will of course support her; how strange it is, to remember when April was born, and now April will have a child. She tells her that her secret is safe with her, and it is.

Though afterwards, Lucia wishes that she had broken the confidence and told Mariah and Richard and her parents. That way, she would have been able to spare April the worst of it. The worst of the first wave, anyway.

April arrives on the train on a sunny day in the middle of June. Richard collects her and brings her straight to her grandparents' house, where Mariah waits with an expression of great martyrdom – 'I do hope she's grown out that awful haircut'. Lucia stands at the library window, watching. She will go out to the car, so that she's by April's side, and she'll stay there, until April decides to break the news. Her beloved niece won't be alone for this. (Maybe, she thinks, if Billy had seen she had some support, he might not have broken things off. She might not have seemed so vulnerable.)

Richard gets out of the car first, and from the expression on his face – part poleaxed, part furious – Lucia realises that the news is out already. April is six months pregnant; maybe even her father can see past whatever April is wearing to disguise the changes in her body. Lucia goes to the passenger door to greet her niece, with some idea of sheltering her; though Mariah is still in the house, on her second gin and tonic.

'Hey, Auntie L,' April says. Her smile is bold but her eyes say something different. 'I thought I'd get it over with. Now

I wish I hadn't.' As she stands, Lucia sees what she means. April is wearing a cropped top and sweatpants, and has tied one of her brightly patterned scarves around her midriff. Her baby bump looks like a gift. And it certainly looks like a baby bump.

'I suppose you knew about this?' Richard says to Lucia. 'I suppose you think it's all right?'

Lucia remembers that her brother-in-law isn't the worst person in the family. 'April's an adult, and she gets to make her own choices,' she says. 'Which I will support.'

She wishes she'd had an Aunt Lucia when she met Billy.

That summer, April and Lucia spend a lot of time together. April comes to the library, where she sits in the reference sections with her sketch book and draws: the people she sees around her, but also, strange trees, flowers whose petals look like the faces of babies, birds in flight. They make Lucia think of the Arthur Rackham illustrated *Peter Pan* which April had loved as a child. Lucia had bought it for her, and Mariah had sniffed at the fact that it was second-hand, and 'too strange' for a child, so it had lived in Lucia's bedroom and she and April had read it when she slept over. When Lucia finishes work, she and April walk home together across the Stray. Outdoors, and away from home, April is sunny and excited. She strokes her belly as though it's a gift she cannot wait to open. Sometimes, in the evenings, Lucia brings out cushions and they sit on the bench under the tree. April dozes or reads – Lucia is distracting her with the books she is thinking of for her book groups, asking her what she thinks – and Lucia knits. When April first came home, Lucia had taken her to the wool shop, where she had picked out a bright turquoise yarn; Lucia is knitting it into a blanket, using the same pattern as she did for April's baby blanket, twenty years ago. Her mother sighs and shakes her head every time she sees Lucia working on it. Mariah tells her off for taking April's side. 'I don't see why my great-niece or -nephew shouldn't have a blanket,' Lucia says. 'Or would you rather it was left on a mountain to starve?'

'Typical,' Mariah says, 'you always take her side. And there aren't any mountains in Yorkshire.'

The wider family has, of course, realised, or assumed, that April's boyfriend is either married, or some sort of unreliable charmer. The conversation about him runs on a loop when April isn't around (and sometimes when she is): why hasn't he proposed/shown his face/taken responsibility? At the end of one such discussion, April yawns and says, 'Does it ever occur to you that I might not want my baby's father to meet my family? I know how you treated Lucia's boyfriend. I hear how you're talking about Rex. Of course I'm not going to bring him here.'

After a moment, it's Lucia's father who speaks. 'If he were any sort of a man, he would come regardless.'

April gets up, slowly, and goes to the door. She turns and says, 'If I were any sort of a woman, I wouldn't come here myself to be put through this spite. One day, I might decide I deserve better.' She doesn't say it as a threat, but as a hope.

April tells Lucia she will name the baby September Lucia if she is a girl, and Luca September if he is a boy. Lucia almost chokes on her tears. Every time she writes in her book of kindness, there are an equal number of kindnesses to and from her niece. It isn't deliberate. In fact, Lucia doesn't even notice until after April has returned to London. Lucia goes to the station with her; Richard waits in the car. As she and April wait, Lucia says, 'I've got something for you.' She opens her purse and takes out the emerald ring. 'It was my engagement ring. I thought it could be yours, if you're in a situation where you want people to . . .' She runs out of steam.

'To not judge me? The worst of that's always going to be here,' April says, and Lucia wishes she'd had the courage then, had the courage now, to leave her parents' house and their hypocrisy and make a life that was all, and only, hers. She feels a fool, for thinking this would help. But April takes the ring and slips it onto her third finger. 'Thank you,' she says. 'It helps so much, to know I always have you.'

On the day the baby is born – 17 September 1990 – April calls Lucia from the hospital. 'She's here!' she says. 'She's perfect! She's so beautiful, Auntie L, I can't stop crying! I can't stop looking at her!'

Lucia, standing in the hallway, cries. 'I'm so glad you are both okay,' she says. She hasn't realised, until now, how afraid she had been. 'Is Rex with you?'

'He was here for all of it,' April says. The pips sound; there is the noise of money being pushed into a slot. 'They have a payphone they can wheel round to you,' she says, then adds, 'Will you tell everyone, Auntie L? I can't bear for them to try to spoil it for me. Her name is September Lucia Merriwether, and she was born just after ten a.m., and she weighs six pounds three ounces, and she has a little fuzz of hair and brown eyes. I'm going to get Rex to send you a photo.'

Lucia stands, for a moment, after she puts the phone down. She wants to enjoy this feeling, before she calls Mariah to tell her the news. Mariah might take it well. But Lucia suspects not. And she is right.

Lucia had hoped that Mariah and Richard might soften towards April as her pregnancy progressed, but they hadn't. Mariah and Lucia's parents, too, stayed stiff. Whenever Lucia has thought there might be a softening – when her mother asked if Lucia had any pictures of April, or her father gave her a bundle of ten-pound notes to pass on, when she was packing for London – Mariah would simply invoke the spectre of What Would the Rotary Club Say and April remained as unwelcome at their home as ever.

September spends her babyhood in the tiny flat in Notting Hill Gate. April ignores all the parenting advice she is given. She sleeps with September in her bed, and she feeds her when she is hungry, and she carries her everywhere. 'We've no room for a pram,' she had said to Lucia when she asked, 'so I'll just carry her until she can walk.' Lucia – who reads baby books at lunchtime – knows that everything April is doing is, theoretically, all wrong, but when she looks at September's perfect, perfect face, the way she plays with her own sweet toes, the brightness in her eyes and her gaze following her mother everywhere, she can only think that April is the best mother she has ever seen. She remembers Mariah, querulous and complaining, and marvels at April's unqualified adoration of her child.

Lucia never encounters Rex. 'He comes when he can,' April explains, 'and obviously he can't be here when you're here, because there's only one bed.'

* * *

April graduates. She completes her degree, it seems to Lucia, one-armed, September always held close. And her exhibition is a thing of strange beauty: doll-sculptures covered in feathers and birds with doll-eyes, tiny hand-sewn creatures in nests of doll-arms and more feathers and twigs, and – oh! – the remnants of the wool from September's baby blanket, which April had asked for. April shines with confidence and pride. Rex comes to the exhibition, too: Lucia has only the most superficial conversation with him, but he holds September and coos at her, and he watches April the way the daisies in the garden watch the sun. Lucia remembers what April said, when she was pregnant, about how she wouldn't want to expose him to her family. So instead of accusations, she asks him, 'Do you think you will ever be able to make things permanent with April?'

'I want to,' he says, and then, as though he's aware of how insipid he sounds, 'I hope to. You know I love them both. It might have been better not to start this, I know, but . . .' He takes September's fist, waves it, kisses it.

'Yes,' Lucia says. She would never wish this beautiful bundle of light out of existence. She buys September books for her first birthday: a newly published book, *The Very Hungry Caterpillar* by Eric Carle, and an old edition of *Peter Pan and Wendy*, illustrated by Mabel Lucie Attwell. April cries when she helps September to open it; she puts it on the shelf, next to her own copy of *Peter Pan in Kensington Gardens*. 'We don't deserve you, Auntie L,' she says.

That year, April and September come for Christmas. Lucia has conducted negotiations with Mariah on the subject: she has given up trying to shame her sister for her treatment of April, or persuade her to come to London with her. But Mariah has never been able to lose to anyone, and Lucia has realised that any move towards April would be a concession Mariah wouldn't make. So instead she talks about how delightful September is, how beautiful and gentle, how much she thinks their parents might like to meet their great-grandchild, if only Mariah and Richard could bear it; and of course, they would stay with Alice and Jacob and Lucia. Lucia mentions that Mariah and Richard still send April money – Richard has insisted – and suggests, obliquely, that April is shirking on her duty by not coming to see her parents. Lucia then writes a carefully truthful letter to April, suggesting that if she and September were to come for Christmas there would be no overt hostility, and that she, Lucia, hopes that when everyone is in the same room, there might be the possibility of forgiveness. April's decision to come is, Lucia suspects, partly motivated by the fact that Rex will be in his marital home.

It starts well. April has dressed September in a checked dress rather than her usual dungarees, and gathered her tufty hair into a little top-knot. She's a picture-perfect baby, and Richard is the first to admire her, to put his finger in the palm of her hand and smile with delight as September grips his finger and conveys it to her mouth. 'She's teething,' April says.

'She's lovely,' Richard responds, and April looks as though she might cry. Alice and Jacob are smiling, at a distance. And Mariah says, 'She's almost as sweet as you were, April.' Lucia takes a moment to parse this to see if it's an insult, and can see from the expression on her niece's face that April is doing the same, but Maria seems sincere.

The days are much like those early art school days when

April came home: there's politeness, and a lot of talk about what's happening in Harrogate, and it seems that the scope of Jacob, Alice, Mariah and Richard's interests cannot extend to encompass April and September's lives in London. Lucia isn't surprised. Mariah and Richard are too busy drinking and fighting to take much notice of what's going on for anyone else. During the last year Richard has had an affair with a colleague; when discovered, he didn't apologise but told Mariah – who moved back in with her parents for two days of non-stop raging – that he wished he had never married her in the first place. He called her a poisonous old crow. She told him he didn't even live up to her low, low expectations. But neither, it seemed, could get up the energy to divorce, so she went home and they remained in their beautiful house, sniping and shouting.

When Christmas morning comes, Lucia thinks April will balk at the expensive identity bracelets that Richard has had made for her and September. It is hardly fashionable jewellery – hardly things that April would choose or wear – and the thought of a one-year-old with a gold bracelet seems ridiculous. But when April unwraps them, Mariah says, 'Richard, we said we weren't wasting money on them,' and Richard says, 'I don't see why a man shouldn't buy something pretty for his daughter and his granddaughter,' and April puts both of their bracelets on immediately.

So overall, on balance, Christmas doesn't go too badly. But then comes New Year's Eve. Lucia offers to babysit, so that April can go out with some of her own friends, but April says she'd rather stay at home. Lucia realises that she is missing Rex. So – oh, Lucia! – she decides to organise a family dinner party.

She plans a menu. She talks her father into buying a couple of bottles of champagne and allows Mariah to dress her up – something Mariah has loved to do, and Lucia loathed, since they were girls. Once the duck is in the oven and the dauphinoise ready, Lucia subjects herself to Mariah's ministrations: 'See how good you would look if you just made a little bit of effort, you might actually find yourself a man at long last.' April brings September in and sits on Lucia's bed, and Mariah unbends a little at the sight of a bathed and sleepy granddaughter, wrapped in the blue blanket Lucia knitted. April sits on the bed and starts to nurse September. In the mirror, Lucia watches. It's such a perfect picture. Lucia feels as though she has spent the last fifteen months looking at the top of April's head; April is always absorbed in her little girl.

Lucia sees, too late, that Mariah is watching April and September, too; but that she isn't seeing love, or fulfilment, or happiness. Lucia remembers – too late, too late – the first months of April's life, when Mariah cried and slept, and Lucia and Richard fed April from bottles and exchanged anxious looks. Mariah was never diagnosed, officially, with anything except 'the baby blues'. Their family doctor had prescribed sleeping pills and fresh air, and Mariah accepted the former and eschewed the latter. Lucia thinks of all the times she has defended April to Mariah and Richard; more recently, how she has championed her: her devotion to September, how their headstrong girl has become a woman they should be proud of. She should have been saying: Mariah, I'm sorry you missed out on such a lot. It isn't too late. She closes her eyes and resolves to do something truly kind for Mariah, every single day, instead of seeing kindness as putting up with her.

Mariah clatters down the hairbrush and says, 'I've done as much as I can with you. April, that child has no business being breastfed at her age. I'm going to get a drink.'

April looks up. 'You've made it very clear that September is none of your business,' she says. Then, when Mariah has left, slamming the door – April winces, holds September close – 'You look lovely,' she says. 'But you always do. Don't take any notice of her.'

'She had a difficult time when you were a baby,' Lucia says. Maybe she should have said more about this, sooner.

'Don't make excuses for her, Auntie L,' April says. 'All the niceness for two people went into you, and all of the spite for two went into her.'

'I don't think it's that simple,' Lucia says. April passes September to her and puts on her own make-up at the mirror; when September is settled in a nest of cushions on the bed, she and Lucia change and go downstairs. Lucia puts on the dress that Mariah brought for her to wear: it feels frumpy despite its shimmer until April ties a bright pink scarf around her waist. April wears a long black T-shirt, which she's embroidered with what appear to be insipid, pretty flowers, until you look more closely and see that they have teeth. April goes to set the table, and as Lucia heads for the kitchen to prep the prawn cocktails – the only thing her father will countenance as a starter – she thinks, at least that's the unpleasantness over with for the evening.

But.

Mariah is drinking, and Richard is drinking, and although her parents are not in any way drunk, they have enough wine to loosen their manners and their tongues a little.

It comes to a head innocuously enough. Richard praises

the duck. Mariah says he doesn't like duck when she cooks it. He says she doesn't cook it, as far as he knows. Their father puts in that Mariah was never much of a one for the kitchen, and adds something unintelligible about what women think they want these days. Mariah spits at Richard that he should have married her mousy little sister, he always seemed to like her better, and Richard says he certainly likes her better now. There's an intake of breath around the table. Lucia and April look at each other: an 'oh-oh' expression. She has always seen herself as April's protector and defender: now she realises she also has an ally in her great-niece.

Mariah puts down her glass, with the great care of the already-drunk. 'I suppose all of you like Lucia better than you like me.'

'Don't be absurd,' their father says.

'You're just different,' their mother says. 'Chalk and cheese. You always have been, right from when you were babies.'

Mariah pulls a face. 'Because I would never settle and Lucia was never a bit of bother.'

'Mariah, you're being ridiculous,' Richard says: Lucia doesn't think this is the most helpful of interventions. But there's something reckless in his eye.

No one says anything. Lucia helps herself to more green beans. No one follows her lead. The serving spoon rattles against the china in the quiet of the dining room. Outside, an early firework laces the sky with light.

Then, April speaks. She pulls herself up straight; looks her mother in the eye. Lucia has an urge to throw something, to burst into song: anything, to stop what's coming.

But everyone is looking at April, who takes a sip of her

wine and then says calmly, 'I wish Richard had married Lucia. I wish Lucia was my mother.'

Lucia opens her mouth to say, *You don't mean that*, but she knows April does. And – as usual, as ever – nothing she says to Mariah, or her parents, will make the slightest impact. So she waits. Mariah is sitting very still.

April isn't finished. 'I used to think I might be adopted. I used to hope that Lucia had got pregnant by mistake and you all bullied her into giving me to Mariah. It's the sort of thing you would do.'

Lucia says, 'April.'

April looks at her. 'It's true. That's what I thought.' Then, just for a moment, she looks like her ten-year-old self: mischievous, eager: 'This would be a great time to tell me I was right.'

Mariah says, 'How could you say such a thing? It's easy to be an auntie, to indulge you and give you everything you think you want. If it wasn't for Lucia you probably wouldn't be in this mess.'

'By mess, I take it you mean September?'

'Of course I mean September. That poor little thing, being dragged up in London with a father who clearly doesn't think much of either of you and a mother who's only ever cared about herself.'

'Oh, for heaven's sake, Mum.' April's anger has a quiet, glittering edge that makes Lucia afraid. 'September is never going to have a moment in her life when she doesn't know that her mother loves every cell and breath of her. That's a million times better than living in an ugly old house with ugly, unkind people.'

Mariah is crying now, the full-on heartbreak of the drunk,

and mascara is running down her face with her tears. 'Richard,' she says.

'Don't speak to your mother like that, April,' Richard says.

April laughs. 'Have you ever told *her* not to speak to *me* like that? You're all so scared of her. You're so scared of her that you would rather not see your own daughter – your own granddaughter – than cross her. All except Lucia. She's stood by me. She's supported me. She's been a mother to me.'

'How dare you. She taught you how to be a little slut, more like.'

And now Lucia laughs, at the sheer injustice of that. She's had one great love, and he thought better of her. He knew – he could see – that her family would destroy her if she married him. And she's a virgin, for crying out loud. 'I'm a virgin, for crying out loud,' she says. She pours herself another glass of wine.

'Lucia!' her father says. 'Language!'

April shakes her head. 'Do you not see, Grandpa? Mama can call me a slut – which is not true, by the way, there's only ever been Rex – and nobody turns a hair. Lucia says she's a virgin and you tell her off? Virgin isn't a swearword. And it seems to be what you want all of the women in this family to be.'

Lucia looks around the table. Mariah is still sobbing. Richard is holding out a handkerchief, three inches in front of her face, which she's ignoring. He is looking between April and Lucia, with an expression halfway between confusion and panic. Lucia's own father has a similar look. Her mother is eating, as though only the act of pressing potato dauphinoise on to a fork and conveying it to her mouth is going to keep the world turning. April isn't crying, but her eyes have a brightness about them that suggests she might. Lucia thinks she might have the same expression on her own face.

'April, darling. It's all right,' Lucia says, because no one else is going to. She's not sure what she thinks will be all right, but they are the only words she can think of. This room – this family – has never been subjected to as much truth as April has delivered just now. Lucia knows, in some unspecified way, that life will never be the same.

'Oh yes. You're as bad as her,' Mariah says. She snatches the handkerchief from Richard as though he's insulted her by offering it.

April rolls her eyes, and a few tears fall. But her voice is strong with fury. 'I'm not as bad as anything. We are not bad. Auntie L isn't and Rex isn't and that poor little baby up there isn't. She has two parents who love every tiny bit of her and she has an auntie who means the world to her and that's all the family she needs.'

'Well, that's us put in our place.' Mariah has regained enough control to look around the table, as though she is rallying her troops. She pours herself another drink. Maybe, Lucia thinks, maybe that's the end. She half-rises, ready to start clearing the plates. It's just after 9 p.m. They will be finished dinner by 9.30; hopefully Richard and Mariah will decide to leave then. When Lucia had proposed the gathering, Mariah had made a great fuss about missing the party her friends were having. Once Mariah and Richard have gone, she and April can drink tea and make each other feel better.

But then April stands, and says, 'Do you know what, I've had it. I'm going to go home tomorrow, and I'm going to pack up my life, and I'm going to go travelling. I'm going to take September to India or America or somewhere where we can get some sun and some happiness and I'm never going to tell her anything about her miserable family in Harrogate.'

Richard says, 'April—'

But Mariah interrupts. 'Well, good riddance to you both. But don't expect to come crawling back here when you run out of money or that man of yours gets bored with you. I don't know why I ever wanted to have a baby, and one day you'll wish you'd got rid of yours, too.'

Lucia will always remember this moment. It's when things break. It's when Mariah breaks them. She looks around the table and sees her parents, both sitting with their mouths open; finally, here is a thing that even they cannot pretend away with nice manners and talk of the Rotary Club. Richard – who, along with Lucia, has long known the unkindness that Mariah is capable of – is looking at her with a sort of horror that Lucia feels too. Tears are running down April's face; her hands are wrapped around her midriff, as though Mariah has tried to tear September out of her body.

And Mariah? There's a flicker – a second's flicker – when Lucia sees her realise what she's done. Finally, she has said something so unforgivable that it can't be written off as Mariah being Mariah, or tiredness, or unhappiness, or drink. There's a sudden uncertainty and, despite the make-up and the perfectly highlighted hair, she looks like April, confessing her love for Rex to Lucia, or September, letting go of a hand and teetering across the floor. And contained in that flicker, too, is a second of hope. If Mariah can see what she's done, then maybe, for the first time, she can also fix what she's done. Or at least try. Lucia thinks that if Mariah, for once in her life, said she was sorry and meant it, then she, Lucia, could—

But before Lucia can even complete the thought, Mariah's expression goes back to closed-off malice. She stands, too quickly, wobbles; she reaches for Richard's shoulder. He shakes her hand away. 'I'm going,' she says. 'Richard.'

It almost looks as though Richard is going to refuse her, but he stands. 'Mariah, I really think—' he says.

'Oh, do you now?'

April shakes her head. 'Don't worry about it, Dad. It's too late.'

Mariah says, 'I wish you joy of your travels, April. I'm sure we will get on perfectly well without you.'

April nods. 'Likewise,' she says.

Lucia is braced for tears and upset. But what happens is worse.

Her parents go to bed soon after Mariah and Richard leave; their goodnights are much the same as usual, though Alice kisses both Lucia and April, drily, on the cheek. Lucia starts to clear the table, but when April comes down from checking on September, she says, 'I think you've done enough skivvying for one day, Auntie L,' and takes the bowl of profiteroles that Lucia has made into the living room. They sit on the sofa, eating their way through the pastries, which are, as April says, too much for one bite, too small for two. Lucia isn't sure why she feels sick: the profiteroles, the wine, the richness of the duck and potatoes, the look of something like hatred on her sister's face. The feeling of the truth being out and not knowing how to recover. The certainty of consequences coming, and the unknowing of what form they might take.

April says, 'I meant it, you know.'

Lucia takes her sticky hand, and thinks of all the time she has spent with April, loving her as much now as she did when she was a baby, a toddler, a child, a teenager. As much as she always will. She feels her tears begin. 'I know,' she says.

As though she's replying, April says, 'You should try sex. It's nice.'

Lucia laughs. 'I liked being in love.'

They sit in silence. It's still not midnight – what a long evening this has become – but there are fireworks over the Stray.

Then April says, 'I mean, I meant it, about going away. Me and September.'

Lucia says, 'I can believe you'll never come to Harrogate again.'

And now it seems that, rather than Lucia holding April's hand, it's the other way round. 'I'm going to go travelling. India or Thailand, maybe. I'm going to tie September on and go and have an adventure.'

'What about Rex?' Lucia doesn't really care much about what Rex thinks, what he wants – it seems to her that everything in his life goes his own way – but it seems a better thing to say than 'but I cannot imagine life without you here' or 'please don't leave me'.

April looks down at their held hands. 'Rex needs to sort himself out,' she says. 'I know he loves me.' She takes a deep breath. 'I don't know whether he'll ever leave his wife.'

'Oh.'

April gives her aunt a 'what can you do' look that makes

her seem much, much older than her years. 'I know they're miserable. I know their marriage won't last. But it feels as though all I do is wait.'

April seems to have gone far away, inside herself or beyond herself.

After a few minutes, Lucia says, 'I know Mariah can be a—'

'A stone-cold bitch? A selfish cow? An evil piece of shit?'

Lucia, to her surprise, hears herself laugh. 'I was going to say a lot. And I'm the last person to defend her. But I do think she'll regret what she said to you.'

'I really don't care if she does wish I hadn't been born,' April says. 'But I'll never forgive her for saying I'll ever wish I had got rid of September.'

Lucia nods. She doesn't think she'll forgive Mariah, either. 'You don't have to leave the country to get away from her, though,' she says.

April shakes her head. 'I just can't sit around and wait for people to realise that they love me,' she says.

April doesn't leave the next day, as she threatened, but the day after. On New Year's Day, Lucia and April and September sleep late, all in the same bed; when they get up they find that Lucia's parents have washed up, for the first time since Mariah and Lucia were old enough to do it. April makes scrambled eggs and toast, and they eat them in the dining room, and then they bundle up and walk around the Stray, September alternately being carried or toddling between them. They exchange 'Happy New Year's with dog-walking strangers; they smile at each other when they pass the people who are clearly walking home in last night's clothes. 'I wonder how Mariah is feeling this morning,' Lucia says.

'I don't,' April says, and then, 'I meant it, you know. I wish you were my mother.'

Richard drives them to the station. Mariah doesn't come. There's nowhere to park, so Richard says he'll stay with the car; he gives April a hug – the most affection Lucia has ever seen him show any adult – and kisses September's head. 'I'll see you soon,' he says.

'You won't, Dad,' April says. Then, 'I know it isn't easy for you. Thank you for the bracelets.'

On the platform, she says to Lucia, 'Come and see me. I'll write to you. Come and visit.'

'India?'

'Why not?'

Lucia laughs. April has always made her bold. 'I've only ever been to Paris.'

'Then it's time we both went further,' April says. 'We love you, Auntie L. Don't we, September?'

The toddler in April's arms puts her hand on her own chest, screws up her face and, with great effort, says, 'Bebember.' April and Lucia laugh, delighted. She has never said her own name before.

When she goes back to the car, Lucia realises they have forgotten September's blanket. She folds it into a square and holds it on her lap as though it is her own child.

July 2024

September had been surprised when Marina said she would love to come to book group. But here she is, smiling round at everyone with something like shyness. She had pulled up in her little black sports car and parked it next to Kit's old Mazda, which September is trying to clean when Kit is at work, but in a way that Kit won't notice, taking out the mats and hoovering them, spraying the inside of the glovebox with kitchen cleaner.

When Kit first moved in, September had been wary of doing anything that might make her seem as though she was being self-indulgent: whenever she heard Kit's key in the lock she had the urge to get up and start cleaning a window. But at first Kit was quiet. She works full-time, so was out a lot during the day, and seemed to sleep a great deal. When she moved in, she told September that she wouldn't get in her way, and September had told her that there really wasn't anything for her to get in the way of. It had taken a week for Kit to stop making her food and scurrying up to her room with it, then scurrying back down and washing up as soon as she had finished. After a week, September was in the garden, reading, when Kit got back from work and had asked her to please, please, help eat up the ratatouille that she and Esin had made with courgettes and onions from the garden, and tomatoes and aubergines from the greenhouse. It was delicious, and she had asked Esin to take some home to share with her housemates, but there still seemed to be an awful lot left. Kit had laughed and agreed. September had heated up some garlic bread to go with it and they had sat at the kitchen table, the radio on in the background, and eaten together. After that, Kit had suggested she cook; she'd made penne carbonara and asked if she could pick herbs from the garden to go in a salad, and told September about her grandmother's huge pine dresser covered in china and what a treat it was to take everything down, wash it up, and put it back. And so they have become housemates, at least; maybe they will be friends soon. Tonight, September has made a meal for Kit and Esin and herself before book group. She's been to the deli for cheese and meat, to the bakery for bread, to the garden for tomatoes and cucumber, and thanks to Kit she knows how to make salad dressing now. Three people eating together at the kitchen table is even better than two. And then there's the sound of Marina's car, and September goes outside to welcome her.

She is used to Marina's two-cheek kissing now, and feels as though she manages it better than last time: she's had some practice with Johnny. Marina knows Esin, from previous visits to the house, after Lucia died. September watches her laughing and chatting with the rest of the group with a mixture of pride – Marina is her solicitor and, she thinks, her friend – and envy for the way Marina can be with people. If Marina had inherited this house, she would have done things differently. Better. She would have known what to keep and what to throw away; what to do about Cassie next door. Marina would certainly not have poisoned her own dog.

Marina might know what to do, about the piece of paper September has found.

Marina has brought a huge box of fancy chocolates for everyone to share, and a bouquet of flowers and a bottle of wine for September. 'Call it a belated housewarming gift,' she says. And then she produces something from her handbag and waves it at September, a question on her face. 'I went to the pet shop and they said Figgy would like a piece of buffalo horn to chew. Is that okay?' Figgy, with her unerring instinct for the possibility of food, looks up, and September smiles and nods. She takes her guest into the living room to leave her coat. Jojo is starting work in there the next week; September has painted patches of colour on the wall. Marina says, 'Oh, good idea!' And before September can stop her, she has pencilled her name on top of the bright yellow-green that September isn't sure she has the confidence for. 'That's my vote.'

September laughs. 'There wasn't going to be a vote.'

'We'll see about that.' Marina grins, and then there's the tapping of fork on glass by Esin that calls them into the library where the rest of the book group are waiting.

This time, they have read *The Prime of Miss Jean Brodie*. September is glad it was short; she seems to spend more and more time reading her birthday books these days, and could barely fit it in. Her nineteenth birthday present was a short story collection, *Interpreter of Maladies* by Jhumpa Lahiri, in which Lucia had written, 'This book has won so many prizes and I think it's wonderful. So many ways to love and be loved. I hope you have found yours.' Then September read *Passing* by Nella Larsen, her twentieth birthday present, the story of a Black woman who is living as white in Harlem in the early 1920s. 'Dear September,' Lucia had written, 'do not be afraid to be your wonderful self.' She raced through *Wuthering Heights*, her twenty-first birthday book, but put it down with the overwhelming feeling that she couldn't bear the thought of such doomed and destructive love as that of Catherine and Heathcliff. Lucia had written, 'For your 21st birthday, let's go somewhere wonderful. You can choose, when we see each other again.' And September thinks of how, whatever she suffered, Lucia suffered too.

She has read *The Prime of Miss Jean Brodie*, Kit's choice, in two afternoons. She envies Miss Brodie's girls their lives, with wealth and possibility all around them. She envies them their teacher, with so much time to dedicate to such a small group, rather than just writing 'could do better' in green pen at the bottom of things the way September's teacher used to. She wished then she was the best at something. She wishes it now.

Kit says, 'I read this when I was about sixteen and I didn't really get the historical context. I thought it was a school story. And I know it is, sort of. But all the stuff about supporting the Nazis came out much more strongly for me this time. I don't think I like it all that much, though it's brilliantly written.'

Dan is unimpressed for different reasons. 'If it wasn't white people, this would be grooming.'

Zain adds, 'Teacher shouldn't be allowed to get away with this sh—' he glances at Esin, corrects himself, 'this stuff, man.' The two exchange a significant look and September wonders what's going on in their school that makes them feel this way.

William has a different take. He says he likes the way the novel shows how important teachers are: he was tricked into thinking she was a good woman, to begin with. 'There are so many good women,' he adds, 'but I suppose they don't make good stories.' A light goes on in September's brain: this is why there are so many orphans. A happy kid with a family tree as strong and stable as the ash tree outside is just not a story. She opens her mouth to say this, but then she sees Kit across the room, and thinks: *I mustn't make this book all about me, too.*

She has another sip of her wine. She never used to like wine, or so she thought. Marina has made her realise that what she didn't like was cheap wine.

Esin clears her throat. 'I wish,' she says, 'that this teacher was a better teacher. Children need good teachers if they are going to be able to have clear eyes in the world.' September thinks Esin might cry: she looks vulnerable, uncertain, in a way September has never seen before. Esin touches her hijab at her throat, as though words are stuck there, and September thinks of how often she used to feel like that, choking back all she wanted to say for fear of losing her job, or her relationship, or her home. She opens her mouth to save Esin, to move the conversation on, even if Kit will get cross with her. But before she can do so, Marina, who is sitting next to Esin, reaches across and takes her hand. 'Say whatever you want to say,' Marina says.

Esin shakes her head. 'You do not need to hear my story. It is a sad one.'

'We do, if you want to tell it,' Johnny says. September looks around at the people gathered in this room, all of whom are focused on Esin, kindness shining from them.

September finds her voice. 'Would my aunt want you to tell us?' she asks.

Esin nods, smiles, and begins. The room falls silent around her.

'I was born in Afghanistan, near Kabul. People do not believe, but it was a happy time and a happy place. I was close with my family: my mother, my father, my older sisters. I was lucky because I could go to school. My father had no sons and so he made sure that he educated us.'

Kit makes a small sound in her throat, then says, 'Sorry. I didn't mean to—'

Esin smiles. 'This is how it was. You will not think it, but my father was a good man for his time. He did not put aside my mother to try to get a son. He showed us that he loved us. This was not the way with every family.' She looks at her hands. 'I loved school. To learn and to read felt like heaven to me. I learned to speak English and when I was fifteen and the other girls were leaving I stayed and helped the teacher with the young ones. When I was seventeen I started to work in a school on the outskirts of Kabul. My mother had died the year before. My sisters were both married. And so I was not expected to marry. My father told me every day that he was proud of me.'

Esin's lips twitch with a small smile when she says this. Then she stops speaking and closes her eyes; opens them. She is sitting up straighter now. 'In 1992, when I was eighteen, the Mujahideen came to power. They decreed that women must not be employed and must stay at home, and

I thought that life was over for me. But,' she spreads her hands, 'the government could not uphold this. There were not enough of them and they did not care much about the small places. So life went on as it had been, except women were even more careful to go unnoticed. Always I watched the ground in front of my feet when I was not in my classroom or my home.'

'I can't imagine,' Marina says.

'No. You cannot. You are lucky. And then the Taliban came. People in this country know that the Taliban were bad, but you do not know how bad.'

It's on the tip of September's tongue to say, *You don't need to tell us if you don't want to.* But then she realises: she's trying to protect herself. If Esin wants to talk she must listen.

'Women could not leave their homes, but that did not keep them safe. Any woman with the smallest slur against her might be put out of her home, and they would wander in the streets, trying to sell anything they had managed to carry away with them. My cousin was touched by a man visiting her husband's home, and when she screamed she was flogged in the street as punishment for being impure. They said he would not have touched her if she was pure. My neighbour's daughter vanished and she was never found.' Esin talks of these events as though she is reciting a shopping list: fact after fact. They land in the room not as statements but as small explosions, each one provoking a sigh or gasp or the occasional low 'no', which September realises has come from her own mouth.

'Of course, I could no longer teach,' Esin continues. 'Even when I was going to leave the house to buy food, my father would pray over me for my protection. But soon, I was not able to leave the house at all. The world had become small and vigilant and no one could be trusted. So I thought, how can I make this life bearable for my father and for me?'

Kit says, 'Esin. You're—' and then she stops. September knows exactly why. There is no word to express how brave, strong, amazing Esin was in this unimaginably frightening situation.

Esin smiles at her. 'My name means "shining light" and I thought, now it is dark I must shine. I spent many hours reading to my father. We knew we only had each other.' She goes quiet. September feels how everyone is waiting for her to begin again; how they will wait for as long as it takes. She feels so proud to be here, part of this group of people.

'Then, one day, someone came to the door. A man. It was allowed, of course, for men to go about their business. I was afraid. I knew that if anyone had said anything against me – and being unmarried was enough to make me a woman you could doubt – then there did not need to be any proof or any discussion. When I could still go to the market, women whispered about how girls were taken and kept in barns for the soldiers to enjoy. But the man was one of the teachers from the boys' part of the school I had worked at. Though I knew him I did not say so. I served him and my father tea and I looked at the floor. I could not assume the man was there for good reasons. I behaved as though he was there to watch me, to find something wrong with the way we were living. But when I was near he lowered his voice and said, he had come to tell us that there was a possibility I could leave the country. Of course, he said, it would be illegal and it would be dangerous, and if I was caught it would not go well. I thought my father would say no, but instead, he said, dangerous for you too. Why would you help my daughter? I kneeled on the floor, as though I was serving them, in case anyone walked past and looked in. The man told us that the school was still running, but in a different way. Only for boys, of course, and teaching about religion and law, only in the ways that were permitted, which were not many. The teachers, he said, did not like this, did not think it was what education was for. And the teachers were afraid of what was happening, and what was going to happen, to women under this new regime. So, through people that they knew in embassies and on borders, they were arranging escapes.'

Esin looks around the room. There are tears in her eyes. 'What I did next I am ashamed of. I left my father.'

William says, 'I think that must have been what he wanted?'

'That does not make it a good thing,' Esin says. 'But yes. He said I should go. I refused, even though I had no right to disobey. Because I thought no daughter would leave her father alone, in the same way that no father would abandon his child. My father said I must go. He said, I am commanding you. I said, we must talk about this more. We must pray. But the teacher said, there is no time. You must come with me now. There are not many opportunities. So my father said, I command you, daughter. Obey me in this. So I left him, and went with the teacher. I carried nothing with me.'

There's a moment of silence. Marina has tears in her eyes. Zain is biting at his lips, Dan's fists are balled in his lap. Johnny has his eyes closed and William is wiping a tear away. Kit looks straight at September with an expression that reads, without judgement, *and we thought our lives were bad*.

Esin shakes her head. 'Compared to leaving my father, the journey was not so terrible. It was long and tiring and frightening, but so many people were so very kind. And when I came to this country I was given some money and a place to stay, but I missed my father and I could get no news of him. I knew that if I wrote I could get him into trouble. I thought I could get a job as a teacher, but I had no qualifications. Then I tried to get a job caring for children, but I had no history of employment and nothing to prove that I was a good person, and people were suspicious of me. So I started to go to the library, to read and to look through the newspapers. A woman who worked there showed me how to apply for jobs. And that, of course, was our dear Lucia.' Esin beams. September wants to smile but she is thinking of Esin, hidden in the backs of vans and the dark corners of boats, knowing she will never again see her father.

'Lucia offered me work. I cooked and cleaned in this house. She said she was sorry it was not more, but it was my start. And she gave me references and helped me find other cleaning jobs. Without her I would not have found any place where I could feel belonging.'

'All this time we have known you,' William says, his voice gentle. 'You know you could have told us.'

'I know,' Esin says. 'But Lucia knew. I think, so long as someone knows your story, you are alive in the world.'

Johnny says, 'Thank you.'

Esin smiles. 'You are welcome.' She wipes her eyes. 'I did not know that I was going to tell you this tonight. I think it is that the thing I think about most often is all of those girls who did not get an education. They were not even allowed to hold a book. It is such a waste for my country. Such a waste of those children. And this Miss Jean Brodie, she is a disgrace, also.'

Johnny offers Esin, Dan and Zain a lift home. William says he will walk. Kit goes to bed. And so Marina and September stand in the fading evening light in the garden. It's almost 10 p.m., but there is still light in the sky.

'Tell me you didn't buy this rust bucket,' Marina says, looking at Kit's car.

'No, it's Kit's. She's staying while she's between places.'

Marina smiles. 'You're just like your aunt, hey?'

September takes a breath. What's the worst that can happen? 'Marina. If I had a name and a phone number, would you be able to find my birth father, do you think?'

Marina hesitates. 'I don't know that that's enough to go on.'

'You found me,' September says.

She thinks of Bobbie at the end of *The Railway Children*. She goes upstairs and takes the piece of paper that she found in the back of one of Lucia's books of kindness, and the blurry Polaroid of the man she thinks must be Rex, with April.

Marina is standing by her car, scrolling through her phone.

'I found this,' September says.

Marina frowns. 'Lucia said your biological father was called Rex, but she couldn't tell us anything else.'

'I presume this is a phone number,' September says. She had googled, and found that phone numbers used to be shorter. 'I know it won't exist any more, but maybe there's something you can do?'

Marina takes September by the shoulders and looks into her face. 'Are you sure you want me to do this? My guy is good, but he might not be able to trace this Rex. He might be dead. He might not want to know you.' Marina squeezes: her face fills with tenderness. 'Something happened, a long time ago, that meant he couldn't be a father to you. The smart money would say that he still can't. Or doesn't want to.'

September nods. 'I know. But I want you to do it, please.' Life might not always be easier when you have a lot of money, but it does mean you can do what you want.

In September's book of kindness that evening, she writes:

My kindnesses
Working on Kit's car
Making food for Esin, who wants so much to help that it's hard for her to be cared for
I don't know how to write this, but listening to Esin felt like kindness. No, like – holding? When we were listening it was as if everyone's attention was making it possible for her to speak? I felt proud of us all. I don't know what I did (if I did anything) but there was kindness there
Inviting Marina

Other kindnesses
Everyone caring for Esin
Esin trusting us
Marina's gifts, and she thought of Figgy

She feels as though she might be getting the hang of kindness, the way Lucia did it. She goes to Lucia's books of kindness, as she often does before she sleeps, and finds a page with Esin's name on it. There are many, from the year 2000 onwards. September notices that Esin appears as a giver of kindness at least as often as Lucia is kind to her. It's the same with April's name, in earlier years.

On 2 August 2002, Lucia had written:

My kindnesses:
Went with Esin and her friend to the GP to get her and her baby registered. Between Esin's translation and my refusal to take no for an answer, we got everything sorted. It makes me sad, how vulnerable these women are.

Library book group for teenagers. I think they really use it as a place to flirt and be together, but I don't mind. Why shouldn't they have somewhere?

Other kindnesses:
Esin had been here to clean after the GP, and she had done all of the ironing. Mum said she refused to take any extra money for it. She had asked my father about the garden, too, and he had showed her everything.

Mum asked about my day. She and Dad rarely do. I suspect Esin talks about me to them.

The next morning, September and William hoe and weed and are quiet together in a way that feels just right. When September brings their tea and biscuits out, she tells William that she and Johnny are going to walk part of the Nidderdale Greenway with Figgy that afternoon. 'Good,' William says. 'I worry for that boy.'

September laughs. 'Dan and Zain are boys. Johnny must be nearly forty.'

William nods. 'Next year, I think. And I will be eighty. So he is definitely a boy to me.'

They each take a biscuit. September asks, 'Why do you worry about him?' Then she adds, 'He told me about Skye. I'm not prying.'

'It is not good, to live only a part of your life. He has his business and he has his house; it is not enough for any man. I am glad he's spending time with you.'

'Oh,' September says, 'we're not . . .' She can feel the heat spreading along her jaw, across her cheeks.

'Did I say you were? But still, it will do him good. You too.'

'I knew Esin had come here as a refugee,' Johnny says, later that afternoon. They're approaching the top of a long, slow hill that has left September breathless. Johnny has a little shine around his hairline but looks as though he could walk for ever. 'She mentioned something about it when we read a novel set in Afghanistan – I think it was *A Thousand Splendid Suns* – but only in passing, and she obviously didn't want to say more. I couldn't sleep last night for thinking about her. She was so young.'

September nods. 'Yes, but I think it's normal not to want people to feel sorry for you. And I have no idea how cautious you must have to be if you wear a hijab. But you definitely have to be careful. You must get used to keeping things to yourself.'

She feels Johnny nod beside her. 'After Skye died I found

it much easier with people who didn't know about her. You can be a version of yourself who isn't broken.' He sighs, a sound that September has rarely heard from him. 'It's not good if you want to get to know people, but it definitely helps in the short term.'

They stop as Figgy dives into a hedge, coming out with a sandwich wrapper and looking very pleased with herself. September lets her pull it apart. Figgy can be quite growly when it comes to protecting her food.

The view is beautiful: so many shades of green and grey and yellow and brown make up the landscape, none of them exactly the same colour or texture. September thinks anxiously of her living room. At the end of book group, Marina had ushered everyone in to look at the paint swatches and invited them to vote. There had been an almost equal division, between the two extremes: a deep orange, almost rust, preferred by Esin, Johnny, Kit and Zain; and a bright lemon-lime that Marina, William and Dan had liked. Jojo had pronounced, with great confidence, that the bright colour was the one to go for. September had agreed. Now she's looking at the scene before them, she's wishing for a heathery blue.

'You can always have it repainted,' Johnny says.

September laughs with the sheer delight of being read so easily. 'How did you know what I was thinking about?'

'You're wearing your stressed face, and Figgy's here, so you're not worried about her, and we've talked about Esin, and you're doing what you can for Kit, so the only thing I could think of was the paint. You didn't seem completely sure when we left.'

September smiles. 'I'm just looking at the view. These colours.'

'These colours are excellent for outdoors,' Johnny says, 'but may I remind you that you couldn't wait to get rid of all those paintings of weather? And also, your house is inside.'

He smiles at her – they are almost exactly the same height – and she thinks how easy it would be to kiss him, not in a hello way, but properly. The way you would kiss someone you thought you might want to love. She thinks of Johnny eating figs, buttering scones, pouring wine: his delicacy, his care. Her mouth goes dry. He's looking at her, curious now. 'September?'

'I don't think you've told me how you knew Lucia,' she says, 'apart from that you did some valuations for her.'

'Oh, yes,' Johnny says. 'I think she found me in the phone book. She was very – analogue. Her sister was moving in with her after her husband had died, and they were clearing the sister's house. Your grandmother? Mariah.'

'What was she like?' September thinks she knows the answer, from the things that William and Esin have said, and not said, about her.

Johnny hesitates before he says, 'She was very different to Lucia. Temperamentally. Lucia was very gentle. Quite reserved. Mariah was – well, her husband had just died. She probably wasn't her usual self.'

September feels a laugh rising through her, like a bubble in a glass. 'Are you telling me my grandmother was an old cow?' It figures, of course. A woman who would willingly lose touch with her only child could not be kind. And whenever Mariah comes up in Lucia's books of kindness, it's always Lucia being kind to her, never the other way round.

Johnny looks uncertain. 'I'm saying I met her at a time of great personal stress for her, and she treated me as though

I was some sort of disreputable antiques pirate rather than someone who wanted to help.'

September laughs. But then Johnny looks more serious. 'I should have thought of this before. I should have told you.'

'What?' By unspoken consent, they are still walking, side-by-side on the path.

'I remember she was quite – angry. In general, I mean. Not specifically. It felt a bit as though if you turned your back she would have torched the house. As soon as her husband died, she wanted the house to be emptied and cleared and put on the market. But there wasn't really any urgency. She didn't need the money.'

September says, 'Grief is weird.'

Johnny shoulder-bumps her. 'You're not wrong. But – well ...' he takes a deep breath, 'I cleared the house of anything that could go to an auction, and I arranged for a skip. I had to hire a bigger van for some of the furniture, and when I went round, Mariah was throwing things into the skip. A lot of good things. I could have sold them. I tried to say so but she told me she had done with this life now and she was going to leave all of the past behind. I went into the house and Lucia was crying. It's the only time I ever saw her cry. She told me that Mariah had thrown out all the photographs and photo albums. All the photos of April and you. She was distraught.'

'But – why?'

Johnny shrugs. 'Mariah said it would save Lucia the bother when she died. But something had obviously gone very wrong with Mariah and April. Lucia had grabbed some boxes and put them by the back door. I took them with me and put them in the loft at the house. Your house.'

September's urge is to run back to the car. 'What about the photo albums?'

Johnny shakes his head. 'I went back and looked in the skip, but I couldn't find them. It seemed strange at the time. It's even stranger to think about it now. They would have been your family albums. September, I'm so sorry.'

September takes a few steps as the knowledge settles in her that the only photos she will ever have of her and her mother are the ones she already owns. Maybe it doesn't matter. Maybe Mariah gave Lucia all the best photographs of April. Although from what little she knows of her grandmother, that seems unlikely.

'Are the boxes still there?'

Johnny shakes his head. 'Lucia went through them. After Mariah died. That's when she found your mother's death certificate and her ashes. That's when she started to try to find you. She had nothing to go on before then. I'm sorry, September.'

'Why didn't you tell me this before?' Although the objective part of September knows that, if the photo albums were lost, then it doesn't matter, the possibility of them, there and gone, makes her heart hurt. It's like the difference between knowing Esin is a refugee and hearing her story. She stops and leans against the fence, looking out across the hills. Johnny comes to stand behind her, close but not too close. 'At first I didn't know whether I should tell you at all. When we sold the paintings and the tables I thought I would tell you at lunchtime, but you seemed so happy and I didn't want to spoil it. When we went to Bettys and talked about Skye on the way, I felt too – strange – to talk to you about it. Because if you had been upset I didn't have a lot in the tank to help you with. And then I thought, what if there had been photos of Skye and someone put them in a skip? Would I want to know?'

September says, 'You would have done.' The hurt in her chest is not getting any less.

She knows that he's nodding. 'Are you angry?'

September breathes in and out, slowly, reaches for Figgy, who is standing at her side. 'I'm angry with my grandmother. It seems as though she's the origin of everything going wrong. I mean, in 1989 getting pregnant was hardly the end of the world, was it? And whatever my mother did –' her hand goes to the identity bracelet on her other wrist, 'surely it was up to her mother to make sure things were right between them?' September cannot imagine anything she could have done that would have made her adoptive mother turn away from her, or reject her if she tried to make peace.

Johnny says, 'I wish I had answers. I wish I had told you sooner.' There's a pause, but September knows he hasn't finished speaking yet. 'I suppose I didn't want to hurt you. It's not a happy memory of your grandmother and I should have done more.'

September shakes her head. She thinks of how, sometimes, when she looks in the dressing table mirror, she feels as though there is someone sitting behind her. Of how Dan and Zain playing the piano always conjures a memory she cannot quite catch. 'You weren't to know then that I would show up.'

Johnny exhales. 'I wanted to be able to give you good things to think about, when it came to your birth family. When I think about Lucia I remember how good she was to me. She let me talk about Skye in a way that no one else did. When Richard died it was around the tenth anniversary of her death, which is too many years for most people to remember, and I was bereft. Lucia invited me to join her book group and I was worried that if I didn't do something to look after myself, I'd end up driving the van off a cliff.'

'Oh, Johnny.' She turns to face him. He touches her arm, shrugs. 'It was a hard time. Lucia gave me something to hold on to. Between reading *Vanity Fair* – which is massive, by the way, if you haven't got to it yet – and clearing Mariah's house, I had things to do. It got me through. But I still should have told you about the photograph albums.'

September has seen hints of this in Lucia's books of kindness. Her great-aunt has noted where she *asked Johnny to come to book group, invited Johnny to have lunch after we'd gone to the auctioneer, told Mariah that I would check with Johnny about the income from the sale, though I won't tell him she suspects him of 'diddling' her.* And Johnny, unlike Mariah, features often when he is kind to Lucia: *Johnny wouldn't take money for petrol, Johnny took me to the auction house so I could check that I was happy with the reserves on everything, Johnny came to walk around Mariah's house with me for the last time even though he didn't need to, because he knew Mariah wouldn't.*

September's breath feels slow and cautious, as though afraid to interfere with her thoughts.

September thinks: *my grandmother threw the photographs of her own daughter into a skip.*

September thinks: *maybe I was better off as an orphan.*

September thinks: *my adoptive parents were good to me and they loved me.*

September thinks: *if I had kept a book of kindness when I was a child, then the things my parents did for me would have filled it in no time.* She remembers her father waiting outside the cinema in his car to drive her and her friends home, and her mother taking her shopping, even though the strip-lighting and music meant she would have to lie down with a headache when they got home. She remembers that her bed was warm even when the house was cold, with a hot-water bottle tucked at the bottom of the blankets; that whenever she was worried about something, all she had to do was say that she wanted to talk, and her parents would stop whatever they were doing – even if it was the sort of thing that would save the world – and give her their full attention. She remembers that she never, ever doubted that she was loved.

'September?' Johnny's hand is on the small of her back, Figgy's nose against her hand. She realises she has stopped walking.

'I'm fine,' September says. 'Honestly.'

Johnny nods, and waits. He never seems to be in a hurry.

September is remembering, again. She is thinking of that childhood book of kindness she might have written. Her parents had told her they would help her to find out about her birth parents. They had never concealed that she was adopted. They had made sure that she felt chosen, and not abandoned. Her parents were good people. Whatever Rex and Mariah and Richard were like, she has that.

She ruffles Figgy's ears in the way that she likes, and stands. She's not sure what just happened, but she feels better. A lot better.

'Okay?' Johnny smiles at her. The sun is behind them now; the air is warm and smells of grass and trees.

'Okay,' September says, and they turn and start to make

their way back to the car. Sometimes, on previous walks, Johnny – who seems to be, at least in part, descended from a mountain goat – has reached for September's hand to help her over a stream or to navigate a rocky path; he always lets her hand fall as soon as she is on even ground again. But now, she reaches for him, and they walk hand-in-hand, quiet. September doesn't know where this relationship is going; that doesn't matter today. What matters is that Johnny told her something he knew would be difficult for both of them, and it has made them like each other more.

September has much more to write in her book of kindness now. She has set up monthly donations to a lot of charities. She has invited Esin to use her house to cook for the refugee group that she supports; once a week, her kitchen is filled with women chopping vegetables, making soups and curries and stews, talking in a mix of languages and laughing, always laughing. September tried to help once, but Esin introduced her as 'the kind September who lets us use her house', and then there was an outpouring of capital-g Gratitude followed by a smiling, stilted silence. Esin and her cooks use up quite a lot of what is growing in the garden. September has found out that churches will take excess vegetables, either to distribute to their congregations or to use in their own soup kitchens. The food bank had told her that they can't take fresh vegetables because many of their clients don't have the money to pay for power, and September spends an afternoon trying to find out whether it's possible to donate money to pay electricity bills. There isn't, but she finds a plumber who works for free at weekends for anyone who needs help, so she sets up a standing order to help him cover his costs.

It's not just about money. She has wondered about donating the piano to the school, but when she asked Johnny about it he says they would need to take out the window and use a winch to move it, and the chances were that the school wouldn't have anywhere to keep it. September is obscurely glad. Sometimes she rests a finger on one of the white keys as she passes. One day, she sits down, and is surprised to find herself wanting to play a sequence of keys – one-two-three, her fingers go, then back down the same keys again – and this makes her both tearful and warm.

The next Saturday morning, Kit says, 'I don't start work until three. You said you wanted help with the loft?'

'Oh. Yes. If that's okay.' After her conversation with Johnny about the photo albums, September has even less hope than she did before of finding anything meaningful from her past. The books of kindness are the best and closest she will ever get to Lucia: they are her diaries.

'Sure.' Kit actually does look quite excited at the prospect. She's even tied her hair up in a scarf, like a land girl. September isn't convinced she could pull that off, so she ties her own, freshly washed hair back in a ponytail and thinks ruefully of her new manicure.

The loft of September's house is not the stuff of a novel. There's a switch near the hatch, and when September pushes it, a series of fluorescent tubes stutter into stark life. The loft space runs the length of the house. The floor is boarded and it's high enough for September to stand, slightly stooping, at the apex. The sides, which slope away, are stacked with boxes of various sizes.

Kit, next to her, says, 'What's the plan?'

September looks around. 'How about I start at that end, you start at the other. Let's take the box lids off and shout out what we've got. See if there's a pattern.'

September's first three boxes all contain files with the Rotary Club logo on them. Kit opens a box of hats – *more* hats, September thinks – then one of men's shoes and another of ties and handkerchiefs. 'They smell a bit musty,' she reports from her end of the loft.

'The whole place does,' September replies. She thinks of the days she used to work on the deli counter, and when she came home Shaun said she smelled like a buffet.

Next, September finds ceramic plant pots, and another animal lamp base – a monkey, this time. She wonders what it did to offend, that it was banned from the living room where its companions lived. Kit says, 'I've got a box of metal pans and another one of . . . oh! I think they're SylvaC pots?'

'What?' September edges along to have a look. Kit is holding a ceramic onion, with a face. In the box there's a similar beetroot, and a cabbage. She shakes her head. 'I don't know.'

Kit says, 'They're probably worth something. Y'know . . . vintage.'

September has a sudden, vivid memory: her grandfather's allotment, pulling up onions and with one of them, a tiny metal toy car. She had been delighted; she'd washed it with water from the water butt and showed her grandfather the places where you could still see the red paint. She can still remember him, laughing at her, ruffling her hair: 'One man's tat is another man's treasure.'

'One man's tat is another man's treasure,' she says.

'Indeed,' Kit says. 'We just need to find the right man.'

Although, at one point, September thinks of renting a skip and getting someone to make a hole in the wall so they can simply push everything from the loft into it, it really isn't too bad. This loft doesn't seem to be full of things that someone has shoved out of the way to get rid of later, but things that have been cleaned and sorted before they are put away. The only things that September puts straight in a bin bag are the old shoes. She expects Kit to argue with her about them, but Kit nods. September wonders whether she, too, has ever stood in a charity shop looking at shoes that hold the shape of other people's feet and wondered how things came to this.

After a couple of hours they head downstairs and into the garden with cold drinks, Figgy flopped and panting at September's side as though she is the one who has been dragging boxes around in a cramped, hot space.

'I think,' Kit says, 'you could sell a lot of that stuff. Vintage fairs, or online.'

September presses the cold bottle against her neck. 'I thought I might ask Johnny.'

There's a beat of a pause. September wonders if Kit is going to warn her off, too, tell her about Skye and the drunk driver. But instead she says, 'I could have a go. My old girlfriend – she used to do vintage fairs.' Kit says this with a casualness that tells September that she really wants to do it: she thinks of herself, saying to her supervisor, 'I could cover some shifts next week if you need me to,' in a way that suggested that she was doing her boss a favour, and not that her electricity would be cut off if she didn't pay the bill within ten days.

'Sure,' she says.

'I'd have to pay you,' Kit says. 'For the . . . treasure.'

'Honestly, you'd be doing me a favour by getting rid of it.' But then September realises that this isn't the right thing to say, and adds, 'A percentage of money from your sales, maybe?'

'Twenty percent?'

September shakes her head. 'Ten, and you've got a deal.'

Kit nods and laughs. 'I don't think that's how negotiating works, September.'

Later, when Kit has gone to start her afternoon shift, September goes back up to the loft and checks the boxes again. Just in case there is something left over from Mariah's house. Of course, there isn't. Though she does find two different illustrated editions of *Peter Pan* which make her ache. It must be the weirdness of some of the pictures.

It makes sense that there's nothing of significance here. If Lucia hadn't gone through those boxes, she would never have found April's death certificate; never found her ashes. The thought of her mother's remains here makes September feel cold all through. If she was abandoned, her mother was too. For all the things she is grateful to Lucia for, saving that box – finding April – feels the most important and the best. Sitting under the rafters, September realises that, given the choice, she would have stayed in her old life for ever so long as it meant April's ashes were found and Lucia could stop waiting for her to come home. She sits there, with her back against a pile of boxes, for a very long time. *This pain*, she thinks, *this sadness. I missed out on this, too.*

* * *

A week later, Marina calls. 'I have news about Rex,' she says. 'Do you want to come to the office?'

'Can you tell me now?' September asks. She hears tears, panic in her voice. Be careful what you wish for.

'I think it's better if you come,' Marina says. 'Could you get here for one? I'll get Hilary to bring us in some lunch.'

'Of course.' September lets Figgy into the garden; they had a walk this morning and Kit will be home at two, so she'll be fine on her own for a while. She looks at herself in the mirror – she's wearing her new black jeans, a grey shirt with a bright pink pattern of flowers, white sandals. She thinks about changing, but then she remembers what she was wearing the first time she went to Marina's office. She looks fine. Also, her nerves are clawing at her to get out, get on, get underway. She needs to be on the move.

September arrives in Leeds just before noon. She thinks of going straight to Marina's office, but sitting in the waiting room is not going to help. So she walks through the arcades. She looks at leggings, at jewellery. Just for the distraction, she has the helix of her left ear pierced with a tiny white gold hoop. She cries at the sudden sting of it, and once the technician is sure that she isn't in pain and the piercing is secure, she brings September a glass of water and tells her to take her time. September does. She lies on the paper-covered couch with her eyes closed, and she lets her whole attention be absorbed by the tingling in her ear. Then she thinks of William in the garden, of Figgy in the kitchen, of Kit sleeping in her car and Esin afraid for her life. She thinks of Dan and Zain, the prejudice that dogs their lives and probably always will. She thinks of Johnny and his ever-broken heart. She thinks of her parents, who she misses, and

Shaun, who she does not. And she realises the thing that she values now is not money, but the fact that she is able to make connections – make meaningful bonds – with people that she would not have met before. The life she has now is not so far from the life she could have had in Leeds, if Shaun had been honest with her: if she hadn't been scrabbling so hard for survival. The WhatsApp group with her old colleagues, the night out they are planning for next month, is proof of that.

As the tingling in her ear recedes, September takes a deep breath and thinks about how soon – today – she is going to find out about her biological father. She gets to her feet, pays for her piercing, and goes to meet Marina.

'I'm not going to small-talk you,' Marina says when September arrives. They aren't in Marina's office, but a small room with comfortable chairs, a coffee machine and a low table. There's a platter of sandwiches and a large bottle of sparkling water, plates and cutlery and glasses on a low table.

'Yes,' September says. 'I mean, thank you.' She sits down and pours some water, just for something to do. Marina was delighted to see her, or so it seemed – though when you are rich, September now knows, people are sometimes just pleased to see your money, though she doesn't think this applies to Marina. But Marina's face is neutral now, and September has no idea whether she is going to give her bad news or good.

Marina puts a buff-coloured paper file on the table. September cannot take her eyes off it.

Marina says, 'When Lucia came to see us she told us that April's partner was named Rex and that he lived and worked in this region, but she didn't know where. He used to meet April in Harrogate, and they would sometimes go on trips to Leeds or York. When April moved to London Rex paid for a flat, but as far as Lucia knew he didn't live there, only visited. But Lucia didn't know any more than that. She said she'd had a phone number for him once – the one you found – but when she rang it, it was a company and she was told he no longer worked there. And she didn't know his phone number, of course.'

September isn't sure that that's an obvious 'of course'. But then she thinks: Kit and Johnny are the only people in book group whose surnames she knows, and that's because Johnny gave her his card and Kit's post comes to the house.

'But our guy was able to trace the phone number to Nottingham, and there weren't that many Rexes in Nottingham then. He found his,' Marina's pause is barely there, but enough for September to realise what's coming, 'his death certificate. I'm sorry, September.'

'That's okay.' Is it? September has no idea. Everything inside her is just a space in which she is wandering, lost.

Marina nods. 'He died of heart failure in 2015.'

'Okay,' September says again. She wonders if she should eat a sandwich. She puts one on a plate, then puts the plate down.

'But,' Marina says, 'Rex had a family. He was married to a woman named Jeannie, who—'

'When did they get married?'

Marina holds her gaze. '1982.'

'How old was he?'

'He was born in 1960. He was nine years older than your mother. That was one of the reasons Lucia wasn't keen on him. I think she suspected he was married, but I don't think April ever told her that.'

September goes cold. 'Maybe April didn't know.'

Marina's gaze meets hers. 'It's possible. It was a lot easier to conceal what you were up to then.'

September nods. She thinks of how easily Shaun fooled her. It's not the same as having a wife somewhere, of course. But if you choose to believe someone, then it doesn't matter whether the lie they are telling is big or small. 'You said he had a family,' she says.

'Yes. His wife was Jeannie and they had three children: Christopher, Gemma and Sapphire. I have an email address for Gemma. Though you might want to think carefully before contacting them.'

'Marina. I have no living relatives. Why wouldn't I contact them?' She knows that Marina has parents who live in Scotland, a brother and twin nieces in Hong Kong, a partner named Khaled who she met on the first day of her law degree. She cannot know what this moment means to September.

Marina touches the back of her hand. 'As far as we know, they don't know you exist. Even if they do, you're their father's illegitimate child. You're not going to be uncomplicated for them.'

September had known the answer before she asked the question, but something in her needed to hear it. Now, fear unfurls inside her ribcage. Here are more people who could hurt her. More people who could reject her.

Marina adds, 'I've got some more information about them. If you want to see it.'

The fear swells into panic. 'I don't know,' she says.

'If you don't know, then we do nothing,' Marina says. 'Think about it. Let me know when you've decided. Another couple of weeks won't make any difference.'

It turns out that Marina was right about the yellow/green paint. The living room glows with life. September often goes in there to read in the morning. The ugly old curtains had to come down for the decoration; Jojo also removed the curtain rails and patched the plaster, so September can do what she likes with the windows. She is going to have some blinds made: she has seen a fabric covered with curling vines that she likes, and someone is coming to take a look and measure up.

Kit seems to be – not exactly looser, because she wasn't exactly stiff before. But maybe something in her is relaxing. September remembers how she herself felt, in the first weeks of living in this house: the sense that it could all be snatched away from her, the certainty that something bad would come. She thinks she still feels it, a little. Maybe she always will. Maybe Lucia did. Although, thinking about it, Lucia was living through her most dreaded thing – the loss of April, of baby September – and hoping for news. The photographs show that she loved April and, later, September: there's no possible question about that. September has sent the Polaroids off to be restored and enlarged. She will be able to see how her mother loved her. She will be able to put that love in a frame and look at it every day. She still hasn't decided what to do about Rex's family. She can't seem to find any grief for Rex – he definitely could have, should have, saved her – but the thought of her half-siblings pushing her away has only got more frightening since she left Marina's office last week.

September doesn't allow herself to think about what would have happened if April had lived. It would be an act of disloyalty to the parents who raised her to wish for another life. But sometimes, when September wakes in her bedroom, puts her foot on the soft rug, goes into the en suite, she thinks: *this could have always been my life.* Jojo is going to decorate September's bedroom next. Johnny says that he thinks even he can't turn the brown velvet curtains into cash for her. It had been odd, standing next to him, next to her bed. She had found herself wondering whether she would ever have sex again, or whether she had inherited a born-again virginity from her aunt along with the house. (She doesn't know why she assumes her aunt was a virgin. Maybe it's the ironed knickers.) And then she had wondered what it would feel like to reach for Johnny. Just at that moment he had looked at her and smiled, and she had thought, *It would feel good.* But she didn't. One day, she might. She sometimes thinks about Penny's warning, to be careful of him; since the Nidderdale walk, she has started to understand that they do have the power to be more than friends, and therefore, to hurt each other. She has finally deleted Shaun's number from her phone.

September is going to move into the third-largest bedroom while the decorating is done. Jojo has promised her that the built-in wardrobes that frame the bed will look 'wicked' once they are rubbed down and painted in something lighter; they have sent her a link to an online shop that specialises in something called 'door furniture'. It got easier to choose doorknobs once September decided that she didn't have to choose only one. There are sixteen handles to replace. From a range of enamelled and painted ones, she chooses four with roses, four with snowdrops, four with tulips and, for reasons she doesn't understand – there are better flowers – four with carnations. She didn't ask the book group to choose her paint colours this time; she remembered the walk with Johnny, and chose a heather green for the walls, and a muted blue for the woodwork and the wardrobes.

As she is shunting her clothes – some of them! – from her bedroom in readiness, Kit comes home from work. 'Do you want me to go?' Kit says. 'You can have your old room back.'

September takes a deep breath; she sees Kit's face fall in readiness for disappointment. 'I want you to stay, until you have the money to rent a place of your own,' she says. And then, because everyone else seems to do it, she evokes her great-aunt. 'I don't think Lucia would want you to sleep in your car.'

Kit does the last thing September is expecting. She rushes at her, hugs her. 'Thank you,' she says, 'thank you.'

September almost says, it's nothing, but she knows that it isn't. 'You're welcome,' she says instead, and she means it, in both senses.

In the garden, she and William are harvesting again. 'Why do gardeners plant so many things?' September asks. 'Do you think Esin has a recipe for courgette pickle?'

William laughs; September has noticed that his wheezing is becoming more pronounced. She doesn't know if she should ask about it, so she doesn't. 'Because when we plant, we don't know which seeds will grow. We never think they all will. But sometimes they do.'

September sits back on her heels. The best jeans she wore

the first day she came here are the jeans she wears for gardening, now. 'So all of these grew?'

'Looks like it,' William says. 'I've never known such a crop.'

When they have worked their way along the rows, September goes into the house to make tea. When she brings out the tray, William has sat down. His hat is tipped over his eyes. September hesitates.

'I was not sleeping,' William says, tipping back his hat and smiling.

September laughs. She wonders if she and William are friends.

'How long have you been helping with the garden?' One thing she has realised is that it's easier to be kind when you know about people.

'I came back to Harrogate after my wife died,' he says. 'Ten years ago now. I grew up here. My sister and her family are still here.'

'I'm sorry about your wife.'

William nods. 'She was a good woman. Kind. We had no children.'

'I'm sorry,' September says again, though William's tone is more thoughtful than sad. She thinks: what he has just said of his wife, you could say of Lucia. 'She was a good woman. Kind. She had no children.' Maybe, one day, people will say that of her. She could certainly never have a child; even if she wasn't approaching the danger zone, age-wise, she could never risk it. Couldn't risk dying, leaving an orphan.

William takes a sip of his tea. 'When Katerina died I realised I had never been alone a whole day in my life. I went from my mother's house to the RAF – you are never alone in the forces. Katerina was the sister of one of my RAF mates. I met her when we were on leave. When we got married, we moved into our own place. She loved her home, loved to make it nice and keep it neat. So when she died I thought, William, now is your time to be alone. Katerina did it, all the days you were away, and she was happy.'

September thinks of how glad she was to have space and silence when she first came here. How, now, she cannot imagine her home without Figgy. Without Kit. But she has not always been that way. 'I had a little flat on my own, for a while, when my parents died,' she says.

'Did you like it?'

'I did.' September thinks of herself, in that light, bright room, where all her things had to be put away because otherwise there wasn't room to pull out the sofa into a bed, where she could watch the TV while she made her evening meal. She had felt – held.

William shakes his head. 'I did not. The days were big. There was too much time. I thought about growing things but I could not find the will. My sister, she came to see me three months after Katerina died and she said, William, if you do not come home with me, every day I will wake up wondering if you have died from loneliness.' He laughs. 'She was right. I packed up my life and I came home to Harrogate.'

'Are you glad you did?'

William goes quiet, then, for a long time. 'I was afraid it would be difficult. But at my age, you are glad to be in the place where you were happiest. Even if it was the place you made your big mistakes.'

'And how did you know Lucia?'

William hesitates for a moment. 'We met in the library. Many years ago. We were friends.'

There's something in his face that stops September from asking more.

For her twenty-second birthday, Lucia had bought September *The Handmaid's Tale* by Margaret Atwood. She had written, 'Let's hope this never happens!' September had found the book, about a dystopian future in which the world is infertile and women who have had children are commodified and abused, claustrophobic and frightening. For her twenty-third birthday, Lucia had chosen *The Vanishing Act of Esme Lennox* by Maggie O'Farrell, the story of a long-lost great-aunt reunited with a family that didn't know she existed. September loves it, and it makes her heart hurt, as does Lucia's message: 'Dear September, I hope that, one day, you and I will meet again.' Her twenty-fourth birthday gift was *The Murder of Roger Ackroyd* by Agatha Christie – 'You might have read this, dear September, but if you haven't I'm so happy to be able to give it to you.' It's September's first Agatha Christie novel, though her mother used to love the Poirot TV adaptations of the books. She feels as though she inhales *The Other Side of the Story* by Marian Keyes, gripped by the narratives of the three women in it, all trying to navigate their way through disappointment and success. Lucia has written, 'Women are strong. I know you are, dear September. I hope you're not required to be, too often.' In *Atonement* by Ian McEwan Lucia has written, 'I hope, now that you are 26, that life has taught you not all mistakes have to last for ever, dear

September.' It suggests to her that there might be another version of her life out there. When she's turned the last page, she calls Marina's office and makes an appointment.

'Okay,' Marina says. 'We've got some photos, from Facebook. Gemma – the eldest child – is quite active on there.'

September thinks of the Polaroid of her and her mother, blurry and pale. 'Show me.'

Marina hands over the folder. The printouts are on A4 paper, and the images are clear. The one on the top is of a man wearing a suit, smiling a straightforward grin that says to the person holding the camera, 'There is nowhere I'd rather be, right now, than having my photograph taken by you.' In the image, he might be somewhere between thirty and forty. He might be thirty-three, like September is now. She has heard, many times since she moved to Harrogate, how like Lucia she is: her eyes, her hair. But she realises, looking at this photograph, that she has her father's smile. The caption beneath the photograph says, 'Today we said goodbye to Rex Victor Randall, 1960–2015. He was always smiling.' Lucky him, September thinks.

The next photograph is a family group, taken outside what looks like a church doorway. Rex is in a suit – September wonders whether they only took photographs on dressed-up days, like her own family did – and a slight woman next to him is in a pale blue dress and a straw hat. She is holding a baby wrapped in a blanket that trails almost to the ground. No – September looks closer – it's a christening gown. There are two older children ranged in front, wearing smart clothes and the exact expressions you would expect from children who have been forced to sit through a church service on a sunny day. Beneath it are the words, 'Look, Christopher and Sapphire! This must have been Sapphire's christening!' September wonders how old she was then; whether she was already being looked after by foster parents, whether Rex was thinking of her. The space within her fills with loss and hunger; she puts the photographs down and eats a sandwich, too quickly.

'You don't have to look at them all,' Marina says. 'Now or ever. This can be the end, September. You can decide not to do anything else.'

'Marina. If you had never had a blood family and then you found them, and some of them were alive, what would you do?'

Marina touches the back of her hand, smiles. 'I would eat some sandwiches, and then I would ask my solicitor to help me draft an email on my behalf to the family.'

'I could email them myself.'

'I know. But I'm here to protect you. Let me.'

It's on the tip of September's tongue to retort that she doesn't need protecting, but she knows Marina is right.

The email that Marina drafts, there and then, is dry and simple.

> I am contacting you on behalf of my client, September Blythe, who believes she may have a connection with your late father, Rex Victor Randall.

'His parents had aspirations for him,' Marina says, drily.

> My client would like to meet with you with a view to sharing information and exploring the possibility of

establishing a relationship. Ms Blythe is financially independent.

Yours sincerely,

Marina Mulhaney

'We don't know what they know,' Marina says, 'and people always think a solicitor's letter means that you want their money.'

'Of course,' September says. But she thinks of how this never would have occurred to her, and she would have told them they were her half-siblings, straight away.

'When do you want me to send it?' Marina asks.

'Send it now,' September says, before she can change her mind.

When September gets home, Kit is in the kitchen. Every surface is covered with china and knick-knacks, from the boxes in the loft. But what a difference. They are clean, for a start. They all have brightly coloured twine holding brown paper labels to their handles and bases. The labels say things like, 'I am a Victorian teacup and saucer, made of fine bone china, hand painted and embossed with gold. I am free of chips and marks. I'd love to hold your tea.' And then a price that seems high to September, who intends never to buy another second-hand thing for as long as she lives.

'I'm sorry,' says Kit crossly, 'I thought you would be gone for longer.' September knows that Kit is at her crossest when she is feeling vulnerable, so she takes her time before replying.

'Kit,' she says, 'you've made these look beautiful.'

Kit flushes and looks away. 'I've got Sunday off. I was

going to take them to the vintage fair. If that's all right with you.'

'Of course it is.' Sometimes it's easy to be kind. She wonders if she can be kinder. 'Do you need some help? At the fair?'

'Are you sure?' Kit asks. She looks confused.

'Only if you want me to.'

Because Kit's smile is so rare, it feels like a rainbow when it emerges. 'That would be great.'

Lying in her third-bedroom bed that night – Jojo is well on with the decorating – September thinks of the wisdom of Marina in sending an email from her. The urge to refresh her phone is overwhelming, even though she knows it's utterly pointless. Marina isn't going to be checking her phone at 1 a.m., let alone forwarding emails to September. At least tomorrow she has a full day: the curtain maker is coming in the morning, to measure up for living room blinds and talk about what to do in the bedroom, and then Johnny is coming to walk with her and Figgy in the afternoon. Plus, she is loving *Small Island* by Andrea Levy, her twenty-seventh birthday present ('Dear September, I remember this world. I'm glad yours is different. Happy Birthday. Love, Auntie L.'). It's set in London in the 1940s and 50s, and focuses on Windrush immigrants as they strive to make a life in an often hostile world. September falls asleep to the thought that her idea of a busy day has changed a lot, since that first letter from Marina arrived.

Jojo has given the bedroom walls their first coat, of Summer Moss, and shows Amy ('The Curtain Queen') the Storm

Coming blue for the wardrobes. September leaves Amy and Jojo to their talk of warm colours and seasons and focal points, and goes to put the kettle on. She and Kit loaded the goods for the vintage fair into the car last night; the kitchen seems bare. If it wasn't for Figgy's favourite dinosaur on the floor next to her bed – Figgy is sleeping in the sun on the big sofa in the living room – it would be as though no one lived here at all. When September goes back upstairs, Amy and Jojo have sketched out something on the iPad, and have a selection of fabrics to show her. She goes for the one with an all-over pattern of tiny flowers in pinks and reds and greens, that make her think of her grandmother's sofa. Amy and Jojo look at each other and smile and September feels as though she has passed another test. Though when she says no to blackout blinds – she likes being woken by the sun – Amy says, 'We can always install them later if you change your mind.'

September makes coffee and they drink it in the garden. September left her phone in the kitchen; she knows that Marina has busy days, and all her time is spoken for. Plus, she tells herself, she's lived for thirty-three years without knowing Rex's children even existed. She can manage another day or two.

Johnny postpones the walk they had planned for today. He texts her to say he's been asked to look at some investments with someone who's only in Yorkshire for forty-eight hours; how about tomorrow instead, if she's free? He has started adding kisses to his messages since their last walk. September realises she had been thinking of their time together as dates; she feels warm with possibility when she sees Johnny's name pop up on her phone screen.

She takes Figgy for a walk around the Stray. There are too many people and dogs to risk letting her off the lead, so when they come home she throws a ball in the garden and Figgy races after it. As Figgy has no retrieval instinct, she bounds after the ball, picks it up, shakes it and drops it; September makes her way across the lawn to pick up the ball and throws it again. It's warm; before long they are under the tree, September on the bench with a can of lemonade and Figgy licking an ice cube at her feet. September is pretending to herself that she's reading, but really she's wondering what her half-siblings are doing. She doesn't know how brothers and sisters work, but she imagines a WhatsApp group with a constant stream of conversation. She considers what she would have felt if it had been Rex's family and not Lucia who had set out to find her. How good it would be, to get that message. She wonders if she has nieces, nephews.

The sound of William closing the gate makes September jump. Figgy – who is usually delighted to see him – only lifts her muzzle and thuds her tail against the grass a couple of times. 'It's a hot day, all right,' William says.

September shades her eyes with her hand. 'Isn't it too hot for gardening?'

'Most of it is in shade now,' he says. 'And anyway, August is no time to neglect a garden. She will be thirsty.'

'I know! I water it in the evening and it's dry as a bone by the morning.'

It's then that her phone rings.

Marina cuts to the chase. 'Rex's family emailed back. I'm sorry, September, it's a no.'

'Oh.' September puts her free hand against Figgy, stroking her coat. 'What exactly did they say?'

'Literally,' Marina says, 'they said no.'
She forwards the email to September. It reads,

No.
Yours sincerely,
Christopher Randall, Gemma Randall-Squires, Sapphire Bloom.

It's disappointing, of course. But somehow, it's a blanket of sadness instead of a punch. They are entitled to keep their happy memories of their family; for all September knows, they might have known nothing about Rex's relationship with April, about her own existence. She wishes she knew more about them.

And then September realises that she has their full names. She goes into the house and sits on the sofa in the living room: it's hot in here, too, but at least the sun has moved around now. She googles the names, each in turn. There are a lot of Christopher Randalls, and with no other information September doesn't know where to start sifting through the many faces that are the results of her search. Gemma Randall-Squires, though, is a pretty active member of her local PTA in Ripon. So September does have a niece, or a nephew. More than one, maybe. She doesn't know what to do with the idea of an extended family, even one that doesn't want to know her. There are photographs of Gemma standing behind a big cheque that she's handing over to the school. She writes articles for the parish magazine, about the need for go-slow zones and food waste recycling. If she has a book of kindness it will be full of good deeds. But they don't extend to speaking to her half-sister – and she doesn't even know that she is her half-sister. Sapphire Bloom is a potter, with, according to her website, work in galleries throughout Yorkshire. There's a photograph of her sitting behind a potter's wheel, smiling. Smiling September's smile. September thinks about signing up to receive her newsletter, but she stops herself. For now, at least. And so she starts scrolling through all the Christopher Randalls, clicking profile after profile. There are a surprising amount of them. Either none of them is Rex's child, or Christopher didn't look as much like his father as his daughters – his other daughters – do. After a while, they all start to blur: Christopher Randall, maths teacher, Stroud. Another Christopher Randall at a charity football match, Edinburgh. Christopher Randall, butcher, Chipping Campden. September thinks she ought to get her notebook, make a list, but she can't stop tapping: link, back to search, next link. One of them must be recognisable as her half-brother.

'Hey,' Johnny says, from the doorway. 'September? The door was open. William said he thought you must have come in. My client had had enough for one day so I just dropped him at his hotel. I thought I'd swing by and say hi.'

'Johnny.' September attempts a smile, but her face won't cooperate. 'I didn't hear you.'

He doesn't say any of the things like 'how are you' or 'are you okay', which would allow her to say 'fine' or 'yes', and go and get her trainers, and go for a walk with him and Figgy. Instead he sits down on the floor in front of her, takes the hand that isn't holding the iPad, and says, 'September. What's happened? What's wrong?'

Later that night, in bed, September thinks about how she had a strangely lovely evening for someone whose entire living family had just rejected her with a single word. Johnny had listened as she told him what had happened. She hadn't expected to cry. She's an adult, and she's had more than enough luck when it comes to unexpected relatives. But it still hurts to be rejected. Johnny produced a handkerchief and mopped her face. When she had calmed down, they talked about walking Figgy again, but decided it was too hot. William brought in baskets of gooseberries and peas and Kit arrived home, and September suggested that she order pizza, and they sat in the garden and ate, listening to the birds and the drifting sounds of happy people on a warm summer evening. 'This is the life,' Johnny said, lying on the grass, and then he opened one eye and smiled a half-smile at September to show that he didn't mean to dismiss her sadness. She half-smiled back. Kit, cross-legged on the ground with her fingers combing through Figgy's coat, looked out over the garden and said, 'I think I might like to have a shop one day, with vintage clothes and china. A real shop, not online. I think you have to be able to touch things.' William, from a deckchair, said, 'I have plenty of suits from the old days I could donate to that shop. They were the one thing I could not part with when I moved in with my sister. She is always trying to take them to the charity shop, but I tell her no.' September, taking another mouthful of wine, had thought about how good it would be if things worked out for Kit. Not everyone could have a rich dead great-aunt, but everyone could have friends. 'Are you my friends?' she asked, and everyone laughed, and Johnny said, 'September Blythe, is it possible that you're drunk?' And then she realised that she was. And what bliss it was, to be drunk on good wine, on a warm evening, sitting on a bench under her own tree in her own garden, with three friends and her dog with her. Who needs a family?

Things don't feel quite so bright the next morning. Kit has already gone to work when September wakes; there's a glass of water by her bed and she can hear a strange swish-swish that at first she cannot place – is it possible that she's on a ship, she wonders, and that sound is the waves? Things certainly seem to be swaying. But she realises that it's just Jojo, painting at their calm, even pace. 'Well, hello,' they say, when September emerges on to the landing. 'Kit let me in. She said you had quite an evening.'

September shakes her head. 'I'm fine. We had some wine.' She remembers Johnny laughing as he tried to pull her up, before they both fell over. It might have hurt if she'd been sober.

'Well,' Jojo says, 'I'll be quiet as a little painting mouse.'

September laughs. 'Honestly. I didn't drink that much. I think I just drank it fast.'

'If we can't get drunk in our own gardens on a summer night,' Jojo says, 'fast or slow, then what is life for?'

September assumes this is a rhetorical question, and goes to make tea and run herself a bath. Figgy is asleep in her bed in the kitchen; Kit probably let her out before she went to work, but September leaves the door open just in case. Soaking in the suds with her eyes closed, September lets herself remember that single emailed 'No'. She thinks of everything that's happened since she opened that first letter from Marina. First she gained a great-aunt, in the process learning that her mother, her grandmother and her grandfather were dead. Then she lost her boyfriend. Then she gained a book group. Then she found a father, then he turned out to be dead as well. Then she gained three half-siblings, and unknown nieces and nephews. Then they pushed her off a cliff.

Still, she has Figgy, and she has a home, and she has books. She wonders how she will feel when she's opened all of her years of birthday presents. There are five left, and the next one looks like a brick.

It's definitely a leggings and T-shirt day, especially as September is going to do nothing but lie around in the garden and make a start on *Ethan Frome* for book group.

She's brushing her hair when the screaming starts.

September can't tell where it's coming from.

When she looks out of the window, she sees Cassie next door, then realises that she's screaming at Figgy.

At first September thinks it's an overreaction – it's not as though Cassie has never seen Figgy before, though she's not sure how she can have got into next door's garden. Maybe she can jump higher than September thinks, though she's never seen her so much as try, always waiting patiently at gates for someone to open them for her.

Then she sees that Figgy has something red in her mouth.

She hurtles down the stairs and grabs a lead and martingale, which is thicker than Figgy's house-collar and gives September more control. She takes a pack of salmon from the fridge – Figgy will do anything for fish. Calling 'I'm coming', she rushes out of her own gate, along the pavement, and in through Cassie's. She wishes that Penny was here, or even that she was Penny, with her ability to control dogs with a look. As she runs up the path, she sees that Cassie is now poking at a growling Figgy with the end of a rake.

She looks scared. September recalls what Penny said, about how Scottish Deerhounds weren't starter dogs.

Whatever was in Figgy's mouth is now between her front paws, and she's growling. 'She won't hurt you,' September says. 'This scared me the first time she did it. It's called resource guarding.' She is hoping that the red thing between Figgy's paws is meat stolen from Cassie's kitchen, though she already knows it's worse than that. She throws one piece of fish in front of Figgy, then another, then another; gradually, Figgy moves away from whatever it is until she is taking fish from September's hand. September slips on the martingale and lead – though she knows that Figgy is strong enough to pull her over if she wants to – and keeps on feeding her, leaning her weight against her the way Penny showed her, until she feels Figgy relax. She walks her away, to the gate. 'I'm coming back,' she calls to Cassie, who is standing over the red thing on the grass and sobbing.

When she returns from putting Figgy in the house, Cassie is quiet, but she hasn't moved. She's transfixed by the mess of blood and fur in front of her. 'It was one of the twins' rabbits,' she says.

'I'm so sorry,' September says. 'I don't know how Figgy escaped.'

Cassie closes her eyes and turns away. 'Will you clear him up? I can't.'

'Of course. I'm so sorry, Cassie.'

'I knew that dog was trouble the first time I saw it,' Cassie responds. 'And of course, it will have to be destroyed.'

Lucia, 2017–20

Mariah moving in is, Lucia knows, a terrible idea. But she has been so lost since Richard died. Lucia had only ever seen their unhappiness. When Richard had a heart attack, at the age of sixty-nine, just before starting the car to drive them to a country pub for lunch, Lucia's first thought was that Mariah might be happy now. But Mariah had lost the person who had, continually and unfailingly, chosen to be with her. After April set out for India, Lucia had wondered if they would divorce. But instead they had leaned on each other; they had made a story in which they, the devoted parents, had been betrayed. Richard and Mariah's friends spoke of April in a sad, head-shaking way that suggested she had been imprisoned for drug-dealing or attempted to murder her own parents. Lucia had never had a lot to do with Mariah and Richard's friends: she started to avoid them altogether after that.

It was the March after that disastrous New Year's Eve that Lucia first raised her concerns about April with Mariah and Richard. They had seemed unconcerned: April had decided to leave home, and that was what she'd done. The fact that she hadn't written to Lucia, when she had promised she would, seemed to carry no weight with them. Lucia even called the number on the piece of paper that Rex had given her, all those years ago. But the woman who answered said, snippily, that no one of that name lived there. Lucia asked if she could leave her name and number in case. In case what? In case you remember anything, Lucia had said. She didn't want to wreck Rex's life; maybe the woman was telling the truth. But, just in case she wasn't, she spelled out her name and her number. She didn't think the woman wrote them down. She thought she heard a baby crying; she thought it sounded like September. She called again and again, hoping Rex would answer. He never did, and as soon as she identified herself, the woman on the other end slammed the phone down. Lucia only stopped calling when the woman threatened her with the police. She wasn't sure that she was doing anything wrong, but April wouldn't thank her for making trouble with Rex's family, when she got back from her travels.

Lucia applied for a passport, just in case April was somewhere in the world, unhappy or ill, and Lucia needed to go to her in a hurry.

She went to London. There was no answer at the flat. She went to the health-food shop where April worked on busy weekends and in the run-up to Christmas. The owner, Lili, told her that April had come in in the first week in January and said she was going to go travelling. She had borrowed a rucksack and Lili had given her her old baby sling. They hadn't seen her since, but they weren't expecting to. Lili shook her head. 'It will do her good,' she said.

Lucia left her name and number, just in case; but she

could not imagine why April would get in touch with Lili before she wrote to, or called, Lucia.

But still, Mariah and Richard had nothing to say about it. Mariah told Lucia that this was just what April was like. Richard said, when Mariah wasn't around, that he expected it all to blow over. Lucia's parents reminded her, often, that April had said she was going to go away and never come back, so Lucia shouldn't be surprised. 'She didn't mean she was going away from me,' Lucia said.

But April didn't come home. She didn't write. She didn't phone. Lucia bought an answering machine and set it up at home; she checked it the moment she got back from work. She wrote a note and taped it to the main enquiry desk at the library. 'If someone calls for Lucia, please come to find me. It's likely to be my niece, who's travelling, and I won't be able to call her back. Thank you.'

In April, she talked to the police, who told her that a woman in her twenties who said she was going travelling and hadn't been seen for four months was not a missing person. The police officer she spoke to knew Richard, so Mariah found out about the conversation, and the resulting argument between the sisters meant that they didn't speak until Christmas. Lucia worked; she kept busy at the book group she still ran in the church hall, for teens; she set up more book groups at the library, too, for anyone who wanted to talk about what they were reading. She filled book after book with kindnesses, and tried not to think about the fact that most of the kindness was going out, not coming in. That wasn't the point. Maybe she was a person whose job in the world was to be kind to others. She wished she could be kind to April, to September. She had thought that nothing could be as bad as those first few months of missing Billy. She was wrong. She bought a book for September's birthday, wrote in it, and wrapped it.

That Christmas – when the air unfroze between Mariah and Lucia enough for them to mention April's name – Mariah told her that April had sent a box of her things back.

Lucia stepped away from the tree; she was fighting a losing battle with the tinsel anyway. 'What sort of things?'

'Oh, you know. Her art. Things from India. Scarves. Ornaments. You know the kind of tat she likes.' Mariah had looked bored, or was trying to, but Lucia knew her sister well enough to be able to tell that it was an act. This must be hurting her, too.

'When?'

'May, I think.'

'Why didn't you tell me?'

Lucia could not process what she was hearing. It meant that April was okay. A wave of relief hurtled through her, followed by one of crushing grief, of a different kind to the one that had been threatening her all year. April didn't send anything to Lucia. 'And why didn't you tell Mum and Dad?'

'I thought I had. And anyway, am I supposed to tell you everything?'

'About April? Yes.'

There must have been something in Lucia's tone – she knew there was, the way her words were forming seemed to be making her teeth vibrate – because Mariah didn't argue. She sighed, rattled the ice in her drink. 'Well, she sent a box. Full of her bits and pieces. Apparently we're not to be spoken to but she can make use of our loft whenever she feels like it.'

'Was there a letter? Photographs?'

Mariah shook her head. 'Why would she send us anything like that now, when she's ignored us for all of this time? She doesn't want anything to do with us, Lucia. You need to accept it. Richard and I have.'

Lucia almost said, *you mean you don't want to admit to her that you were wrong*, but she knew it wouldn't do any good. Any opposition only made Mariah dig her heels in. That's how they've ended up where they are.

'Nothing else?' Lucia's mind was scrambling to make sense of it. She wasn't sure when she gave up on the tinsel and sat down on the floor. All she knew was that she was on the rug, cross-legged like a child, looking up at Mariah. Hoping.

'That chap of hers kept writing to us.'

'Rex? What did he say?'

Mariah shook her head. 'We sent the letters straight back. We didn't want to read them.'

Lucia's teeth were grinding against each other. 'But they might've told us something about where she is.'

Mariah got up. Her glass was empty. 'We know where she is. Or was. She was in India, or wherever she went. She came back. She must have had to clear out of her flat. She sent some things. Then presumably she went off again.'

Lucia shook her head. 'But the letters—'

Mariah walked around her sister on the way to the drinks cabinet. 'Lucia. Think about it. Why is he going to send letters to us? Because she's seen sense and dumped him. Because she won't have anything to do with him. He must be pretty desperate if he's writing to us. Nip it in the bud, Richard said. So that's what we did. We wrote "return to sender" on every envelope and put them back in the post.

And when the box came we opened it, saw it was her art and bits and pieces, and put it in the loft. That's it. Nothing to get excited about.'

Lucia had an urge to drop forward on to all fours and bite her sister's leg. And then she imagined telling April about it, and how they would both laugh. She remembered pretend-biting baby September's glorious fat feet, putting them in her mouth and making yum-yum noises after the bath, while September laughed and laughed. Her heart tore itself open with longing.

'I thought they were missing.'

'Well, you were the only one who did.' Mariah handed Lucia a glass. 'Here. You look as though you could do with a whisky.'

Twenty-five years later, as Lucia watches the delivery men tramp in and out of the house with box after box of Mariah's things, she thinks about that evening. She's fairly sure that Mariah has forgotten it. But Lucia has never understood why April cut her off, along with the rest of her family. She has worried at the thought of it, all these years, and never been able to understand where she went wrong. Should she have got on the train with April, there and then? Over the years she has written down more and more kindnesses, as though one day she might have done enough, and April and September will come back to her. Instead, she's going to be stuck in this house with her sister, who never wants to talk about April and September. Lucia doesn't know whether it's guilt or denial, or whether Mariah has rewritten history so thoroughly that she is the injured party and April at fault. But she has had to come to terms with the fact that Mariah will never discuss April with her.

Heaven knows, she's tried often enough. Still. She's nursed her parents. And then she rattled around in the house – the house she felt wasteful and ridiculous in, just her, with all this room she didn't want – but she knew she wouldn't leave because this was where April would come to find her. Now that she's retired, the days feel long. She has started a book group of her own, that meets at the house, from the library attendees she considered friends; she's going to look out for others, invite them to come along. She knows she needs to make a family of her own. And she's rung the school to see if anyone wants to use the piano.

Mariah made the case for them moving somewhere else: two little bungalows, side by side. Lucia had refused to be persuaded. 'April will come home,' she said.

She and Mariah plod on. Mariah won't volunteer at the library, or even go to the Rotary events she is still invited to. She watches television; she gardens, for the most part inexpertly. On the evenings that Lucia's book club meets, she goes out for supper with a friend. Lucia is always relieved. Mariah is never, precisely, rude to Esin, her cleaner, who always comes on book club days: but she asks her where she is from in a way that makes Lucia uncomfortable. She thinks of how Mariah has never changed her attitude, and remembers how Billy was treated when he came to this house. For years, she dreaded meeting him, in the street or at the library, if he moved back to Harrogate; but now, she thinks, it would be good to see his face again. She wonders if this is what being old means.

And then, one evening in early 2020, at the age of eighty and in an uncharacteristically understated manner, Mariah goes to sleep and does not wake up. Lucia finds her in the morning. The doctor says Mariah had a heart attack in her sleep. Lucia feels an ache for her sister, who was the only person left who knew her for her whole life long.

Of course, Mariah and Lucia have talked about their deaths. There is no one to leave everything to, Mariah had said, and Lucia had thought she was probably right. April and September might be out there somewhere, but they had no desire to come back to Harrogate. They had no intention of being found. Because their family solicitor had closed their Harrogate office, a bright young woman came out from the Leeds office and talked them through it all. Everything could be put into trust; the drawn-down interest would be more than enough for the upkeep of the house and holidays, and anything else they wanted, and they could always withdraw money if they needed to. When one of them died, everything would be left to the other. When the surviving sister died – well, they needed to think about that. Mariah and Lucia promised that they would. They drew up a list of charities. Lucia chose educational charities, a charity that supported Black children into university, another that helped young single mothers. Mariah called her politically correct and left a bequest to the Rotary and the Church.

Lucia is surprised by how few people come to her sister's funeral. *Well*, she thinks, *we are all getting older.* And then: *maybe I wasn't the only one who found Mariah hard work.* What a relief. Next to her, Esin looks concerned, but Lucia squeezes her arm. Her friends Johnny and Kit from book group are there, too, sitting amongst the handful of friends of Richard and Mariah who did come. The vicar reads out the invitation to come back to the house, at the end of the service. Lucia has a caterer providing food for forty, and it looks as though there will be a lot left. Never mind; she'll find someone to take it.

It's when she's leaving the church that it all seems to hit. Lucia has no one. She wonders who will be in the pews when she dies. Esin is holding her arm; she is aware of being steered out of the church, across the churchyard to where the grave waits.

Back at the house, people drift and chat. Kit and Johnny peruse the bookshelves in the library; Lucia is dimly aware of Esin, thanking the caterers and handing them the envelope that Lucia had given her. She's looking out over the ash tree she remembers planting with her father, when she becomes aware of a presence at her shoulder.

'Lucia.'

She has never forgotten, will never forget, that voice.

'Billy.' She has wondered how she would feel if she ever saw him again. Now she knows. She will feel warm, from her now-arthritic toes to the top of her head. Being in her seventies might have changed her body but her feelings are still young. She turns. He's smiling. His face – oh, his face – is just the same. His hair is grey-white now, close-cut. He is smiling. He is wearing a three-piece suit. She doesn't know what to do.

Neither does he, it seems. Then he laughs, and says, 'Your face. I am so happy to see it.' He glances around. 'I should not be laughing, after a funeral.'

Lucia hears herself laugh. 'I never thought I would see you again.'

'I came back,' Billy says. 'A few months ago. I did not

know that you would welcome me. But then I saw in the newspaper that your sister had died, and I thought, I will come to tell you I am sorry.'

'She wasn't very nice to you,' Lucia says.

'I did not take that personally. But I did not like the way she treated you, Lucia.'

Lucia laughs again. Some of Mariah's friends look over. She doesn't care what they think of her. The aftermath of a death needs laughter. And she never has to see them after today. 'She didn't really improve with age,' she says. And then she thinks about April, that terrible New Year's Eve. And she knows, more strongly than ever, that April did not choose to break contact with her. She thinks of the boxes of papers in the loft. They used to be Mariah's, and private. Now they are hers. There has to be something in there that will help her to understand what happened to her beloved April and her perfect September.

August 2024

The vintage fair is bigger than September expects it to be. She had imagined a church-hall jumble sale, of the sort that her parents used to organise for good causes of one kind or another. But this splendid Georgian hotel ballroom is filled with pristine tables laid with jewellery, china and paintings. There are racks of clothes: coats, suits, band T-shirts. Not all the stalls have vintage wares: there are greetings cards, silver jewellery – September buys a set of oval bracelets of different textures that jangle on her wrist – and screen-prints of birds, cats, people dancing. Kit sets out her stall with confidence and care but shrinks away when people come near, so September finds herself slipping into her old, customer-service mode. It feels good to be useful, though all she does, really, is greet people, invite them to look. As soon as there are questions, usually about provenance or price, September hands over to Kit. When people buy, she finds bubble-wrap and tape and packages things up, putting them into paper bags which she gives to Kit; Kit ties a ribbon round the handle before giving them to their new owner. Kit takes payments on her phone but logs sales in a notebook, with a pen with a chewed end. September feels proud of her.

The last hour is quiet. Kit goes and buys tacos from one of the food vans in the courtyard; September didn't realise how hungry she was. She didn't realise, either, until she starts to eat, that she hasn't given a thought to her half-siblings, or to Figgy, since the first customer arrived. Sometimes, while being as polite as it's possible to be to someone who works in the supermarket where she buys her groceries, September wonders how she ever managed long days on her feet, answering the same questions over and over, feeling headaches gather as she beeped purchases through a till. Today has reminded her that work used to give her little time to think about anything but being tired, and how much she had earned by now.

Kit says, 'Thank you.'

'It was a pleasure.'

'You're really good at this.'

'Thank you.' September almost says, there's nothing to it, or old habits die hard. But then she thinks of all the things that Kit has seen her do. September knows next to nothing about books. She's never had a fancy afternoon tea. She can't handle a dog. No wonder Kit is surprised that September is halfway good at something. 'How have you done?'

Kit runs her eyes down the page of her notebook. 'More than three hundred pounds.' She looks really pleased. 'Less fifty pounds to hire the table, and your ten percent. I feel as though I should pay you for today.'

'You've paid me in tacos, and taking my mind off Figgy,' September says. Another of those kindnesses that balance, in and out.

Kit nods. 'I'm so sorry about that. Poor Figgy. Cassie can't really make you have her put down, can she?'

'I hope not.' She thinks about the bloodied body of the rabbit but doesn't mention it to Kit, who doesn't eat meat. 'I feel bad for the kids, too.'

Kit nods. 'Yeah.' Then she says, 'What are you reading? Did you finish *Small Island*?'

'Yes. I loved it.' *Small Island* by Andrea Levy, her twenty-seventh birthday present, was about the Windrush generation trying to settle to life in London. Lucia had written, 'It really used to be like this, September. I'd like to think the world is kinder now.'

Then September had decided that her twenty-eighth birthday present, *Vanity Fair* by William Makepeace Thackeray ('I promise it's worth it, darling September! Love Auntie L') is more of a winter book. So she'd opened her twenty-ninth birthday book, and begun that. '*Why Be Happy When You Could Be Normal?*' she says.

Kit's face lights up. 'What do you think?'

'I like it. I mean – it's awful.'

Kit laughs. It's as rare and as lovely as her smile. 'I thought that, too.'

September doesn't want to spoil this oddly enjoyable day: 'And it's not about me.'

Kit ducks her head in acknowledgement. But September means it. There's nothing about this vindictive mother, this horrible adoption, this frightened child that speaks to anything about her previous life.

The letter from Cassie's solicitor comes at the end of that week, and coincides – except, of course, it isn't coincidence – with a post on Facebook in which Cassie writes about the hell of living with a dangerous dog as a neighbour. September only lurks on Facebook but Dan sends her the link. It's an unkind post. There's a photograph of Figgy, taken over the fence, and Cassie has written 'This brute of a dog got into my garden and destroyed my child's rabbit. The owner, September Blythe, does not seem to have a problem with this. She offered to buy a new rabbit, as though that's the answer. Just because you are wealthy doesn't mean you can buy your way out of trouble. My children and I are too afraid of this dog to spend any time in the garden. I fear for our mental health, and we mourn our gentle bunny, gone too soon.' There's a lot of sympathy from Cassie's friends under the post, a few links to scaremongering articles about dangerous dogs. But Dan has added a comment that says, 'I know this dog and she's the best. Can't help her instinct', while Zain has gone with, 'Isn't there enough hassle in the world without you adding to it?'

The solicitor's letter lays out, in no uncertain terms, the trauma that Figgy has caused by killing the rabbit. The children are distraught at the loss of their pet; Cassie cannot sleep; though the family recognise September's swift action to restrain Figgy, and her immediate desire to make amends by replacing the rabbit, they regretfully feel that they must request that Figgy be humanely destroyed.

As September reads the letter, Figgy is snoring in her basket, her legs aloft and twitching. September feels a simultaneous rush of love and failure. She took Figgy on and she failed her, and now Figgy might have to be put down. She thinks about calling Marina; calling Penny; calling Johnny. She wonders what Christopher or Gemma or Sapphire might do, might advise: surely this is what siblings are for? She'll never know.

September sits on the kitchen floor next to Figgy in her basket and makes a list. She can make the fencing higher and stronger. She will find a dog walker who will take Figgy out for an extra walk every day, or maybe pay Dan and Zain to do it, as they're saving for college. She'll ask Penny for advice, and if Penny says Figgy would be better off elsewhere then maybe she will have to consider it, though she cannot imagine having to say goodbye to her beautiful, gentle dog who cannot help her instincts.

When Kit comes downstairs, she shows her the letter. 'I'm not a legal expert,' Kit says, 'but that's bullshit.' She rubs Figgy's ears the way she likes, and then hugs September. 'Try not to sweat it. I'm not saying it wasn't an awful thing to happen, but people like Cassie are always up in arms about something. She'll get a parking ticket next week and this will all be forgotten, or she'll want something from you and she'll knock on the door as if nothing's happened.'

September really wants this to be true. 'I hope so.'

Kit picks up her bag. 'I know so. She went to the police with so-called concerns about people coming and going from here at all hours. The police came to see Lucia and of course they did nothing, because it turned out that what Cassie was complaining about was Dan and Zain letting themselves in to play the piano. But the next week, she was at the door asking to use the garden for some church thing she was organising.'

'I really hope you're right.'

Kit smiles. 'Of course I'm right. What are you doing today?'

'Esin and I are making jam again. William has me on slug patrol. And I might see if Johnny fancies a walk.'

'Good. I'll see you later.'

When Kit has gone, September takes her time grooming Figgy, talking to her. She texts Johnny who says he's at an auction but can pick her up at four. Having a dog to walk makes it easy to spend time with him; she's certain that her growing feelings for him are reciprocated. Johnny knows a lot of people and is always busy; she's not sure he makes time for anyone else in his life at least a couple of times a week. 'Of course,' she says to Figgy, 'it might be you he wants to hang out with,' and kisses her on the head. 'I won't let Cassie harm you,' she adds, and feels the sadness in her diminish a little. And now, she has fruit to pick.

September, Johnny and Figgy drive to a car park on the moors and walk to a waterfall. September thinks she might have been there before: she has a memory of her own laughter, certainly, when she rounds the corner and sees the water hurling itself from rocks above to rocks below. Figgy snaps at the flies in the air and pushes her nose into the edges of the stream; Johnny takes September's hand as they cross the slippery rocks, and though he lets go when they are on less treacherous ground, it's a lovely moment. They talk about Cassie's letter and Facebook post, the vintage fair, Johnny's auction triumphs and disasters of the last couple of weeks. September decides against mentioning the great big 'no' from Rex's children. She isn't going to feel sorry for herself about it. When they get back to the car, Johnny says, 'We could get fish and chips, if you like, and go back to my place. I'd like you to see it.'

* * *

Johnny's place is halfway between a house and a building site. 'It used to be a barn,' he says.

'Really?'

Johnny laughs, and stands back and looks at it with her. 'What gave it away?'

'Well, the fact that it's in the middle of a field, for one thing.'

He laughs again, and then he looks at her, as though he's measuring something. 'Come on. These will get cold.'

They eat their fish and chips sitting on a sofa that looks out over the moors; the side wall is mostly window. 'I love this view,' Johnny says, 'partly because I love the view, and partly because when I'm looking at it I don't have to see what's behind me.' He didn't offer her cutlery, so they are eating with their fingers. The fish flakes, white, from the batter; September thinks of the meals she and Johnny have had together. The figs, the afternoon tea, the pizza in the garden.

She nods. 'It's a good view, this way.'

Behind them is the detritus of a house being renovated: floorboards up, a box of taps, an open toolkit, a workbench stacked with things September doesn't recognise. She thinks of how hard it is when no one knows about your past. 'Was this your place with Skye?'

Johnny smiles. 'No. When Skye died we were still living in a place that was one step up from a student flat. If the lease hadn't been up I would probably still be there now. I moved home for a bit, and then decided to try my luck in Yorkshire. A mate gave me a job.' He falls silent, gathering up scramptions of batter with his fingertips.

'Would she have liked it here?'

She thinks he hasn't heard, or he doesn't want to answer. But then he says, 'Honestly? I don't know. I've lived more of my life without her than with her, now. I'd like to think she would. But I honestly have no idea. The Skye I remember wouldn't be the Skye I knew now. I like to think we'd have grown together.'

September thinks of her birth mother in the Polaroid, holding her so tightly, blooming with love. That love would never have changed. But it's different with couples. 'Has there been anyone else?'

Johnny is feeding Figgy fish that he's pulled the batter from. Laughter erupts from him. 'I didn't become a born-again virgin, if that's what you mean.'

September holds out fish for Figgy. She doesn't know whether to laugh too. 'I'm sorry.'

He rubs her arm. 'Don't be sorry. I was laughing because I spent a year hardly going out of my room and the next two trying to shag myself into forgetting. It didn't work. I've done a bit of dating since but . . .' He shakes his head. 'Skye's parents told me she would have wanted me to find someone else, and they're probably right. But I think I've left it too long. I don't know how to be with someone any more.'

'I think you would get the hang of it.'

Johnny laughs, but then goes serious. 'Yes. But I don't think I want to inflict myself on anyone.'

They look out of the window for a long time. 'You should find yourself a nice builder,' September says. 'Two birds with one stone.'

The way he looks at her warms her. She's about to say more – that being rich makes everyone different towards you, that life can never be the same – but she remembers: *it's not about you, September.*

When they set off back to Harrogate, she notices his bike, parked in a room that is about forty percent kitchen. She's not an expert, but it looks like a good one. 'Maybe I should get a bike,' she says. She wouldn't have one like Johnny's, which looks as though it's all business. But she can imagine something with a basket on the front. She'd cycle around the Stray and then into Harrogate, lock it up, buy flowers and something nice for lunch, and cycle home again. She tries not to think of the possibility that Figgy wouldn't be there to meet her.

'Are you going to tell me that you never had a bike now?' Johnny asks.

'Of course I had a bike. I didn't grow up in Dickens.'

'Just checking,' he says, and as she and Figgy follow him out of the door, September thinks: *You would be just the same with me if I was poor again.*

The latest book group book is *Ethan Frome* by Edith Wharton. September thought she had started it too late to get it finished: when Johnny dropped her and Figgy home, there was an email from Marina which September needed to absorb and reply to. Marina thinks that if Cassie was serious about having Figgy destroyed, she would have gone to the police. 'A pet rabbit being eaten by a dog is not a legal matter,' Marina writes, 'but that's unlikely to stop Cassie from instructing her solicitor to send more letters. I suggest that I write back and say that there is no legal basis for their request and Figgy won't be destroyed, but we are happy to hear their other suggestions. Things might have calmed down by themselves by then. They often do.' September agrees, and then she brushes Figgy's coat and tells her that if she does have to go to another home, she'll make sure it's the best it can be. After a bath – she thinks she might have the bathroom decorated like the one at Bettys, with trailing branches on the wallpaper and white orchids in white pots – she goes to bed with her book. Her heart feels too full of worry, her brain too busy spiralling through possibilities, for reading to be possible: but she's soon drawn into the cold and misery of the small-town life that Ethan Frome is leading. She finishes the book the next morning, after breakfast. Then she takes Figgy for a walk into town, when Kit goes to work. 'I finished the book for tonight,' she says. 'Have you?'

Kit nods. 'Did you like it?'

'I did,' September says. 'It made me think about how suddenly life can change.'

Kit says, 'You know that time I said to you about how books aren't always about you?'

September laughs. 'I haven't forgotten.'

Kit looks sideways at her, half-smiles. There are times when September thinks that Kit and Figgy need to be treated in the same way. Be gentle with them; reassure them; wait. 'I think it might be more than that. I read this and I thought about how the point of books isn't that they're all about you, but if an author has written about something that you recognise, then maybe what you're feeling is – okay. Normal. You don't need to be scared.'

September thinks of her siblings who don't want her, her mother who died and went unfound. 'Or not so sad.'

'Exactly.'

They are approaching Bettys. Kit says, 'I should have enough for a deposit soon.'

September feels her heart lurch. Because there is no point in being less than honest with Kit, she says, 'You can stay for as long as you like. I mean, I want you to stay. For as long as you like.'

She feels her loneliness, her worry, swelling. She's been trying not to think about Christopher, Gemma and Sapphire, but it isn't always easy. Then Kit gives September a quick, hard hug, almost over before it's begun. 'I won't start looking until Cassie calms down a bit,' she says.

Two weeks pass, and September is reading, in her room. The book group is reading *Jane Eyre*; she is going to try to get through it this time, though she can't say she is loving it any more than when she tried the first time. Esin is downstairs; the hoover is humming and there's the sound of her singing, loud above it. It's a miracle that Esin hears the doorbell, but she does: the hoover stops, there's the sound of voices. September slides her feet into her shoes and makes her way downstairs. She's not expecting anyone. She can only think her visitor might be Cassie, or someone Cassie sent. Esin has become much more of a fan of Figgy since what they now euphemistically call the Rabbit Incident. She is of the opinion that you don't punish an animal for its instinct, and you cannot know what Figgy's life was like before. September wonders if this is what Esin thinks of her.

But it's not Esin's job to deal with Cassie. September walks down the hallway; Esin has stepped outside, has the door half-pulled to behind her. Figgy joins September; September takes hold of her collar. Figgy will be fine but Cassie might not be.

But as she approaches the door, she hears Esin saying, 'I only work here. I cannot say more. It would not be right.'

September pulls the door open. 'It's okay, Esin,' she says.

It isn't Cassie on the doorstep. It's a woman September has never seen before. Not in real life, anyway. She's slight and pale, with dark hair in a plait over her shoulder; she's wearing jeans, rolled up, Birkenstock sandals, a long shirt. She looks nervous.

She looks like Sapphire. Her sister.

September has to remind herself to breathe. Someone she is related to – a living relative – is standing on the doorstep. Someone who said 'no' to her might have changed that to a 'yes'.

'September?' The uncertainty in this woman's voice spurs September to words.

'It's Sapphire, isn't it?' she says. Her voice is steadier than she thinks it will be. She doesn't feel steady inside.

Sapphire nods. 'I'm so sorry about that email. They didn't tell me before they sent it. Christopher and Gemma.'

'Oh,' September says. 'There wasn't a lot to go on.'

Sapphire's face breaks into a smile. 'Right? The trouble with being the youngest is that your opinions never count.'

'I can imagine.' She wants to talk, ask questions, but what if she says the wrong thing? What if Sapphire has come here just to tell her that she wasn't consulted about the email? She hates the thought that this woman, who smiles like her – a living, breathing person who smiles like her! – might turn and leave.

But Sapphire gives a half-laugh, half-sob. 'God,' she says, 'you look like my dad.'

They take cold drinks out to the garden and sit on the bench under the tree. Figgy lies at September's feet. Sapphire says, 'I always wanted a dog. My mum said they were too much bother.'

September says, 'My mum – my adopted mum – said they were too expensive.' Then she asks, 'How did you find me?'

'Chris and Gemma told me about the email and I googled you. I couldn't find anything, but I set up an alert. I got a notification about your neighbour's post. She shares quite a lot, so between that and Google Street View . . . here I am.'

September laughs. 'Well, at least Cassie is good for something.'

Sapphire says, 'I've often wondered where you were. But I didn't have anything to go on, until your solicitor got in touch. Not even your name.'

'You knew I existed?'

Sapphire smiles, but not in a happy way. 'Oh, yes. You caused quite the splash.'

19 January 1992

Jeannie isn't expecting Rex home for another couple of days. Being married to an area manager is all well and good when it comes to the salary and the car, but she does miss him, and he seems to find it hard to fit into family life when he comes home. So she always makes an effort: she gets the jobs done so that there isn't a list waiting for him when he returns; she puts meals in the freezer so she isn't always stuck in the kitchen, and they can cook together, if they want to. Rex makes a great curry if he's in the mood for it.

But today, she hears the car pull up on the drive as she's upstairs, hoovering the kids' bedrooms. She looks out of Christopher's window and sees Rex get out, then stand next to the driver's door for a couple of minutes, as though he's forgotten something. Jeannie wonders about putting a brush through her hair before she goes downstairs, but heaven knows they've been together for long enough: ten years now, since she was twenty and he was twenty-two.

He's still standing by the car when she opens the front door. Now she's close to him, she sees that he looks pale, shocked, scared. Her first thought is that he's lost his job.

'Rex?'

'Jeannie.' He glances back at the car then ushers her into the house. 'I need to talk to you.'

'What's happened?' He's standing at the window, looking out on to the street: she wonders who could be following him.

He looks at her. 'You're going to be very angry with me,' he says, 'and I'm sorry. I just didn't know what else to do.' He takes a deep breath and she wants to say: *No, don't tell me, I'd rather not know anything about it*. But she doesn't. And then Rex does something she has only ever seen him do at his mother's funeral. He starts to cry. 'Jeannie. I have a daughter. Her mother died. She's in the car. I didn't know what else to do.'

The thing that Jeannie has read about in magazine true-life stories, about the sense of leaving your body and watching yourself during times of crisis, happens to her now. 'How old is she?' She's wondering whether Rex has had someone from his teenage years get back in touch when she knew she was dying, whether there's going to be an older child to bring into their lives. But she isn't that lucky.

'Fifteen months.'

'Fifteen months.' Jeannie closes her eyes. She counts backwards from ten. By the time she gets to zero she has willed herself to be the capable mother who manages everything while her husband is away.

'I'm sorry.'

'Don't you dare apologise,' Jeannie says. And then she thinks, *for better for worse*. 'You can't leave a baby in a car on their own. You'd better bring her in.'

The first thing Jeannie thinks when Rex walks up the path with the baby is that she cannot remember him having held either Christopher or Gemma so tenderly. She can't remember him being that interested in their children at all: though of course, during the early days of their marriage, he had been working his way up the ladder and she had stayed at home with the children, something they had both agreed was best for their long-term future. Watching him hold this child – this child who is so very small – Jeannie realises something that hurts more deeply than infidelity; more than the fact that this child exists. She sees with utter certainty that Rex loves this baby more than anything in his life. That he must have loved her mother, too. 'What's her name?'

Rex looks at Jeannie, then back at the child in his arms. 'September. Her mother was April. She had meningitis.' And he starts to cry.

And something in Jeannie breaks. 'And why would you bring September here? Doesn't her mother have a family?'

Rex sits down and settles September into the crook of his arm in a way that tells Jeannie he has cradled this child many times before. 'Because – because I'm her father. Because I didn't know what else to do.'

'Do you think I know?' Jeannie wishes for a drink, a cigarette, a time machine, though whether she would go back to fifteen minutes or fifteen years ago she can't tell. 'Making this my problem isn't the answer.'

Rex nods. 'I just thought – I thought—'

'You really didn't,' Jeannie says. 'Not with your head, anyway. Do you expect me to take her in?'

'I don't know.' And Jeannie thinks: *That's exactly what he wants. He doesn't know it, but he wants me to raise this baby while he goes back to his normal life, except he'll be grieving for this baby's mother rather than loving her.*

She knows already that she won't do this. She has her self-respect. But for now, because she can't see what else to do, she takes September from his arms. She had forgotten about what babies are like: their heft, their scent, their plump softness. 'You'd better go up to the loft and find the highchair and the cot.'

August 2024

Sapphire is a year younger than September, so she wasn't even around when their father brought this secret child home. Her older siblings, though, were in what she describes as 'the thick of it'. When Christopher and Gemma were children, Rex had been largely absent, their mother devoted to them. (I don't remember that about her, Sapphire says, in a matter-of-fact way that makes September want to hug her.) There had been happy family times, at weekends and on holidays, but Christopher and Gemma don't remember their parents as being either happy or unhappy,

Then, one day in January 1992, Jeannie had not been there to collect Christopher and Gemma from school. A friend's mother had walked them home and waited to see that the door was answered, which it was. Jeannie had thanked her and brought the children in. Rex had been in the kitchen. He was crying; he was holding a child that was also crying. Christopher remembered reaching for Gemma's hand.

Rex had said, 'Christopher, Gemma, this is your—' and their mother had said, quietly, 'Don't you dare, Rex. Don't you bloody dare.'

Christopher and Gemma had been allowed tea in front of the television that afternoon, which was a rare treat; no one checked to see if they had homework. In the kitchen – the door closed, for all the good it did – their parents had argued, cried, and, worse, sometimes gone very, very quiet.

The child had been there for a week, maybe two; Christopher and Gemma could never quite agree. The day after September had first appeared, they had come downstairs to find Rex trying to feed a mashed banana to her as she sat squalling in the highchair that had not been in the kitchen the day before. Rex had explained that they were looking after his friend's baby while his friend was ill. Christopher had told Sapphire, years later, that he had assumed the 'friend' he spoke of was one of the men his dad went running with sometimes, so had asked why the baby's mummy couldn't look after him. His father had started to cry, standing in the kitchen, a spoonful of banana in one hand: and then Jeannie had swept into the room, said, 'Rex, I will only be able to do this if you don't expect me to feel sorry for you', and taken Christopher and Gemma to school.

Not long afterwards, the child disappeared. After a while, she was not exactly forgotten, but never spoken of. And the following year, Sapphire was born.

When Sapphire told her this, September thought of the christening photo. How strange to think, now, that she had met all those people.

Sapphire does not remember her parents as being happy. She remembers her father as largely absent, and her mother as almost always discontented. Though Jeannie didn't drink often, when she did she would get incoherent quickly; she would call Sapphire her consolation prize, which as a child

Sapphire had thought sounded like a good thing. But her father had once overheard it; he had come storming through to the kitchen and told Jeannie that she shouldn't speak to Sapphire that way. Sapphire thinks she might have been eight by then. So September would have been nine. At least her parents – her adoptive parents – were happy. Her birth father was married to someone else.

'So your father brought his – brought me home to your mother?'

Sapphire smiles. 'Right? I honestly think he was desperate. I asked him about it, years later. Mum was ill and he came to my graduation on his own. We had a lot of wine with lunch. I said, I want to know about September. He said that he had loved her mother and she died. He said he brought you home because he didn't know what else to do. He cried when he told me.'

'I'm sorry,' September says. 'But I don't understand how I got from there to being adopted.'

Sapphire looks at her hands. 'This bit is awful.'

September takes a breath. 'I just want to know how I came to be abandoned.' A father who took her home, to face the fury of his wife and upturn the lives of his children, wouldn't consent to leaving his daughter in a hospital A&E department, surely.

Sapphire says, 'Christopher and Gemma say they came back from school and you weren't there. The highchair and the cot were back in the loft. When they asked our mum where you were, she said you had gone to live with your auntie.'

25 January 1992

Jeannie tries. She really does. And to be fair, September isn't the problem. She's a sweet child who likes to be held. She sleeps and eats and chatters nonsense. Sometimes she cries and looks around, her expression seemingly puzzled, and Jeannie thinks she must be searching for her mother.

If Rex had held it together – if he had even taken the time to understand what he was asking of Jeannie, of Christopher and Gemma, who would have to be told the truth sometime – then maybe things would be different. But it seems to Jeannie that he doesn't even try. She insists that he tells her about him and April. It hurts – oh, it hurts – but she doesn't want to be ambushed by anything ever again. He tells her everything: how they met, in Leeds, how they fell for each other, how her family didn't approve of him, though her aunt was kind. He tells her that the pregnancy was accidental, and made everything with her family worse. And when he talks about April, a light goes on inside him. Jeannie doesn't think he can help it.

Every detail is agonising. When she first took the baby into her arms, she thought nothing would ever be harder.

But knowing that there is a whole group of people – a family – who know about Rex and April, have watched their relationship develop, might even be worse.

It seems impossible to bear. But she bears it.

Somewhere deep, she finds a spark of satisfaction that April's family so clearly saw through Rex, although presumably he didn't bother to mention he was already married, given how little he has considered her.

She asks him whether September's place shouldn't be with April's family. Surely they will want her. Whatever has gone before, surely contact with their lost daughter's child would bring them comfort? But Rex shakes his head. 'I've tried,' he says. 'Before I brought her home I tried to talk to them about September. They wouldn't talk to me. They don't want to know.'

Well, Jeannie thinks, *maybe now he will think better of me. Maybe now it's obvious to him that this is his real family. I've taken in a child that isn't even mine.* She remembers how he used to look at her, when they were first married, as though she was his birthday.

And then he wrecks any chance there is. He rubs his hand across his eyes and says, 'If you're not willing to accept this, Jeannie, and I wouldn't blame you if you're not, then I'll take September and I'll go. You'll never have to see us again. I'll make sure you have enough money. Your life will be the same. I'll start again.' He doesn't even look at her as he says it. He's watching September, sleeping in his arms.

At that moment, Jeannie stops feeling let down by him, stops feeling broken-hearted, and starts to wonder why she has wasted so much of her life on this man. But she's stuck with him: she won't let Christopher and Gemma suffer because of what he's done.

It is so much easier when he's at work, and she can pretend that September is the third child she always wanted and Rex said he wasn't sure about.

I can manage, she tells herself. *I can do this*. She drives Christopher and Gemma to school and leaves September strapped in her car seat while she drops them off. She buys some new baby clothes, because she had given all of Christopher's and Gemma's away. She goes to the Citizens Advice Bureau and gets some leaflets about adoption, because if she is going to do this, then she will do it properly.

Then comes a day when September will not stop crying. Jeannie walks and walks around the garden with her: she doesn't want to go out, to have to talk to her neighbours about this mysterious baby. She thinks about going to the doctor, explaining who the baby is, getting sympathetic looks. She thinks about the fact that she knows nothing about September's family, in practical terms: what health conditions might be lying in wait, what allergies she might have inherited. So far, Christopher and Gemma seem to like having September around, but that could change, and will Rex expect Jeannie to prioritise this baby over his older children? From the way he has been behaving around September, that seems likely. It's already happening.

The last of Jeannie's strength gives out.

She looks at September, half-sleeping so long as Jeannie keeps walking, but squalling as soon as she stops; and she sees only that this child and her mother have robbed her of her life, of her happiness. She feels a bloom of pain. How stupid she was, to think she could raise another woman's child with her husband: to fool herself into believing that she wanted to. And how cruel it would be, to September, to have her live a Cinderella life with them, or to send her back to a family who hadn't wanted her when her mother was alive. Better to have a fresh start, for all of them.

August 2024

What Sapphire has said feels like the wrong ending. But she continues: 'At that lunch, Dad told me that your family found you. He had sent a few letters, when your mother first died, which came back unopened. But he tried one last time and they called. He had been away on a work trip. Jeannie called him and told him that April's parents had opened his letter, that September's aunt Lucia wanted to take you and bring you up. He said he wasn't sure. My mother said he should think about it but that she had promised she would let April's family know the next day. She told him that if he wanted their marriage to work he needed to give September up, and that it was only fair that the family who had lost April shouldn't lose September too.'

Sapphire sighs and looks at her hands. 'He agreed. From the way he said it I don't think he felt he had any choice, really. And when he came home a couple of days later, you were gone. He hadn't agreed to that: he had assumed he would have time to say goodbye. My mother told him that April's parents had wanted to collect you as soon as possible. She said they asked that he didn't contact them again; that they thought it best September had a completely new start, without anything to confuse her. He said that if he'd known that was the condition he would never have agreed. But it was too late. You were gone.'

'But,' September says. 'But that's not what happened.'

Sapphire nods. 'I know. That's why I'm here.' She takes a breath. 'My parents were never happy after that. Dad died of a heart attack in 2015, so more than twenty years later. My mum got ill not long afterwards. Cancer. Gemma said that it was only hating my father that kept her alive.' September thinks of her own parents. Their understated love, the fact that, after her mother died, her father would often shake his head and say, 'Your mother would know what to do.' She waits.

Sapphire takes a breath. 'I moved back home for the last two months of her life. She was in a lot of pain and she took a lot of medication. She had nothing to do but lie there and think about her life and I don't think she liked it much. Sometimes when she was a bit out of it, she would ask me to bring the baby. Gemma had just had Hector' – September tucks away the fact that she has a nephew called Hector, to think about later, when there is space in her blistering, wondering heart – 'so I thought she wanted to see him. But Gemma brought him and Mum kept saying, "Not that one. The other one. Rex's one."'

'Me.'

Sapphire nods. 'She woke up that night and I went in to her. I said, "What did you want to say to Rex's baby?" And she said, "I shouldn't have left her like that." I said, "She's probably had a lovely life, with her mum's family." And that's when she told me what she'd done.'

'Told you what?'

What Sapphire says next all comes out in a rush: 'One day, she dropped Christopher and Gemma at school, and then she drove to the hospital and she left you there. She said she found the waiting room of paediatric A&E and put you in the little play area, and left you there. She had put your bracelet in your coat pocket.'

Sapphire opens her bag. 'There were letters. It's my dad's writing, and they have "return to sender" on them. I found them in the last of Dad's things, after my mother died.'

September takes them. There are four: they are sealed. Sapphire says, 'I wasn't sure I wanted to know what was in them. I really loved my dad.'

September holds the envelopes on her lap. She exhales. Sapphire looks at her and smiles. There's a moment of shared silence in which September realises that neither of them can take any more emotional revelations today.

Sapphire is making a fuss of Figgy. 'She's a rescue,' September says. 'I feel bad because the woman at the shelter told me that she wasn't a starter dog. But I got her anyway. Then she killed next door's rabbit and they're not exactly being understanding. Hence the Facebook post.' It seems easy to be honest with Sapphire. September isn't sure whether that's because she is a stranger, or because she's her half-sister.

Sapphire pushes her face into Figgy's neck, where the hair is shaggy and dense. 'I'm so sorry.' She raises her face to September, her eyes wet.

'It's okay,' but then September feels tears start. 'I mean, it's not okay. But thank you.'

'Oh, God, I've set you off.' Sapphire wipes her eyes, half-laughing.

September, bold – she has never met a blood relation before, who knows what the rules are? – touches Sapphire's shoulder. 'I'm so glad you came.'

Sapphire drops her head for a moment, takes a breath. 'I am, too. I partly came because I didn't agree with what Chris and Gemma did. But also because I'm pregnant, and I want my baby to know their family. All of their family.'

September feels her world stop. She knows this moment will change everything. 'You mean you want me to be a part of it?'

Sapphire nods, smiling, crying, laughing. September realises she already knows her well enough to know that this is normal: that here is someone who feels their feelings. 'My husband knows, of course. But you're the first other person I've told.'

When September goes in to make tea, Esin comes downstairs, her tread hurried. 'September? Are you all right?'

'Yes,' September says. 'Sapphire is my half-sister.' This feels like the first important thing. She has a living relative.

And then she adds, 'My father really, really loved me.'

Esin opens her arms and September walks into them and is held, and cries. She cries for that little girl, left in a hospital waiting room with only her name on a bracelet. She cries for her mother, who did not get to give her all the love she had, and for her father, who didn't know that she had not, after all, been folded into her mother's family as though he, Rex, no longer existed. And then there are footsteps at her back; Sapphire's arm around her too. 'I'm sorry,' she says – September hears that she is crying too – 'I'm so sorry.

I wanted to find you but I didn't know how. We only ever knew that your name was September.'

'I was so small,' September says. 'I wasn't even sixteen months old.'

Sapphire squeezes her a little tighter. 'I know it's not worth a lot,' she says, 'but I do think she regretted it. My father believed what she said about your aunt, but he never forgave her for not giving him the chance to say goodbye to you. And she – well, when she was dying, you were the person she asked for. It could only have been to say that she was sorry.'

Esin says, 'My Lucia. She would have loved you. She did love you, with all of her heart.'

September sobs out, 'I didn't get the chance to love her back.'

'No,' Esin says, 'but she would be so glad you are here now.'

9 January 1992

Dear Mr and Mrs Merriwether,

I've left several messages for you, and you haven't called me. I can't blame you; I know you have never liked my association with April.

I write to you with the most terrible news. When I came to see April and September after Christmas – on the 5th of January – April was unwell. She had a fever and seemed delirious. I dosed her up with paracetamol and fluids, and she slept for twelve hours. I thought she had picked up some sort of flu. But when she woke up she complained of a headache. It got worse, to the point where she was screaming with the pain. I called an ambulance.

April was admitted to hospital on the evening of 6th January. She died in the early hours of the 7th. She had meningitis.

I am so very sorry. I'm sorry to have to tell you like this. Please call me as soon as you receive this letter.

Yours,

Rex Randall

13 January 1992

Dear Mr and Mrs Merriwether,

I have had no response from you. I have arranged April's funeral. I feel sure, whatever your feelings about April and me, that you – and certainly Lucia – would like to come?

I haven't been able to contact you, so I've arranged a small private service at the crematorium. I will keep her ashes for when you are ready to receive them. Then you can have your own memorial and inter her ashes as you would like.

September and I are managing as best we can, but after the funeral I'll need to think about what to do in the longer term. To begin with I'll take September to my family home in Nottingham and throw us on my wife's mercy. From there, I don't know what will happen.

Again, I'm sorry to have to write to you about this. I've tried Mr Merriwether at his work but have been told in no uncertain terms not to call again.

I loved April very dearly and I miss her terribly. Please don't let your disappointment with me and April blight September's life.

Yours,

Rex Randall

1 February 1992

Dear Mr and Mrs Merriwether,
I hope you will forward the enclosed letter to Lucia.

Dear Lucia,
I'm so very grateful to you for taking September. I know how much you love her. Jeannie told me what happened and of course I can understand that you want September to have a fresh start after this horrible loss. I know you thought April deserved better than me, and I'm sure now that you were right. But should you ever change your mind about me, or should September want to see me, I'll do whatever you and September need. I know a man who had an affair and a child doesn't deserve sympathy or much consideration, but I will play an active part in September's life should that ever be possible. I will of course take my financial responsibilities seriously too. Please let me know how to contribute, and please kiss September from me.

Yours,
Rex

12 May 1992

Dear Mr and Mrs Merriwether,
I know you would prefer not to hear from me.

However, I felt it only fair to let you know that I need to clear the flat that April and September lived in, as the lease will soon be up. I'll arrange to send April's things to you when that is done. I'll enclose her ashes and a copy of her death certificate.

I'd prefer not to be doing things this way. However, I am doing my best to respect your wishes.

Yours,
Rex Randall

The simplicity of the story is what hurts most. There are so many places where her life could have been different. There was no great conspiracy, no plan.

There was her grandparents' obstinacy where Rex was concerned; there was the argument that April had with her parents, where she said she was going to go travelling; there was the fact that Rex worked away and Jeannie could give him a version of events that wasn't true.

Her mind is a whirl of could-have-beens.

She opens her book of kindness.

Kindnesses done to me:
Sapphire came to find me
Sapphire told me everything
Sapphire wanted me to know about her baby
My father loved me and he thought I was having a good life
My adoptive parents chose me and loved me
Lucia loved me for my whole life, even when I wasn't here

September 2024

William is clearing dead foliage from the vegetable plot. He looks up when September rounds the corner of the house, takes off his hat. He puts a hand out to Figgy; he always carries a treat now. 'This poor dog, being threatened with letters. Nature is nature,' he says.

'Marina thinks it won't come to anything,' September says. 'I hope she's right. Did you know my aunt well, William?'

William smiles. 'Oh yes. I knew her when she was a young woman and I knew her when she was an old woman. I missed the middle part.'

September starts to pull up weeds. 'Tell me something about her.'

William stands up and stretches. 'Well,' he says, looking around him, 'she hated this house.'

'Really?'

'Really.'

'Why didn't she sell it? Live somewhere else?'

'I suppose she might have. But she thought this was the place where you and April might come home.'

September imagines Lucia looking out of the window,

hoping. But of course, that wasn't what she did. The knowledge comes on September like a downpour; she is soaked with understanding. Lucia did good deeds because she needed to fill the days: if she was good enough, April would come home. September loves her aunt so much in this moment that she doesn't know how to hold it. She sits down; closes her eyes. The garden – her garden, Lucia's garden – smells of damp, of grass, of the late-blooming honeysuckle that grows in the half-shade.

William works on for a moment, and then he comes to stand next to September; puts his hand, briefly, on her head.

'Some days I wish Lucia had lived to see you. And other days I think, that does not matter. What matters is that you found your way.'

'Not really. She looked for me.'

'She looked for you. And you came. You could have sold this house, never even been to it. Said thank you very much, old lady, and gone on your way.'

September laughs. 'Bought a motorbike.' She stretches out her hand. 'This was my mother's ring, you know. It was a gift from Lucia. April sent it back to her. I don't know why.'

William doesn't say anything for a long time. Then: 'I am so glad you came here. I hope Lucia knows about it, wherever she is.'

September thinks of something and immediately wonders why she has never thought to ask before: 'Do you know where my aunt is buried?'

'I do. Do you want me to show you?'

William washes his hands and takes off his gardening apron. September picks blue and white cornflowers from the border.

They walk to a churchyard that September passes most days. Figgy likes to sniff around the gate but September has never taken her in: she's not sure of cemetery etiquette when it comes to dogs.

William leads her to a corner where there's an oblong marble headstone, longer than it's tall. It's engraved with names and dates. It takes September a moment to realise: *this is my family.*

The headstone reads:

HERE LIES JACOB DAWSON,
7 MAY 1920–30 JULY 1995
HIS WIFE ALICE BARFIELD DAWSON,
29 NOVEMBER 1924–8 AUGUST 2009

RICHARD ALEXANDER MERRIWETHER,
10 JULY 1938–3 OCTOBER 2017

MARIAH DAWSON MERRIWETHER,
BELOVED WIFE OF RICHARD.
1 FEBRUARY 1940–21 JANUARY 2020

APRIL ALICE JANE MERRIWETHER,
SORELY MISSED,
10 APRIL 1969–7 JANUARY 1992

LUCIA DAWSON,
17 FEBRUARY 1942–12 SEPTEMBER 2022

September stands and looks at the words for a long time. Here is her birth mother. Here is her blood family.

She waits for grief; for tears; for regret. What she feels is none of those things. It's as though, deep inside her, two tiny parts that have never fitted before click together, and she is whole.

She takes the dying carnations that are lying by the headstone and places her own flowers.

'When Lucia found your mother's ashes, she had them laid here,' William says. 'That was a sad day and a good one.'

'Were you here?'

'No. She did not tell anyone. But that night was book group, and we had been reading *The Old Man and the Sea*, and she said no one should underestimate peace. After that she was different. She wanted to find you. But she knew where your mother was.'

'Yes.' Now September knows where her mother is, too.

As they walk back to the house, William says, 'I underestimated your aunt. I think she forgave me for it. But it will be a thing I always regret.'

'Did she – did she like her life?' Those pages and pages of good deeds first looked, to September, as though her aunt cared only about the world around her and nothing for September. Then, after Sapphire's visit, they had seemed like displacement activity. It had never occurred to September that maybe her aunt was unhappy. It hadn't seemed possible, when she had so much money, such a big house to live in. Until now. She knows better now.

'I think she did. It was maybe not the one she wanted. But she loved her job and she liked to help people.' He sighs, seems lost for a moment.

'Yes.' September remembers *Ethan Frome* by Edith Wharton, in which a young man makes a reckless mistake and in so doing condemns himself and others to a life of misery; of that horrible moment when a life turns from one thing to another, and nothing can go back. Her mother's death – April's death – was that for her and for Lucia.

'I'll willingly go to the cemetery with you whenever you want,' William says when they return to the house. 'Though of course you don't need me to.'

'I'd like that.'

William says, 'I'm sorry. I thought you would know. I could have taken you sooner. The day you came.'

September shakes her head. She thinks of her own parents, cremated and scattered at the cemetery, unmemorialised, as they had wished. 'My parents – they aren't anywhere. I suppose I didn't think about a grave for Lucia.'

'It seems to me,' William says, 'that the parents who raised you are in everything you do, September.'

Something that her adoptive parents did: they equipped her. They expected her to keep on moving through her life, to realise how lucky she was, to keep trying. They expected her to keep her own book of kindness, though they might not have expressed it that way. If they had kept their own books of kindness, there would easily have been as many as Lucia's.

The more September thinks of Lucia, the more she admires her. The more she reads the books of kindness, the more she understands that Lucia was not a do-gooder or a saint, but someone who was trying to get through the days. She had the hope that April would come back; she had kindness; she had the book club; she had her job – and she loved her job.

3 July 2017

I hung some heavy curtains so Mariah isn't woken by the light. They are horrible, but she chose them so I didn't say anything. Why would you have brown when you can have brightness? I suppose we will never understand each other now. She didn't help, but I knew she wouldn't, so I asked Johnny to come early to book group and we got it done in no time.

I walked on the Stray and took seeds for the birds. I felt like a silly old woman, sitting on the bench, but people smiled.

I had a long talk with a woman who had a greyhound on a lead. His name is Harris and he can't be trusted not to chase things. He looked at me as though he understood me. (I am a silly old woman.)

I had a phone call from Peter from the library, who is finding retirement difficult, too. He has suggested we go to Bettys and behave like tourists.

The next morning, after she has walked Figgy, September decides to go to the library. She passed it, she realises, on her way to the house on that very first day. If she had looked to her right as she walked down towards the Stray, she would have seen the cherry trees in the gardens outside. They would have been blossoming then; today, their leaves are glowing golden in the early autumn light.

The library September and her parents used to go to was an unprepossessing building, concrete and square, and the cold had seemed to creep up through your shoes. The librarians had always seemed stern to September, though her parents had liked them.

This library, though, is something else altogether: it's a library that does not apologise for itself, a library that knows how important books are. There are carvings of cherubs on the front of the building, and stone steps leading up to the entrance. September is walking somewhere else where Lucia walked. Somewhere her aunt chose to walk.

She starts on the top floor. There are skylights in the ceiling. There are people at the desks in the reference library, industrious and calm. September recognises the smell from the library near her home: paper, books, a clever sort of dustiness. She walks around the shelves. There are files and files with different aspects of Harrogate's history. She notices one for the Rotary Club, and knows that if she takes it down from the shelf, if she goes through the papers, she will likely find her grandfather's name. She chooses not to. He chose not to look for her.

A woman wearing a lanyard approaches her and asks if she can help. 'I was just looking,' September says.

'Yes,' the librarian agrees. 'It's quite something, isn't it? These bookcases are the original ones, you know. They've been here since the library was built in 1905.'

'Really?' September puts her hand out. She doesn't know why it means more to touch something Lucia touched, here, when she lives in a house full of things that her aunt had been surrounded by all her life. Maybe it's something to do with choosing. Lucia chose this place.

She must have wanted to work. September thinks of her aunt here, shelving books and helping readers, and she feels a warmth spread through her. She thinks of her own supermarket days; how even in the worst of times, the fact that she had to be somewhere else, doing something else, got her through. She holds the thought of Lucia in her heart. She stands, for a long time, next to the doors that say 'Reference Library', the font old-fashioned and the wood darkly shining. Lucia read these words, too. Maybe there is more than one way that books can save you. She goes down to the desk in the foyer and asks whether the library needs volunteers.

September is planning a birthday party. Thirty-four might not be the most exciting number, but for the first time ever, she can celebrate on the right day. On the day she was born. The seventeenth of September. Not the twenty-fifth, as someone chose for her, once.

Her guest list is only people she has met since she came into her inheritance. She thought about putting something in the WhatsApp group with her old supermarket colleagues, but decided against it. There's been a natural dropping-off of contact, which she doesn't mind. So all of the book club are coming; and she's invited Marina, Penny, her hairdresser and her manicurist. She even messaged Sapphire and invited her along. She hasn't had a reply yet. How would it be, she wonders, to have your half-sister at your birthday? She feels like a little girl when she thinks about it. She's asked everyone to bring someone: so that will be twenty-three people, including her. She sort of hopes that Johnny won't bring a guest.

She's had invitations made; she'll give them out at book group tonight, though she's already WhatsApped everyone who she wants to come with the date. The invitations are in a russet-coloured calligraphy, and say 'no gifts, please' at the bottom; apparently, this is a thing you can do. She's booked a caterer. She's ordered helium balloons. When she told Kit, Kit pulled a face and said, 'I didn't realise you were going to be twelve. And they're terrible for the environment.' But she'd smiled, and offered to arrange September's cake from work. When September said she would pay for it, Kit laughed and said, 'Let me have this one thing, all right?'

So the party, a week from now, is all ready. September feels ridiculously excited.

But first, the garden.

She and William are checking the rabbit-proof netting along the bottom of the fence, which they installed, along with higher fencing, the week after Figgy caught the rabbit. It means Figgy can be in the garden without September watching over her all the time.

When her phone pings, she thinks it might be a reply from Sapphire. But it isn't: it's a message from Marina: Can you talk? September's first impulse is to ignore the message, because if it's bad news about Figgy she really doesn't want to hear it. But she texts back: Yes. Her phone rings a moment later. 'It's good news and bad,' Marina says. 'They aren't going to try to insist on Figgy being destroyed. They've obviously listened to their lawyer. They say they do want her to be rehomed. But they have no power to insist.'

No, September thinks, but that won't stop Cassie from trying. 'So we just get on with it?'

'Yes,' Marina says, but she doesn't sound happy about it. 'I'm going to write to them to say that you undertake to keep Figgy under supervision and control, and reiterate that when you realised what had happened you took immediate steps to rectify the situation, and although what happened is regrettable, it's the only time Figgy has ever escaped from the garden. But you might want to think of getting CCTV installed, just in case anything happens in the future and you need to make your case. In my experience, if neighbours decide to be difficult, they are hellish difficult.'

September knows she should be glad that it's sort-of sorted. She can't quite get there, though. It all seems so unfair. If Cassie liked September – if September had agreed to join one of her committees, or go to one of her clubs, or abandon Lucia's 'miscreants and ne'er-do-wells' – the whole thing would have been sorted out much more easily. Of course, she wishes Figgy hadn't gone for the rabbit, and she's sorry for the rabbit, and the kid. But she suspects Cassie of spite, and it makes her skin contract every time she steps into the garden. This happens whether or not Cassie is lurking with her phone to take photos.

At least there's book club, even if it is *Jane Eyre*. Esin chose it, because she wanted to re-read it: it was the first book Lucia recommended to her when she said she wanted to read some English classics. 'I found that I admired this woman so very much,' she says. 'Lucia told me that she was brave and strong and knew her mind, like me.' She beams. September wishes she could agree. She picked up where she left off and got to the end, but she didn't feel any better about Jane's journey from orphan to wife via endless drama. The trouble with books being called classics, she thinks, is that if you don't like them, it feels like your fault, not the book's.

'I just don't like it,' she says, when Esin asks her what she thinks. 'I don't like her. Jane.'

'Why not, do you think?' Esin's questions are always gently expressed.

'I honestly don't know. She just grates on me.' September shrugs. 'I suppose it's like, you don't like some people in real life.'

'But she keeps going, innit? Never give up,' Dan says.

William clears his throat. 'It makes me a bit sad that she only gets the hero when he's damaged. He has to be brought down to her level.'

'You're assuming that disability's bad,' Kit says, and William nods.

Zain offers, 'It's like, before, he was a nine and she was a four. And then he gets injured and she works out what she wants and they're both sixes now.'

Esin says, 'What they are inside is what matters. I like her because she holds true.'

Johnny says, 'I think I feel like Dan. She keeps going, and that's what I like about her. No matter what life throws at her.'

'But don't we all do that?' Kit says.

September feels her brain, her heart, grasping after a thought, a feeling. She almost has it, but then Marina says she needs to get back to Leeds because she has an early meeting tomorrow, and whatever September was about to take hold of blows away.

September wakes on her birthday – her real birthday – because Figgy is licking her toes, which are sticking out from under the duvet. Then there's a tap on her bedroom door.

'Hey,' Kit says. 'Happy birthday.'

She's carrying a tray bearing two cups of tea and two plates with croissants. One of the croissants has a lit candle in it.

September laughs and blows out the candle. 'Thank you, Kit.'

Kit puts down the tray on the dressing table and shrugs. 'It was Figgy's idea. I brought mine in case you want company but I can eat it downstairs if you like.'

The air in September's bedroom is cool in the mornings; the sun comes round later. She pushes back the duvet. 'Come on. Get in.'

Kit hesitates, and then gets into the bed, bringing the tray with her. She puts it between them. That rare smile. 'I'm not making a habit of this.'

September nods. 'My birthday treat. I understand.'

Eating croissants in bed is, they agree, a terrible idea; but they do it anyway. Figgy lies at September's side of the bed, like a lumpy rug.

Kit says, 'Imagine if you'd been called something like Melody or Kate. The local authority would have had no clue.'

'Well,' September says, 'they looked at developmental milestones. It said in my adoption papers that given that I knew my own name, and the fact that I had no signs of malnutrition and good clothes, then it was likely that I had been born in September.' She drinks the last of her tea. 'I think they looked at my teeth as well. Teeth tell you a lot.'

She has said it lightly, wonderingly; she got her adoption file when she was eighteen, so it's nearly half a lifetime away. But she feels Kit inhale, a sharp, shocked sound. 'God, September. That's awful.'

September thinks: *it was awful*. She remembers getting her file, reading through it with her parents. It had felt devastating, to see events from a time before she remembered, written there in black and white: the details of the searches the local authority had made, the developmental checks she had gone through, the fact that her foster mother reported that she pulled at her blouse, as though in search of breast milk.

But now, it feels different: as though there are two Septembers, September Blythe and September Lucia Merriwether. The second feels for the first. The first still cannot believe that the second is even possible. The second is proud of the first. The second has a house, and a dog, and enough money to never have to worry. She has a friend who put a candle in a croissant for her. She has a sister who wants to know her, and soon she will have a niece or nephew for whom September will be a simple fact of life; someone who has always been there. And maybe Gemma will mellow, and she will meet Hector some day.

When they've finished their tea, Kit starts to put things back on the tray. 'I'm so grateful to you for letting me stay here. But I think I need to find a place of my own soon.'

'I know,' September says. She thinks: *I need a place of my own, too.*

Kit hesitates at the door. 'What are you going to wear for the party?'

'I don't know yet.' September has a haircut booked for early afternoon; she supposes she could go shopping. But there are plenty of dresses in her wardrobe, and she'd rather be here.

The party is more than September expected. Kit comes downstairs in a black vintage dress that she bought at the fair she and September went to: she's mended the torn beading on the bodice, and she looks like something from an F. Scott

Fitzgerald novel. 'I'll answer the door,' she says. 'You go and sit down. Enjoy your first real birthday.'

They have pulled the sofas back against the walls in the living room, and left the blinds open to get the last of the light. September lights candles. She walks through to the library, where the shelves feel like friends. She thinks of the shelves at the library where she will volunteer, there since the building was built. Older than her. Older than her aunt. That restored and enlarged Polaroid – that first photograph of her – is in a frame, now, on the little table that she kept.

Dan and Zain arrive first. They have brought their mothers as their guests. Both women are earnest in their thanks for September's support for their boys. 'I wish I could do more,' she says. Even as she says it, she realises that maybe she can. Zain's mother talks about his musical ambitions but shakes her head at what a hard world it is, music, and maybe she should be encouraging him to become an accountant like his father. She smiles as she says it. September says, 'I think we both know that won't work.'

Dan and Zain return from the kitchen with glass bottles of Coke with straws in the top for them and their mothers. 'We've not said anything embarrassing to your friend,' Dan's mother says.

'And I haven't said anything embarrassing about you to your mothers,' September says. They all laugh.

'We made you a playlist,' Dan says, brandishing his phone. 'Mostly old people music, but we snuck some bangers in. No reason why a birthday can't be educational.'

William and Esin arrive together. September isn't sure that William could be any smarter than he is at book club, but he has a yellow carnation in his buttonhole. Esin's dress and hijab both sparkle.

Marina is somehow more glamorous in a shirt-dress and slingbacks than she is in her work suit. She and her husband bring champagne and flowers. Johnny is wearing cords rather than jeans, and his shirt has the regular creases in it that suggest it's fresh from the packet. September feels warm at the sight of it. 'I'm so glad to know you,' he says, as he kisses her cheek. Penny's hair swishes and curls and, when September tries to tell her she was right about Figgy, Penny says, 'No, I wasn't. Look at how healthy and happy she is. People like your neighbour don't understand that animals have instincts and humans make mistakes.'

Dan and Zain play 'Happy Birthday' on the piano; everyone sings along. September looks around at these people, who were Lucia's friends and now are hers; who have never asked her for anything.

September didn't hear the doorbell ring again, but Kit obviously did; she walks back into the library with Sapphire and a tall man. 'I'm sorry we're late,' Sapphire says. 'I was teaching a workshop and it overran.'

She comes over, embraces September and introduces her husband, Barney. 'I know you said no gifts,' she says, holding out a package, 'but I thought if I made something you wouldn't mind.' September unwraps the parcel. There's a mug, the perfect shape for cradling, painted in shades of blue. There's a letter 'S', swirling and ornate, on each side. 'S for September,' Sapphire says. 'But also Sister.'

Then Johnny taps on a glass and Kit brings out a cake, and they all sing 'Happy Birthday' again.

And just when September thinks this day couldn't be better,

Esin and William approach. They're holding a bag. Inside it are six wrapped rectangles. 'We know you said no gifts,' William says, 'but Lucia, she used to say that books were necessary. So we each chose our favourite necessity for you.'

Johnny stays to help Kit to clear up. They won't hear of letting September do anything. So she sits on the sofa, and she opens her gifts.

Kit has given her *Tipping the Velvet* by Sarah Waters, and written in the front that it's 'the next best thing to *Fingersmith*'.

Esin's gift is *We Are Displaced: My Journey and Stories from Refugee Girls Around the World* by Malala Yousafzai. 'I have found this only recently,' Esin has written, 'but it speaks to me like no other book.'

William has chosen *To Sir, With Love* by E. R. Braithwaite: 'I see myself in these pages.'

Dan's choice is *Boy Swallows Universe* by Trent Dalton. He's written, 'Read this next!'

Zain has given her *Ready Player One* by Ernest Cline. His message reads 'You've got the Easter egg' which September assumes she'll understand when she's read it. She feels a happy buzz of anticipation.

And from Johnny, there's a copy of *Treasure Island* by Robert Louis Stevenson. In it he's written, 'You make me want to have adventures again.'

She takes all the books up to her bedroom and puts them on the bedside table, next to *Jane Eyre*.

Jane Eyre. She picks it up; something tugs at her heart, her mind. There's a feeling: the feeling she had at the cemetery, when those two disconnected parts of herself clicked into place and made her make a deep and whole sense that she'd never made before.

September knows now why she didn't like *Jane Eyre*.

It's like fitting a key into a lock, and opening the door into the life she is meant to have.

September opens the last of her birthday books. First there's *Harvest* by Jim Crace, a historical novel set in a small English village, which would have been her thirtieth birthday gift; she reads the first few pages and finds the storytelling hypnotic. In it, Lucia has written, 'I know this isn't cheerful, but it's beautiful. I hope that wherever you are, you are part of a community that stands strong. Love, Auntie L.' September realises that Lucia would have chosen *A Secret Garden* by Katie Fforde in the year of her sister's death. The inscription reads, 'Darling September, something lighter, but still wonderful, that I hope will make you smile. I wonder if you have a garden? I love mine. Auntie L.' The final gift – *Beyond Black* by Hilary Mantel, which is about a travelling medium passing on cheerful messages from the dead, while being plagued by spirits from her own past – says, 'I loved this, though book group wasn't so sure. I like the idea of ghosts. I will take care of you, always. Auntie L. xx'

September is anxious before book group begins. She's spent a lot of time, in the two weeks since her birthday, talking things through with Marina, who has come to book group to offer moral support, she says, though September notices she has Post-it notes throughout her copy of *A Tree Grows in Brooklyn* by Betty Smith, and joins in with as much pleasure as anyone else. It's the first time, September thinks, that they have all loved the book they have read, unreservedly; at the end of the discussion, the room feels full of an easy contentment. Marina winks at September, as if to say: *There is never going to be a better moment than this*.

September thinks about how, last year, she thought today was her birthday.

She says, 'I wanted to say something. About me and about *Jane Eyre*.' Kit smiles at her, rolls her eyes. 'I kept thinking about it. And after my party I realised something.' She takes a deep breath. 'The thing about Jane Eyre isn't that she's an orphan, or that she gets tricked by Mr Rochester, or that she turns down St John's proposal. The thing about Jane Eyre is, when things aren't right she moves on. She lives in a world where she has almost no control, but still she manages it.' She feels a bit silly about saying the next thing, but she does it anyway. 'It's "Reader, I married him", not "Reader, he married me."

'When I first came here I could not believe my luck. A place of my own, and so much space. A room for everything. It was so different to my life before. And I felt upset because I never knew Lucia, and sad because of everything my life might have been. But I thought, I'm safe now. I can stay here for ever and not worry.'

Johnny is sitting forward in his chair; Kit is half-smiling. Marina is doing what September thinks you might call cheerleader eyes. September keeps talking.

'So I didn't like Jane Eyre, because she listened to her instinct. Because she knew that a cottage was better than a big house. She came to understood what contentment was. And I didn't want to admit that for me, contentment isn't . . . it isn't this.'

Faces fall around her and she says, 'I don't mean you. I don't mean this moment. I mean – this house. It's too big. It's too much. I worry every time Figgy goes into the garden. I was going to put in a new kitchen and a new bathroom but it will still be the house where Lucia waited for my mother to come back. And all the time my mother was dead and I had no idea that I had an aunt who loved me.'

Esin is clasping her hands together. Dan and Zain look at each other and nod.

'So, I'm going to sell this house. I'm going to buy a flat in Harrogate. I'm going to find something to do with myself that's useful. I've got more money than I will ever need, so I need to think about how to use that properly. I don't want to be someone who just dishes things out to good causes. I need my money – Lucia's money – to be used in the best possible ways. But for now, Marina is going to help me set up some bursaries for music students and,' she cuts her eyes at Kit, she knows she can't make it sound too easy, 'I could be persuaded to invest in a business.'

She looks at Esin. 'I want to know how to do more to help women who come to this country and don't have a friend.'

And at William: 'And I'm putting myself on the list for an allotment. I'm going to need an adviser.'

There's a moment of silence. She looks at Johnny. 'I'm glad that this house gave me safety. But I want adventures.'

Esin says, 'I think Lucia would be very proud to see this.' There's a rumble of agreement around the room.

'And there will still be book group?' William asks.

September smiles. 'Always,' she says. And she goes to make some more tea for everyone.

The For Sale board goes up outside the house the next week, and Cassie smiles at September over the fence. September has already had her offer on the flat she wants to buy accepted. It's a garden flat close to the library. She and Figgy will be able to walk on the Stray as easily as they do now. The rooms are bright, with tall windows: a living room, a kitchen-diner, three bedrooms, a bathroom. The big bedroom with the en suite will be for her; the smallest one will have shelves built in for her books, and there will be room for a chair for her and a bed for Figgy. The other bedroom will be for when people come to stay. By people, she means Sapphire and the baby. And maybe, eventually, that baby will want to come and stay with Auntie S by themselves.

From here, she will be able to walk to work. She's not sure if she can call it work, really, when she's volunteering, but William says work is work, and she respects his wisdom. Her duties will be varied, and once she has passed the induction she'll be able to sign up for shifts. She feels nervous about everything she doesn't know about books; but then, she remembers how little she knew about books this time last year. Dan's family is going to house the piano; she'll donate many of the books to the library; Esin is taking her to the refuge she works at tomorrow. Kit is putting together a business plan for September's consideration.

Marina says September could think about investing in property. September hated the idea, to begin with; she remembers all her years of dealing with unscrupulous landlords, of feeling sick with nerves at the possibility that, any minute now, her home could become unaffordable or unavailable to her. But Marina has floated the idea of charging low rents, of offering flats to people who wouldn't normally find it easy to rent. Young mothers, refugees finding their feet, people employed on zero-hour contracts. They are going to figure out how it could work.

September has got the keys to her flat from the estate agent and is waiting for Jojo to come and take a look. She knows exactly how she wants her living room to be: she has forwarded Jojo the photos she took in the bathroom at Bettys. That spring-like wallpaper, those velvet chairs. Jojo sent back a thumbs up. As for the rest, September only wants the place to feel like her own. The more she thinks about it, the more she's sure that that's what Aunt Lucia would have done, if she could.

She has arranged to meet Johnny afterwards, at the cafe round the corner; as she said to him, it's important to work out where she will buy her croissants. So she's surprised when he knocks on the door. He kisses her, both cheeks, the way he always does; the way she's used to, now. 'Is Jojo here yet?' he asks.

'No. Are you and Kit checking up on my decorating ideas?'

Johnny doesn't laugh. 'No. I wanted to talk to you and I thought it would be better to do it in private.'

September nods. 'I thought we were dog-walking tomorrow? Figgy's not going to say anything.'

'I might have lost my nerve by tomorrow.'

The windowsills are deep and wide; big enough for the two of them to sit side-by-side. 'What is it, Johnny?'

He takes her hand; a grip, rather than a hold. 'Jane Eyre,' he says. 'What you said about it.'

Oh, God. 'I was only talking about me, Johnny.'

'I know.' He squeezes her hand quickly. 'I know you were.

And you're right. I always thought Lucia was content because she was kind. And she was. But it would make sense that she didn't like the house. Until you know that she was waiting for April to come back.'

They sit quietly, until Johnny says, 'Jane Eyre. You're right. She knows when she's being true to herself. And I – I haven't been.'

'What do you mean?'

'I mean, I don't want to go on the way I am. I want to do what's right for me. And I think what's right for me is you, September.'

She takes a breath, lets it fill up her own spaces of loneliness and longing, of old grief and new happiness. She raises his hand to her mouth, kisses his palm. He looks at her and smiles. And then he kisses her palm. And then he takes her face in his hands and kisses her, properly, and she laughs and they kiss and touch and then he says, 'I could love you,' and she says, 'I could love you too.'

Perhaps it's time to start a book of love.

Epilogue

Sapphire's baby is born in April. Her name is Ruby Bloom.

Kit sets up a tiny shop called the Vintage Cupboard and sells from there, from fairs and online. After much negotiation, she agrees to take a start-up loan from September. She pays it back within a year.

William dies in his sleep the following summer. He never tells September that he loved Lucia, or that the ring she believes was her mother's was her aunt's engagement ring. But he does tell her what good friends they were, once they met again, and how they would drink tea on the bench under the tree and talk about how you never know where life will take you.

Figgy lives a long and happy life with September, and never eats another rabbit.

September pays for Esin to take a qualification in teaching English as a foreign language. Esin is able to use it to support fellow Afghan women at the charity where she volunteers – but she also gives up her cleaning jobs and teaches at night schools. She insists on cleaning September's flat.

Dan finds that he loves sound engineering even more than he loves writing and performing, and he moves to London where he finds a great job.

Zain meets a girl on his first day of music college. They marry when they have finished their qualifications. He sets up her YouTube music channel, manages her tours, and could not be prouder of her career.

Johnny and September are perfect together.

When the majority of Lucia's books are donated to the library, September has bookplates made. They read, 'From the library of Lucia Dawson, who loved books, and April, and September.'

The Books

Lucia's birthday gifts for September
1st: *The Very Hungry Caterpillar* by Eric Carle and *Peter Pan and Wendy* by J. M. Barrie
2nd: *Burglar Bill* by Janet and Allan Ahlberg
3rd: *Dogger* by Shirley Hughes
4th: *Alice's Adventures in Wonderland* and *Through the Looking-Glass* by Lewis Carroll
5th: *Pollyanna* by Eleanor H. Porter
6th: *The Wind in the Willows* by Kenneth Grahame
7th: *The Borrowers* by Mary Norton
8th: *A Little Princess* by Frances Hodgson Burnett
9th: *Black Beauty* by Anna Sewell
10th: *Matilda* by Roald Dahl
11th: *Little Women* by Louisa M. Alcott
12th: *To Kill a Mockingbird* by Harper Lee
13th: *Jane Eyre* by Charlotte Brontë
14th: *Noughts and Crosses* by Malorie Blackman
15th: *Fingersmith* by Sarah Waters
16th: *Northanger Abbey* by Jane Austen
17th: *Behind the Scenes at the Museum* by Kate Atkinson

18th: *The Yellow Wallpaper* by Charlotte Perkins Gilman
19th: *Interpreter of Maladies* by Jhumpa Lahiri
20th: *Passing* by Nella Larsen
21st: *Wuthering Heights* by Emily Brontë
22nd: *The Handmaid's Tale* by Margaret Atwood
23rd: *The Vanishing Act of Esme Lennox* by Maggie O'Farrell
24th: *The Murder of Roger Ackroyd* by Agatha Christie
25th: *The Other Side of the Story* by Marian Keyes
26th: *Atonement* by Ian McEwan
27th: *Small Island* by Andrea Levy
28th: *Vanity Fair* by William Makepeace Thackeray
29th: *Why Be Happy When You Could Be Normal?* by Jeanette Winterson
30th: *Harvest* by Jim Crace
31st: *A Secret Garden* by Katie Fforde
32nd: *Beyond Black* by Hilary Mantel

From Lucia's life
Bird at My Window by Rosa Guy
Of Love and Dust by Ernest J. Gaines
Ring of Bright Water by Gavin Maxwell
A Wrinkle in Time by Madeleine L'Engle
The Owl Service by Alan Garner
The L-Shaped Room by Lynne Reid Banks
I Know Why the Caged Bird Sings by Maya Angelou
Fire from Heaven by Mary Renault
Story of O by Pauline Réage
Illustrated Peter Pan by Arthur Rackham
Peter Pan in Kensington Gardens by J. M. Barrie

Marina's recommendation
Little House on the Prairie by Laura Ingalls Wilder

The book club at September's house
The Color Purple by Alice Walker
Rebecca by Daphne du Maurier
Silas Marner by George Eliot (*The Mill on the Floss* also mentioned)
Oliver Twist by Charles Dickens
The Prime of Miss Jean Brodie by Muriel Spark
A Thousand Splendid Suns by Khaled Hosseini
Ethan Frome by Edith Wharton
A Tree Grows in Brooklyn by Betty Smith

The book club's birthday books for September's 34th birthday
Tipping the Velvet by Sarah Waters
We Are Displaced by Malala Yousafzai
To Sir, With Love by E. R. Braithwaite
Boy Swallows Universe by Trent Dalton
Ready Player One by Ernest Cline
Treasure Island by Robert Louis Stevenson

Acknowledgements

This is my eighth published novel. I am so very grateful to Oli Munson, my agent, for building my career, having my back, and generally being the best supporter, champion and friend that an author could wish for. You're the best, Oli. Also at A. M. Heath, Harmony Leung has smoothed my path more times than I can count. Thank you.

Marion Donaldson, my editor, is insightful, thorough, and kind. She has coaxed the best possible version of this book from me. Thank you, Marion. Thanks too to Imogen Taylor, whose early editorial input shaped September's journey.

Everyone on my team at Headline is professional and dedicated. Thank you, Zara Baig, Hannah Bowstead, Caroline Young, Oliver Martin, Alara Delfosse, Ana Carter, Victoria Lord, Becky Bader, Grace McCrum, Ruth Case-Green, Sinead White, Sarah Bance and Kate Truman.

Many people helped with the research for this novel. I'd like to extend special thanks to the adoptees, social workers, Afghan women and Windrush descendants who asked to remain anonymous. I will never forget your generosity and honesty and I hold your stories in my heart. Barry Speker

OBE DL helped me to wrangle my way through the legal implications of September's situation, and talked me through adoption-related legalities too. Matthew Davies taught me about hallmarks and saved me from myself. Brian Wright helped me to understand what Billy's early career in the RAF would have been like. The Harrogate library staff past and present could not have been kinder or more helpful. Special thanks to Alison Wheat. Ruth Marshall helped me to understand why gardening is so wonderful, as did Beth Hill, who showed me round her fantastic garden allotment. All mistakes are my own.

Beloved Mr Butland wandered round Harrogate with me as I searched for September's house and investigated the library. He even selflessly joined me for afternoon tea at Bettys.

I workshopped an early version of this novel on a Save the Cat! Beat Sheet workshop brilliantly run by John Yearley. It accelerated my thinking, challenged me and helped me to get to the story I wanted to tell. My fellow participants, Nancy, Maggie, Natalie, Karoline, Arif, Leland and Neobe, were supportive and had amazing ideas of their own. It was inspiring to spend time with you all.

I don't know what I would do without the CoT. Carys Bray, Sarah Franklin, Shelley Harris, you know. Thank you for taking care of me.

Many of the writers I work with have become supportive, kind friends. Big thanks and love to the talents who are Sarah, Hilary, Zoë, SJ, Kathryn, Maureen, Emma, Anna, Tessa, Erika, Jodie, Fiona, Catherine, Jane, Cat, Kate, Katy, Sophie, Jennifer, Kay.

Hilary, Rachael, Tessa: thank you for the cakes!

Part of this novel was written while in the care of Rebecca and Hamish at the peerless Garsdale Retreat. Thank you, my friends. You're the best.

Mo and Lou both beta-read this novel twice, in quick succession, and gave me honest and kind responses which quelled my wobbles. Thank you. Thanks, too, to Susan and Alan, who read it later and were enthusiastic and encouraging.

The friends and family of any writer have a lot to put up with. Thank you for your support and love: Mum, Dad, Alan, Ned, Joy, Chris, Beloved Auntie Susan, Scarlet, Bex, Jude, Kym. And of course, Harris the greyhound, for think-walks in all weathers and snoozing supportively in the studio as I work.

My best friend of 35 years, Lou, to whom this book is dedicated, did not live to see it published, though she read it (twice) and helped with some early plot wrangling. In writing, and in everything else in my life, I wouldn't be who I am without her. Thank you, Lou, wherever you are.

**If you enjoyed *The Second Chance Book Club*,
don't miss Stephanie Butland's heartwarming novel . . .**

Loveday Cardew's beloved *Lost for Words* bookshop, along with the rest of York, has fallen quiet. At the very time when people most need books to widen their horizons, or escape from their fears, or enhance their lives, the doors are closed. Then the first letter comes.

Rosemary and George have been married for fifty years. Now their time is running out. They have decided to set out on their last journey together, without ever leaving the bench at the bottom of their garden in Whitby. All they need is someone who shares their love of books.

Suddenly it's clear to Loveday that she and her team *can* do something useful in a crisis. They can recommend books to help with the situations their customers find themselves in: fear, boredom, loneliness, the desire for laughter and escape.

And so it begins.

Available now from

REVIEW

If you lost your heart to

THE SECOND CHANCE BOOK CLUB

stay in touch!

Visit Stephanie's website at
stephaniebutlandauthor.com

Follow her on X @under_blue_sky

Like her on Facebook:
facebook.com/stephaniebutlandauthor

Follow her on Instagram
@StephanieButlandAuthor

REVIEW